Blood Orange

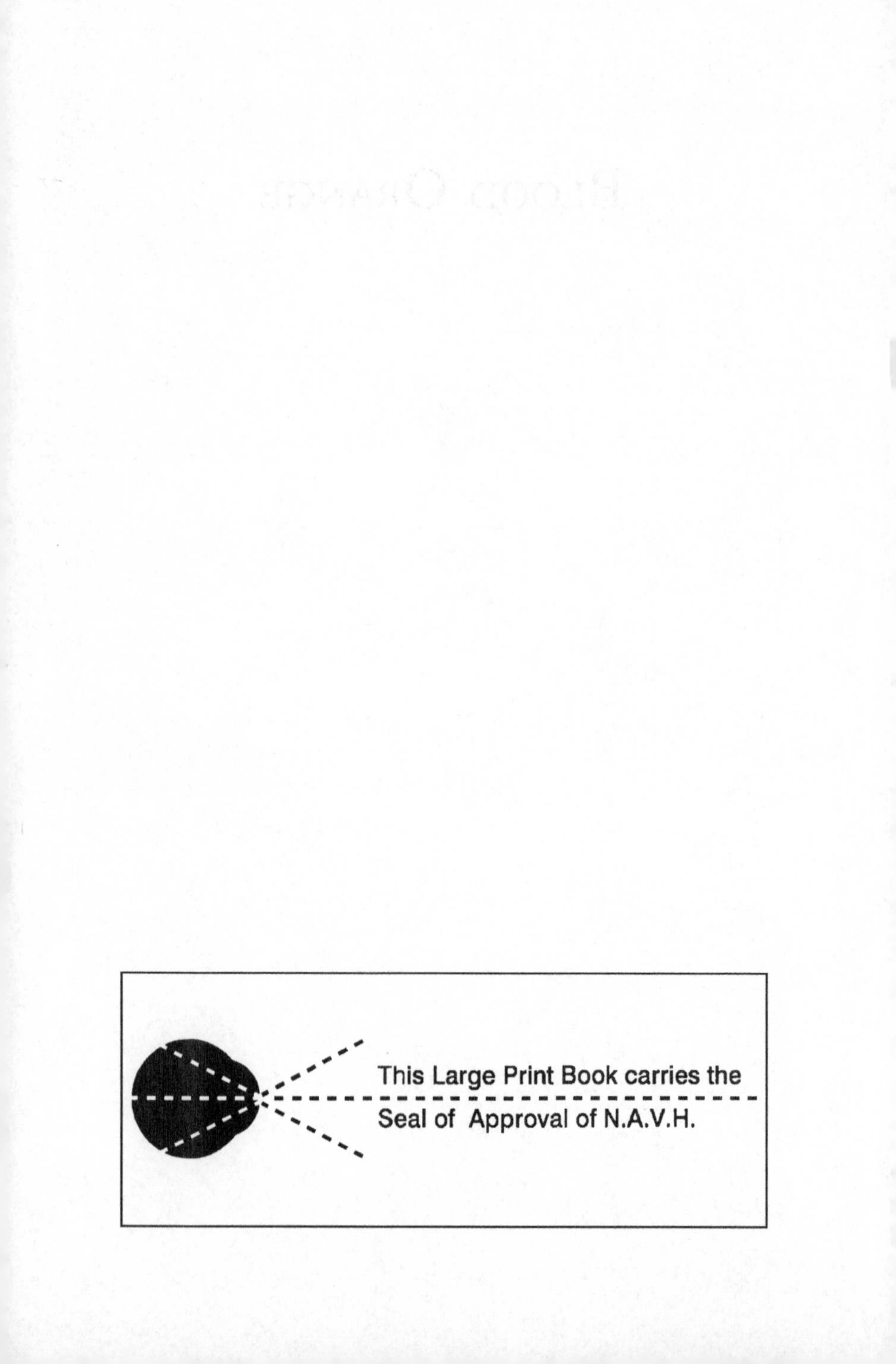
This Large Print Book carries the
Seal of Approval of N.A.V.H.

Blood Orange

Harriet Tyce

THORNDIKE PRESS
A part of Gale, a Cengage Company

Farmington Hills, Mich • San Francisco • New York • Waterville, Maine
Meriden, Conn • Mason, Ohio • Chicago

Thorndike Press, a part of Gale, a Cengage Company.

Thorndike Press® Large Print Reviewers' Choice.
The text of this Large Print edition is unabridged.
Other aspects of the book may vary from the original edition.
Set in 16 pt. Plantin.

**LIBRARY OF CONGRESS CIP DATA ON FILE.
CATALOGUING IN PUBLICATION FOR THIS BOOK
IS AVAILABLE FROM THE LIBRARY OF CONGRESS**

ISBN-13: 978-1-4328-6523-8 (hardcover alk. paper)

Published in 2019 by arrangement with Grand Central Publishing, a division of Hachette Book Group, Inc.

Printed in Mexico
1 2 3 4 5 6 7 23 22 21 20 19

For my family

Prologue

First, you light a cigarette, the smoke curling in on itself and up towards the ceiling. It catches at the back of your throat with the first draw before seeping into your lungs and easing into your bloodstream with a tingle. You put the fag down in the ashtray before turning to set your scene. Kneeling over the back of the sofa, you tie the rope onto the shelves, the smoke sliding up your face and stinging your eyes.

Next, you wrap a silk scarf round the rope to soften it and pull at it once, twice, to make sure it's secure. You've done this before. You have practiced, tested. Measured it to a perfect calibration. So far, and no farther. No drop. Only a little death wanted here.

The screen is set up, the film you selected ready to play.

And the final cut, the orange you have laid out on a plate. You pick up the knife, a sharp one with a wooden handle, a steel-dappled blade, and you push it into the fruit. A half, a quarter. An eighth. The peel orange, the pith white, the flesh bleeding out to red at the edges, a sunset spectrum.

These are all the textures you need. The sting of the smoke in the air, the figures dancing on the screen before your eyes. The padding of the silk soft against the coarse rope. The thumping of the blood in your ears as you come closer and closer, the sweet burst of citrus on your tongue to pull you back from there to here, before the point of no return.

It works every time. You know you're safe, alone.

Behind the locked door, just you and the glorious summit you're about to reach.

Only a few beats away.

1

The October sky lies gray above me and my wheelie bag's heavy but I wait for the bus and count my blessings. The trial is finished, kicked out at halftime after a legal argument on the basis of insufficient evidence. It's always pleasing to get one up on the prosecution and my client's over the moon. And the biggest plus of all, it's Friday. Weekend. Home time. I've been planning for this — I'm doing things differently tonight. One drink, two at the most, then I'm off. The bus pulls up and I make my way back over the Thames.

Once I arrive at chambers, I go straight to the clerks' room and wait for them to notice me amid the ringing phones and whir of the photocopier. At last Mark looks up.

"Evening, miss. The solicitor called — they're well pleased you got that robbery kicked out."

"Thanks, Mark," I say. "The ID evidence

was crap. I'm glad it's done, though."

"Good result. Nothing for Monday, but this has come in for you." He gestures down to a slim pile of papers sitting on his desk, tied together with pink tape. It doesn't look very impressive.

"That's great. Thank you. What is it?"

"A murder. And you're leading it," he says, handing the papers over with a wink. "Nice one, miss."

He walks out of the room before I can reply. I stand holding the bundle, clerks and pupils moving past me in the usual Friday rush. A murder. Leading my first murder. What I've been building up to all my professional life.

"Alison. Alison!"

With an effort, I focus on the speakers.

"Are you coming for a drink? We're on the way." Sankar and Robert, both barristers in their thirties, with a collection of pupils trailing behind them. "We're meeting Patrick at the Dock."

Their words sink in. "Patrick? Which Patrick? Bryars?"

"No, Saunders. Eddie's just finished a case with him and they're celebrating. That fraud, it's finally come to an end."

"Right. I'll just put these away. See you in there." Clutching my brief, I walk out of the room, keeping my head down. My neck's flushed warm and I don't want anyone to spot the red blotches.

Safely in my room, I shut the door and check my face. Lipstick on, flush toned down with powder. Hands too shaky for eyeliner but I brush my hair and reapply scent; no need to carry the stench of the cells with me.

I push the papers to the back of the desk, straighten the photograph frame I've nudged out of line. Friday-night drinks. But I'm only going for one.

Tonight it's going to go to plan.

Our group fills half the bar's basement, a dingy place frequented by criminal lawyers and their clerks. As I walk down the stairs Robert waves his glass at me and I sit down next to him.

"Wine?"

"Wine. Definitely. Only one, though. I want to be home early tonight."

No one comments. Patrick hasn't said hello. He's sitting on the opposite side of the table, engrossed in conversation with one of the pupils — that Alexia — holding a glass of red wine. Distinguished, handsome. I force myself to look away.

"Looking good, Alison. Had a haircut?"

Sankar's buoyant. "Don't you think she's looking good, Robert, Patrick? Patrick?" More emphasis. Patrick doesn't look up. Robert turns from talking to one of the junior clerks, nods and toasts me with his pint.

"Well done on the murder! Leading it too. You'll be a QC before you know it — didn't I tell you, after you did so well in the Court of Appeal last year?"

"Let's not get carried away," I say. "But thank you. You seem in a good mood." My voice is cheerful. I don't care if Patrick noticed me coming in or not.

"It's Friday and I'm off to Suffolk for a week. You should try having a holiday sometime."

I smile and nod. Of course I should. A week on the coast, perhaps. For a moment I imagine skipping through the waves like a figure in the playful portraits seen in a certain kind of holiday cottage. Later I'd eat fish and chips on the beach, wrapped up against the October chill blowing off the North Sea before lighting a fire in the wood-burning stove in my perfectly appointed house. Then I remember the files squatting on my desk. Not now.

Robert pours more wine into my glass. I drink it. The conversation flows around me,

Robert shouting to Sankar to Patrick and back to me again, peaks and troughs of bad jokes and laughter. More wine. Another glass. More barristers join in, waving a pack of cigarettes around the table. We smoke outside, another, *no, no, let me buy some more I keep stealing yours* and the search for change and the stumble upstairs to buy some from behind the bar and *no Marlboro Gold only Camels but for now who cares yes let's have some more wine,* and another glass and another and shots of something sticky and dark and the room and the talk and the jokes whirling faster and faster around me.

"I thought you said you were leaving early." Focus now. Patrick, right in front of me. He resembles a silvered Clive Owen from some angles. I look for them, tipping my head one way, another.

"Christ, you're pissed."

I reach out for his hand but he moves sharply away, looking around him. I sit back in my chair, pushing my hair off my face. Everyone else has left now. How did I not notice?

"Where is everybody?"

"Club. That place Swish. Fancy it?"

"I thought you were talking to Alexia."

"So you did notice me when you came in. I wondered . . ."

"You were the one who was ignoring me. You didn't even look up to say hello." I try and fail to hide my indignation.

"Hey, no need to get stressed. I was giving Alexia some career advice."

"I bet you bloody were." Too late now, all the jealousy is spilling out. Why does he always do this to me?

We walk together to the club. I try to take his arm a couple of times but he pulls away and before we reach the entrance, he pushes me into a dark corner between two office blocks, grasping my jaw for emphasis. "Keep your hands off me when we go inside."

"I never put my hands on you."

"Bollocks, Alison. The last time we ended up in here you were trying to grope me. You made it so obvious. I'm just trying to protect you."

"Protect yourself, more like. You don't want to be seen with me. I'm too old . . ." My voice trails off.

"If you're going to talk like that you should just go home. It's your reputation I'm trying to protect. All your colleagues are in here."

"You want to get off with Alexia, you're just getting me out of the way." Tears leak out of my eyes, any dignity long gone.

"Stop making a scene." His mouth is close to my ear, the words quiet. "If you make a scene I will never speak to you again. Now get off me."

He pushes me away and walks round the corner. I stumble on my heels, putting my hand against the wall to hold myself up. Instead of the rough texture of cement and brick, there's a sticky substance smeared right where I plant my palm. Steady on my feet now, I smell my hand and retch. Shit. Some joker has smeared shit all over the alleyway wall. The smell does more to sober me up than anything Patrick has hissed at me.

Should I take it as a sign to go? Hell no. There's no way I'm going to leave Patrick to his own devices in that nightclub, not with all those hungry young women desperate to make a good impression on one of chambers' most important instructing solicitors. I scrape the worst of the mess onto a clean bit of wall and walk with assurance to Swish, smiling at the doorman. If I wash my hands for long enough I'll get the stink off. No one will ever know.

Tequila? Yes, tequila. Another shot. Yes, a third. The music thumps. Dancing now with

Robert and Sankar, now with the clerks, now showing the pupils how it's done, smiling, joining hands with them and spinning and back to dancing on my own, my arms waving above my head, twenty again and no cares. Another shot, a gin and tonic, head spinning backwards falling through the beat as my hair falls round my face.

Patrick's in here somewhere but I don't care, not looking out for him, certainly have no idea that he's dancing very closely with Alexia with the smile on his face that should just be for me. I can play that game. I walk over to the bar, a wiggle in my stride. Looking good. Dark hair artfully pushed back from my face, fit for nearly forty — the match of any twentysomething in that room. Even Alexia. Especially Alexia. Patrick'll see oh he'll be sorry he'll be so sorry he lost this chance messed this one up . . .

A new song comes on, with a heavier beat, and two men push past me to get onto the dance floor. I sway on my feet, then fall, unable to stop the momentum, my phone dropping hard out of my pocket. I knock into a woman holding a glass of red wine that spills everywhere, all down her yellow dress and onto my shoes. The woman looks at me in revulsion and turns away. My knees are damp in a pool of spilled booze and I try to gather myself a little before standing.

"Get up."

I look up, then down again. "Leave me alone."

"Not when you're in this state. Come on."

Patrick. I want to cry. "Stop laughing at me."

"I'm not laughing at you. I just want you to get up and get out of here. That's enough for one night."

"Why do you want to help me?"

"Someone has to. All the rest of your chambers have found a table and are knocking back Prosecco. They won't notice us leaving."

"You'll come with me?"

"If you get on with it." He reaches out his hand and pulls me up. "Go outside now. I'll meet you there."

"My phone . . ." I look around the floor.

"What about it?"

"I dropped it." I spot it under a table near the edge of the dance floor. The screen is cracked and sticky with beer. I wipe it off on my skirt and trail out of the club.

He doesn't touch me as we walk to chambers. We don't talk, don't discuss it. I unlock the door, getting the alarm code right on the third attempt. He follows me into my room, ripping at my clothes without kissing me, before pushing me facedown onto the desk. I stand back up and look at him.

"We shouldn't be doing this."

"You say that every time."

"I mean it."

"You say that every time too." He laughs, pulls me close and kisses me. I turn my head away but he puts up his hand and twists my face back to his. My mouth's rigid against his lips for a moment but the smell of him, the taste, overtakes me.

Harder. Faster. My head thumps into the files on the desk as he thrusts into me from behind, pauses for a moment, moves himself.

"I didn't say . . ." I start but he laughs, makes a hushing sound. One hand's pulling my hair and the other's pushing me down onto the desk and my words turn to a sob, a gasp. Again and again against the desk and then the files fall and as they fall they catch the photograph frame and it falls too and the glass smashes and it's too much but I can't stop him and I don't want to stop him but I do, and on and on and no don't stop don't stop, stop it hurts, don't stop until a groan and he's done, standing and wiping and straightening.

"We have to stop doing this, Patrick." I

get off the desk and pull up my underwear and tights, tugging my skirt neatly down to my knees. He's doing his trousers back up, tucking his shirt in. I try to do up my shirt.

"You ripped off a button," I say, fingers shaking.

"I'm sure you can sew it back on."

"I can't sew it on right now."

"No one will notice. No one's here. Everyone's asleep. It's nearly three in the morning."

I look around the floor, find the button. Push my feet into my shoes, stumble into the desk. The room's spinning, my head foggy again.

"I mean it. This has to stop." I'm trying not to cry.

"As I said, you always say that." He doesn't look at me as he pulls his jacket back on.

"I'm finishing this. I can't deal with it anymore." Now I'm crying in earnest.

He walks over, holds my face between his palms.

"Alison, you're pissed. You're tired. You know you don't want this to stop. Neither do I."

"This time I mean it." I back away from him, trying to look emphatic.

"We'll see." He leans forward and kisses

me on the forehead. "I'm going to go now. We'll speak next week."

Patrick leaves before I can argue any more. I slump into the armchair in the corner. If only I didn't get so drunk. I wipe the snot and tears away from my face with my jacket sleeve, until my head slumps onto my shoulder in oblivion.

2

"Mummy, Mummy, Mummy!"

My eyes are shut and I'm warm and lying in my bed and how lovely that Matilda's there to say hello.

"Mummy! You slept in your chair. Why did you sleep in your chair?"

Chair. Not bed. Chair.

"Open your eyes, Mummy. Say hello to me and Daddy."

Not a dream, either. I open one eye, shut it again. "Too bright. It's too bright. Please turn off the lights."

"The lights aren't on, silly Mummy. It's morning."

I open my eyes. It's my chambers, place of my working week, full of briefs, case law, the detritus from the night before. My daughter shouldn't be standing here in front of me, one hand outstretched on my knee. She should be tucked up in bed at home, or sitting at the kitchen table eating her breakfast. She is here, though. I reach my hand out and cover hers before trying to get myself into some order.

I'm curled up to one side in the armchair, and as I straighten up, I feel my left foot has fallen asleep. I move my legs and wince as blood returns to my extremities. That's not the bit that hurts most, though. Flashes of the night before burst through my head. I can see the desk over Matilda's head, shadows of Patrick pounding into me as she leans over and hugs me. I put my arms around her and inhale the scent of her head. It calms the pounding of my heart, a little. There's nothing to worry about. I've just fallen asleep in chambers after a bit too much to drink, that's all. That's all that's happened. And I've finished with Patrick, too. It's going to be all right. Maybe.

Finally I feel strength enough to look at Carl. He's leaning in the doorway, disappointment in every feature, the lines from nose to mouth strongly pronounced. He's in jeans and a hoodie, as usual, but the silver in his hair and the sternness in his face give him the air of someone decades older than me.

I clear my throat, my mouth dry, looking for the words that might make this all go away.

"I came back from the club to pick up the new brief and then I wanted to have a little sit-down and the next thing I knew . . ."

Carl is unsmiling. "I thought so."

"I'm sorry. I really meant to get home sooner."

"Come on, I know what you're like. But I really hoped that this time you'd behave like a grown-up."

"I'm sorry, I didn't mean —"

"I hoped you'd be here, so I thought we'd come and get you and take you home."

Matilda starts to wander round the room. Before I realize what's happening she crawls underneath the desk. A sudden cry, a scramble out, straight to me.

"Mummy, look, Mummy, my hand, my hand it hurts, it hurts . . ." The sobs drown her words. Carl pushes past me and takes hold of her hand, wiping it with a tissue, which he holds up to me. There's blood on it.

"Why is there broken glass on the floor?" His voice is tight, even as he soothes Matilda.

I get up slowly, move underneath the desk and fish out the photograph frame that was knocked off the night before. Matilda smiles out at me from behind jags of glass.

"My picture was on the floor. Why was it

on the floor?" She sobs even louder.

"I must have knocked it off by accident. I'm so sorry, sweetie."

"You should be more careful." Carl is angry.

"I didn't know you'd be coming in."

He shakes his head. "I should be able to bring Matilda to your office." He pauses for a moment. "And that's not the point. I shouldn't have had to bring Matilda to your office. You should have been home last night. Like a proper mother."

There's nothing I can say. I tidy up the rest of the glass and wrap it in an old newspaper before putting it in the bin. The photograph of Matilda itself is undamaged and I take it from the broken frame, leaning it up against the corner of my computer. I tuck my shirt down into my skirt. Carl's face is furious, his brow knitted, before the rage subsides to an expression of deep sadness. I feel a tightness in my throat, a sharp sensation of guilt and remorse, strong enough to dull the acid taste of my hangover.

"I'm sorry. I didn't do it on purpose."

He's silent for a long while, tiredness etched on his face.

"You look exhausted. I'm so sorry, Carl," I say.

"I am exhausted. Far too late a night waiting up for you. I should have known better than to bother expecting you home."

"You should have called."

"I did. You weren't picking up."

Stung by his tone, I pull my phone from my bag. Twelve missed calls. Fifteen texts. I swipe delete. Too much, too late. "I'm sorry. I won't do it again."

He takes a deep breath. "Let's not argue in front of Tilly. You're here now. We're together." He walks over to me and puts a hand on my shoulder and for a moment I put my hand up to his, before he takes a tighter hold and shakes me. "It's time to go home."

Then he catches sight of my phone. He picks it up and examines the crack. "Honestly, Alison. You only had it mended a few months ago." He sighs. "I suppose I'll have to sort it out for you again."

I don't argue, meekly following him out of the building.

The journey's quick to Archway, cars and buses slipstreaming down the empty streets. I lean my head against the window, looking out at the ruins of the night before. Burger wrappers, bottles, and here and there a small street-cleaning cart trundling along, its brushes turning as it erases the traces of Friday night.

Gray's Inn Road. Cast-iron railings obscuring the view into the expanses of lawn. Rosebery Avenue, Sadler's Wells — books I read long ago spring into my mind. *No Castanets at the Wells, Veronica at the Wells.* What was the other one? That was it. *Masquerade at the Wells.* I know all about that, the masks, the doubling. My hands clench, the knuckles whitening. I'm trying not to think about how the rest of Patrick's night might have gone. Did he believe me when I said it was over? Did he go home or go back out, to look for my replacement? Carl reaches over from the steering wheel and puts his hand over mine.

"You seem tense. We'll be home soon."

"I'm just so sorry, Carl. And tired. We're all tired, I know."

I turn farther away from him, trying to push the guilt away, still looking out the window. Past Angel now, the restaurants of Upper Street that start well and end badly in a Wetherspoon's on Highbury Corner. The hanging baskets trailing off along Holloway Road, student dives above curry houses and the curious row of latex clothing shops catering for tastes Patrick most likely shares.

"Did the trial go well?" Carl says, breaking the silence as we start to drive up the hill towards home. I'm taken aback at the tone of his voice, more friendly than before. Maybe he's stopped being angry.

"The trial?"

"The one you've been doing this week, the robbery."

"I got it kicked out at halftime . . ." My words come out from very far away, as if through meters of water, my head heavy and floating.

"So you're free next week? Be nice for you to spend some time with Tilly."

Not submerged anymore. Jerked suddenly above the surface, spluttering and fighting for breath. He's still angry.

"Are you trying to make a point?"

"You've been very busy recently."

"You know how important this is to me. To us. Please don't have a go."

"I'm not having a go, Alison. I just said it would be nice. That's all."

Traffic slowing at the top of Holloway, and the turnoff before Archway. Home. Where the heart is. I reach into my pocket to make sure that my phone's still there, but stop myself from checking to see if Patrick has texted. I get out of the car and turn to Matilda, a smile firmly on my face. She takes my hand as we walk into the house.

I shower, scrubbing all traces of Patrick from me. I try not to think about my head pushed against the desk, him insistent above me, the pressure that drove hard edges into all of my soft surfaces. I eat the bacon sandwich that Carl leaves congealing for me on the kitchen counter, focusing on the sounds of Matilda playing in the garden, kicking through leaves and scooting round the lawn, back and forth, *fort, da.* She is a pendulum chiming between this reality and the other one that still isn't texting me, however firmly I tell myself to stop checking. I start to open the murder file, then close it. The temptation to hide in the brief is almost irresistible, to retreat behind statement and summary rather than confront the reality of my own life and the mess I keep making of it, the ways I upset Carl and Tilly. But I know I'll only make matters worse if I start working now. Later.

Friends for lunch, Carl cooking — nothing but the best for these people he's known since university. A leg of lamb spluttering in the oven, the tang of rosemary sharp in the air. The kitchen scrubbed clean, a frame waiting for its picture. Carl has laid the table already, napkins folded rigid on the side plates that crowd into the knives and forks. The blackboard in the corner is wiped clean of the week's activities — no longer a litany of swimming, shopping, and the times for Carl's men's group meetings, it now simply says *Love the weekend!* in Matilda's careful print, with a drawing of two stick people holding hands, one tall, one small.

The kitchen counters are clear, the cupboard doors closed, an array of white surfaces blank against me. I attempt to rearrange a bunch of white lilies that Carl has put in a vase but fat splotches of yellow pollen fall on the table. I wipe them up with my sleeve and move away quickly.

I join Matilda in the garden, admire the spider's web that covers the blackcurrant bush and the collection of twigs in the holly tree that's definitely a nest, *Mummy, you can see that. Maybe a robin lives there?* Maybe.

"We'll have to get some food, Mummy. For the bird so she can feed her children."

"All right, sweetie. We'll go and buy some peanuts."

"Not peanuts. They told us about it at school. Birds like balls of fat with things stuck in them."

"That sounds revolting. What kind of things?"

"I don't know, seeds, worms maybe?"

"Let's ask Daddy, sweetie. Maybe he'll know. Or we can look it up."

Carl calls us in. The guests have arrived, and he's taking the lamb out of the oven. I admire it and move to the fridge to sort out drinks, both of us falling naturally into the roles we always play when Dave and Louisa come round. We've weekend-lunched with them since before the children, days when light falls to dark as we sit at the table drinking bottle on bottle, stuffed on Carl's cooking. I give a glass of juice to Flora, their daughter, and uncork the wine.

"Dave is driving. I'll have some, though." Louisa holds out her hand for the glass that I've just poured.

"Are you drinking, Alison?" Carl puts some crisps in a bowl, having covered the lamb with foil.

"Yes. Why not? It's Saturday."

"I'd just have thought, after last night . . ." He doesn't need to finish the sentence.

"After last night what?"

"You might have had enough? Anyway, it was just a thought. Don't worry about it."

"I'm not." I pour myself more than I mean to, splashing sauvignon blanc over the sides of the glass. Louisa crooks her head to one side, intrigued.

"What happened last night?"

I look at her face, hoping I'm imagining the edge in her tone. "Nothing, it was Friday, you know . . ."

"Mummy was so tired she fell asleep in her chair in chambers! We had to go and collect her this morning. Daddy said we needed to look after her," Matilda pipes up.

I cover my face with my hands, rub my eyes.

"Mummy fell asleep in chambers? She must have been very tired. Why don't you and Flora take some of these crisps through to the other room?" Louisa says, pushing a bowl of crisps into Matilda's hand and ushering them to the door.

Yes, tired, that's all. Tired to the bone.

"So they finally gave you a murder? That's great news. You must have had to do some massive favor for that clerk of yours to pull it off." Dave smirks.

"All earned through her own hard work, Dave. I'm sure she deserves this." Louisa glares at him, raises her glass to me.

"What's it about? Lots of blood and gore? Go on, give us the juicy details."

"Dave, not in front of the children . . ." Louisa says.

"To be honest, I haven't had the chance to look at it in detail. I'm going to start tomorrow, try and get to grips with whatever it's about." I raise my glass back to Louisa and down its contents.

"I thought we might go out for the day tomorrow," Carl says, face downcast. "Tilly, didn't I say we'd all go out for the day?"

"Yes, I want to visit that castle, the one with the maze. You promised we'd all go, Daddy." Matilda's bottom lip sticks out, her treat disappearing before her.

"I wish you'd checked what I was doing first . . ." I swallow the words. I can always work when we get home, after she goes to bed. It'll be fun. She'll run round the maze and I'll follow, turning right, left, right until we know we're lost and shout for help, laughing all the while. "Of course we'll go to the castle, darling." The more we play happy families, the more it'll come to pass.

Dave's work. Lou's work. Carl's therapy clients — no names, only some vague details about his new weekly group meetings for sex-addicted men that make Dave and Louisa laugh nervously. I half listen — I deal with enough sex cases at work to be that interested. No more talk of my murder. Holding my glass by the stem I take one drink, another, hoping I'll drown the anxious voices muttering in my ear about the trial and how long it'll take to prepare.

"Shall we do some karaoke?" I say.

"Let's have some cheese. I bought some port." Carl, the host with the most. He keeps house better than I ever could.

"Brie?" I offer as I cut off a chunk.

"Alison, look what you did. You cut off the nose," Carl says.

I look at the brie, then at the piece on my knife. My throat closes and I put the cheese back on the board, pushing the pieces back together. I can hear Carl sigh but I'm too tired to deal with it.

"Seriously, anyone want to do some karaoke?" Singing will lift my mood. I'll do Adele.

"We're going to have to go soon. Isn't it a bit early for karaoke?" says Dave.

"God, you're always so sensible. Go on then. I'll do it on my own."

"Don't get annoyed — it's nearly seven. We've been here for hours," Louisa says.

Nearly seven? It *is* late. Time's slipped away again. I can't remember half the conversation that we've had. I push myself off my chair, neck the contents of my glass. As I tip it hard towards my mouth, two tendrils of red snake down from the corners of my lips and onto my white top. I slam the glass back down on the table and stalk towards the door.

"Well, I'm going to do some karaoke now. You be boring if you like. It's the bloody weekend."

I'm in good form tonight. The children watch wide-eyed with awe as I hit all the high notes in "Wuthering Heights." They're enthralled. Heathcliff would let me in for sure. I roll in the deep with Adele, take a nod to Prince and his little red Corvette before hitting my musical peak, "There Is a Light That Never Goes Out." Someone said once that I sound spectral when I sing it, and it's always my showstopper. No "My Way" for me, this is my way to finish, outclassing Morrissey himself. Possibly. I hold the last note as long as I can and collapse back on the sofa, spent. I'm almost surprised not to receive a round of applause, so clearly in my mind are Carl and David and Louisa avidly listening and admiring my singing.

". . . how you put up with it." Louisa's voice, clear in the sudden silence after the end of my song. Then a shushing noise. Can they be talking about me? I haven't been that bad . . . I lean back into the cream leather sofa and close my eyes. The door slams and I jump, but only a little before settling back into the cushions, eyes tight shut.

■ ■ ■ ■

A little later I come to with a start. There's no noise in the house. I go into the kitchen and start to clear the rest of the dirty plates and glasses from the table to the sink. Carl's used the good glasses, the heavy ones that look solid but chip as soon as one touches the other. I carry one load over and come back for the next.

I'm confused about the way the afternoon's ended up; I was so sure that everyone would want to join in. There's a fear lurking in the corner of my mind that I've mishandled it all, somehow, my mind clouded with drink, my judgment askew. It's not how it used to be. As I carry the glasses past the kitchen door I catch sight of the print of Temple Church hanging in the corridor — Carl gave it to me when I first got tenancy and I'd been so pleased with how thoughtful he was. I should be more sensitive to him. His confidence has never been the same since his redundancy, even though the counseling training went so well, and his part-time practice as a psychotherapist has really taken off. He never set out to be a househusband.

"Don't carry them like that. I've told

you," Carl says. I jump, nearly dropping the glasses. They chime against each other.

"I was just trying to help."

"Don't. Go and sit down. I can't bear it if you break something."

There's no point arguing. I look at him through my bangs. A vein is throbbing on his temple and his cheeks are flushed. The color gives him youth, suddenly, and the boy he was stands in front of me, just for a moment, hair dark and floppy, eyes creased in a smile. The vision recedes along with the hairline and I'm left with reality again, a cross man in his forties with thinned, graying hair and an impatient expression on his face. But enough of the memory lingers, the boy superimposed on the man, and a small surge of love stirs in me.

"I'll go and read to Matilda."

"I don't want you to upset her."

"I'm not going to upset her. I'm just going to read her a story." I try to stop my voice sounding plaintive. The surge has subsided.

"She knows you're drunk. She doesn't like it."

"I'm not that drunk. I'm fine."

"Fine? When you've pissed off my friends so much that they've left early in embarrassment? When I had to scrape you off the floor of chambers this morning?"

"I was on the chair. And it's not that early."

"You know what I mean."

I do. I don't agree, though. "I don't think that's fair. They didn't leave because of me. They'd have been welcome to do karaoke."

"Jesus, Alison . . . I don't even know where to start."

"This isn't fair."

"Don't shout at me. I'm not going to talk to you when you're like this."

"I know I've pissed you off, and I'm sorry. We always used to have fun together, though. I hadn't realized everyone had got so boring. Whatever. I'm going to read to Tilly." I walk out of the kitchen before Carl can say any more.

She's sitting in bed reading a Clarice Bean book. Six years old but still my baby. She hugs me and murmurs, "Night night, Mummy, I love you."

"I love you too," I say, and tuck her under her flowery duvet. Carl comes through as I'm about to turn off the light and for a moment we stand united, looking at the child we created. I turn to him and hold out my hand and he pauses, about to take it before he backs away, his hand partly outstretched but the fingers curled tightly into his palm.

"I made you a cup of tea. It's in the living room."

"Thank you." He's gone before I can finish the words but this is a start, the smallest of moves. Maybe he's inching back in my direction. Though I know it's more than I deserve. It was only twenty-four hours ago I'd promised to myself that I'd have one drink and then go home. For a moment I feel a deep sense of despair. I can't even keep to one drink, I can't make it home to my family as I ought to. I stare into space for a long while, remorse gnawing at my guts, before I shake myself out of it. I drink the tea and go to bed, overwhelmed by emotion and exhaustion. It's been a long week. I fall into sleep soothed by gentle clinks and splashes as Carl washes up. At least I offered to help.

3

They leave before I wake up, off to the castle together as the brief note Carl leaves me announces. *I couldn't wake you. We had to leave. You've got work to do anyway. I finished the washing up.* No kisses at the bottom. Cross, not crosses. I am too — I promised to go with them. They should have taken me. When I realize they've gone I try to call but his phone's off. I lie in bed, listening to his voice on the voicemail message. *Can't take your call. Can't take your call.*

Won't, more like.

Finally, I get through. "Why didn't you wake me?"

"I tried. You stirred, told me to fuck off. I thought I'd better just leave you to sleep."

I don't remember that at all. "I didn't wake up till eleven. It's not like me."

"You were wiped out from the night before."

"I wished you'd tried harder to wake me

up. Or that you'd waited."

"I did try, Alison. But you weren't having any of it. We left at nine. There wouldn't have been any point going if we'd gone any later."

"Right. Well, I'm really sorry. I didn't do it on purpose. Can I speak to Matilda?"

"She's playing at the moment. I don't want to upset her by making her stop. She was really sad you weren't there but she's better now. Just leave it."

"I don't understand it — I never sleep so late. I didn't mean to. Please tell her I'm sorry, at least."

"It is what it is," he says. A pause, then he changes the subject so firmly I can't argue. "Are you getting some work done?"

"I'm about to start. Going to make a stew for supper."

"Well, I'll let you get on with it." He hangs up before I can say goodbye. I hold my finger above the call icon before moving it instead to home and canceling the whole process. We'll talk later, over a nice dinner. I'll make Tilly understand I'm sorry, that I didn't want to miss the trip. I shake my head clear and get out of bed, pull on some pajamas, and go downstairs to work.

Two coffees later I open the brief, blinking

through the fog of a headache that's lodged itself behind my right eyeball. *Regina versus Madeleine Smith.* The Central Criminal Court. Transferred from the magistrates' court at Camberwell Green, the closest court to the scene of the crime — a rich residential area in south London.

My phone beeps. I jump for it, hoping that Carl is ready to make up.

Any thoughts on the case yet?

Patrick. Pleasure sweeps through me, then anger. How dare he text me on the weekend, especially when I've finished with him. Then his message sinks in.

What case? I text back.

Madeleine Smith. Ur first murder, no?

I didn't think I'd mentioned it to him. It slowly dawns on me and I turn to look at the brief. There it is on the back sheet, the instructing solicitor in my first murder. Saunders & Co. Patrick's company. For a moment I wonder exactly what I have done for the case, how far I've gone, how many times. How hard, how fast. But I know that's not why. Patrick won't fuck with work. Just me.

Another beep.

Hmmm yes, ur welcome. He's being stroppy.

I finished with you on Friday. I feel like I'm fifteen again.

I know I know. But this is work. Conference nxt wk. Client wants to meet u ASAP. I'll book w/clerks.

The end of the conversation. Not the end of the affair. Nothing about Friday, nothing to worry about. If he'd shagged someone else he'd have told me. Not that I should care. I look again at my text: I finished with you on Friday. Delete it. Delete the whole exchange. Maybe I should refuse to work with Patrick for the good of my marriage, but this is what I've been working up to all my career. I push him out of my mind and open the files, start reading. I'm doing my job, that's all.

Later, I put the brief away and start to cook supper. I chop an onion slowly. The last sunlight catches the blade of the knife and I hold it out, angling it from one side to another, letting the reflection dance off the walls and ceiling. It's one of the big kitchen knives we were given as a wedding present, me quickly handing a coin over to the donor, my friend Sandra from school. "I don't want to cut love — we've known each other too long," I said as she smiled and pocketed the silver.

Madeleine Smith hasn't just cut love, she's hacked and chopped and stabbed at it repeatedly, leaving fifteen separate injuries on her husband in their bedroom in Clapham. There are several from which he could have died, though according to the prosecution case summary the pathologist has concluded that the most likely is the stab wound to his neck that almost severed the jugular vein. The red stains are vivid on the white bed sheets where the body was found, shown in pictures provided by the scene-of-crime officer.

I select another onion and slice it finely.

The stew has cooked to perfection by the time that Carl and Matilda return home but Matilda takes one look and says that she is hungry, but she doesn't want to eat meat.

"You ate lamb yesterday," I say.

"When I was talking to Daddy today I asked him about how chickens are killed and I didn't like what he said."

"You don't like very many vegetables," I say.

"I know, but I don't want animals to die."

I look at Carl for help but he shrugs.

"Okay, sweetie, I'll make you an omelet. But maybe you should think about it some more," I say, and she nods. I stir the stew round, hold out the spoon to Carl. "Do you want some?"

He takes the spoon and looks at it, smells it. Then his mouth twists and he pushes it back into my hands. "No, not really. Not that hungry."

"I wish you'd said . . . You're not going vegetarian too?" I try not to sound cross.

"No, it's not that," he says. "It just smells a bit . . ."

"A bit what?" I suppress my anger less.

"A bit . . . Look, don't worry about it. You made the effort, that's what counts. And as far as Tilly going veggie, I'll support her in any choice she makes. It'll be fun, won't it? We'll find lots of new foods you like." Carl smiles at Matilda. He walks over to the stove, stirs at the stew. "It was worth a try, Alison, but maybe let me stick to the cooking? I know what Matilda's favorites are. And I'll make her that omelet."

I don't reply, and move past him to pick up the casserole dish and take it off the heat, putting its lid slightly to one side for the stew to cool down. I'll take it in for lunch, freeze the leftovers. Its cloying, meaty scent will dog me for weeks. The chunks of carrot I'd so carefully chopped into batons poke their heads through the viscous gravy. It looks like sick. I feel sick. My offering, not even burnt, rejected.

Matilda comes over to me and I kneel down and hug her.

"I'm sorry I didn't come with you today, sweetie." I speak to her quietly, words meant for her alone. I put out my hand and stroke her cheek before pulling her into a hug. She hugs me back hard. I push her out gently to arm's length, holding her shoulders so I can make eye contact. "I promise that very soon, we will go out. Just you and me. We'll go wherever you like. I promise. Okay?"

She nods.

"I promise." Then I pull her back and hug her again. She relaxes into me, head warm against my shoulder. A knot inside me loosens.

Carl watches me bathe Matilda. I brush her hair and dry it, read her a story and sing to her as she falls asleep. After we shut her bedroom door he says, "It's very important to keep promises to children."

"I'm not going to break it."

"Make sure you don't."

"There's no need to threaten me, Carl. I'm doing my best. Can't you be more supportive?"

"Don't push me, Alison. You're in no position to be reproachful."

Anger blazes in me, subsides. "I know. I'm sorry. I'm sorry . . ."

He reaches over and runs one finger down the side of my face. I catch his hand in mine and kiss it, then put my other hand round the back of his neck to pull his face closer. We're about to kiss. Then he pulls away.

"I'm sorry. I can't." He walks into the living room and shuts the door. I wait for a moment to see if he'll change his mind, then I return to the study and close the door behind me. I try to work, using statement and statute to dull the sting of rejection, while the stench of stew lies heavy in the air.

Later that night, as I spoon the cold slop into small plastic containers, Carl comes into the kitchen and shuts the door behind him.

"I've thought about it all day, whether I should show you this," he says.

"Show me what?" Something in his tone makes my hand shake and spill gravy down the side of the box I'm filling.

"I need you to understand what it's like sometimes, why we get so worked up."

"What do you need me to understand?" I put the big spoon back in the casserole and fasten the lid on the box.

Carl doesn't reply. He fiddles with his phone. I put the boxes into the freezer, tessellating them neatly, pushing the half-finished bags of frozen peas to one side. As I thump at the ice on the sides of the freezer, I hear the opening bars of "Rolling in the Deep" and smile, about to join in the singing in my head. But as I mentally draw breath, I hear myself already singing. If singing is what it can be called. I slam the freezer hard shut and turn to Carl. He holds his phone out to me, wordlessly, a look of something like compassion in his eyes.

Last night, I'd been glorious, singing without a care in the world. So what if no one else was joining in, they didn't know what they were missing! I was a star, riding a wave of music that had carried me away from all the petty wrangling that had dominated the end of the afternoon. Today, I see what they saw: a hammered woman, with her bra hanging out of her dress and her makeup running halfway down her face. I watch her, appalled. Her voice tears through me — the notes I'd hit so well, she misses by a mile. The rhythm off, the dancing worse. And worst of all, the looks on the children's faces when she tries to get them to join in and dance with her. No, that's not the worst — the worst is the muffled voices on the recording. There's even laughter. Dave, Louisa — Christ, is that Carl's laugh, too?

"Why the hell didn't you stop me?"

"I tried, but you wouldn't listen."

"Instead you thought you'd video me making a twat of myself?"

"I wasn't doing it to be unkind. I just needed you to see what it's like, having to live with you, sometimes. Not all the time, but when you're like this, it's really hard."

I look again at the phone. The woman on-screen — the *me* onscreen — is clearly set up for a long night. She staggers across the sofa, sitting down heavily to sing Prince. Then, the finale, the Smiths song I was so sure I'd aced. It's not a heavenly thing to watch. My hands are cold, trembling as I hold the phone. A flush prickles up my face, shame writhing in the pit of my stomach. I close my eyes but I can still hear my voice shrieking and slurring over the words I thought I'd sung so clearly the night before. Struggling to control my shaking hands, I press pause, and am about to press delete when Carl takes his phone back from me.

"I was just trying to have some fun," I say.

"It isn't fun if it's upsetting everyone else," Carl says, looking down.

"I didn't realize people were upset."

"That's the thing, Alison. You never do."

He leaves the room and I keep spooning stew into boxes. Once I finish I wipe down the counters and start the dishwasher. I turn off the light and stand in the dark for a long time, listening to the humming of all the appliances, hoping it'll calm my mind and drown out the sound of my own voice. I can still hear it shattering like broken glass.

4

Carl makes breakfast for Matilda in the morning, getting her ready for school. Given I'm not in court I'd planned to take her in but he's being so efficient I don't want to get in the way of it. I go down to the kitchen to get a coffee.

"If you give me your phone I'll get it fixed for you. There's that shop near the therapy center," he says.

I try to look nonchalant, running through the dangers in my mind. I'm always careful. Very careful. Messages, emails — all deleted the moment they've been read. As long as I warn Patrick in time. I shrug. "If you can be bothered. It's not that bad."

"It's worth fixing the crack before it gets any worse. You don't want to have to buy a new one."

I know he's right but the prissiness of his tone grates on me. I swallow it down — he's doing me a favor, after all.

"Make sure you've done a backup. In case something goes wrong," he says. He sits down and waits while I back up the phone wirelessly, wipe it, and hand it over.

"Thank you — it's very kind of you."

He takes it from me and leaves, Matilda hugging me briefly before trotting off at his heels.

As soon as Carl is out the door I call Patrick's office to get hold of him before he calls my mobile. His associate partner, Chloe Sami, answers the call and puts me through. Before I can speak, Patrick says, "I've booked the conference for tomorrow."

"I've read through the brief. No more papers from the prosecution yet?" My voice is cool. I can always talk to Patrick about work.

"No. But she needs to meet you, start building confidence in her team."

"Okay."

"I think you're perfect for this," he continues. "You'll make the jury see it from her point of view — they'll relate entirely to you. And it's complicated, legally speaking. You're very strong at that." Patrick sounds professional. It's an objective assessment, not a compliment, but a small shiver of pleasure runs through me nonetheless. "Right, the conference is at two o'clock tomorrow," he continues. "I'll meet you at Marylebone station at half twelve. Madeleine is living at her sister's in Beaconsfield."

"I wish you'd told me you were instructing me in this case when I saw you on Friday."

"I thought it would be a nice surprise for you. Anyway, I've got to go now," he says.

"Hang on, Patrick. Just to say, don't call me on my mobile today? Or message? I don't have it with me."

"We've just spoken. Why would I need to be in touch?" He hangs up. His words have a sting but I don't want to call back. I put it out of my mind and get to work.

The rest of Monday passes, the remnants of the hangover too and with it the fear. Mostly. There's still a tender spot behind my right eye, a small reminder of the pain I've caused to myself and to Carl and Tilly. *Never again,* I think, hoping the words aren't as hollow as they sound. I read the papers, highlighting and noting. He gives me back my phone at the end of the day, good as new.

On Tuesday morning, I emerge booted and suited, with Matilda dancing along beside me. As I walk her into school, a group of mothers form a huddle against me, lithe in their gym clothes. I shake my head, trying to throw off the paranoia. I smile at one, wave at the others, say hello to a couple of fathers who walk past. Eventually the women smile back before talking to each other again, heads close together. *Yes, her, for once. Amazing, isn't it, that she's made the effort. It's always that poor husband of hers.* I shake my head again. That's not what they're saying to each other. Why would it be? Matilda pulls my hand and we walk down the stairs into her classroom.

"Bye, darling. Have a good day." I lean down and hug her.

"Are you going to pick me up?"

"It'll be Daddy today. I've got a meeting."

"Okay. Bye!"

She hangs her coat up on the peg and walks away towards a clutch of her friends. I stand and stare after her for a moment. They smile at Matilda and move over to make space for her in their circle. I wave goodbye and she waves back before I walk swiftly out and through the playground, head down.

"Matilda's really happy, Alison, that's what matters." That's what Carl says to me every time I worry about the other parents. Followed by "They're always lovely to me."

I bet they are — not that I ever say that — and finally, "You just need to make more effort, that's all." Those were his words this morning, as he checked Matilda's schoolbag and signed her reading book. I didn't argue — he's probably right. "I'll pick her up today. My last client is at two," he finished. At least that's one less thing to worry about.

I make it just in time for the bus and sit down in a seat hemmed in by strollers. My black case is right by my leg, containing the brief — photographs and pages of evidence summing up a brutality which it'll be my job in the next months to understand more fully than the workings of anything else: my mind, my marriage, or my failings as a mother. I can't wait.

Once I arrive at chambers, I say hello to the clerks and unpack my wheelie bag, putting the brief on my desk. I sit down and look unseeing out the window. Fifteen years of practice building up to this, my first murder. I started with the usual: drunk drivers, shoplifting smack heads, recidivist robbers in the hell that was Balham Youth Court, pathetic pedophiles wringing their sweaty hands over indecent images of children, a rake's progress of crime from the hapless via the helpless to those who could never be helped, whom even I occasionally agreed might be better locked up and the key thrown away for good. All so much in common, abusive childhoods leading to abuse of alcohol and drugs, deprivation and a desperation that sometimes externalized itself in raging demands: *I want that phone, no, give me that fucking phone or I'll stab you/ punch you/drop you off this railway bridge in the path of an oncoming train.*

That last robbery trial, some ten years ago, was one of my favorites. It was a multi-handed trial in Nottingham where all the defendants blamed each other for making the threats and ended up with five years' custody apiece. It was a good team of lawyers, though, and we drank the pub nearest to the Travelodge dry every night.

So. Madeleine Smith. I leaf through the file until I find the newspaper cuttings reporting on the case, with a passing nod to the restrictions required of a *sub judice* hearing. The main report shows a picture of Madeleine being shouldered by two police officers, her hands cuffed in front of her. She is a thin blond woman with a tired expression.

Madeleine Smith, 44, was arrested by police following the discovery of the body of her husband, Edwin, stabbed to death in their bed. He was a senior partner at the American asset management company Athena Holdings. Police were alerted after a cleaner entered the £3.5 million property in Clapham, London, and raised the alarm. According to sources the suspect was found sitting on the floor beside her husband's body, and submitted quietly to arrest. Neighbors expressed astonishment at the events that have occurred: "She was lovely and always volunteered to help with the street party that we have every year. I just can't believe it," said one source, who asked not to be named.

I pause, make myself a coffee from the espresso machine that I bought Carl for Christmas last year. He's never used it, telling me how wasteful the capsules are.

These are the facts of the prosecution case as provided in their brief summary: On Monday, 19 September, Edwin Smith is found dead in his bed by his cleaner; his wife, Madeleine, is sitting on the floor beside him. He has been dead for approximately twelve hours, and the cause of death is loss of blood from the fifteen stab wounds found on his neck and torso. It appears that he has been stabbed in his sleep, as there are no signs of defensive injuries on the body, nothing to show that he tried to fight back or stop the attack. A twelve-inch chef's knife is found on the bed next to his body, the blade of which is consistent with the injuries noted before. Blood loss is extensive — it has soaked through the bed and the floorboards, leaking down through the ceiling of the living room below. Madeleine's clothes are also covered in blood.

The police and an ambulance arrive immediately, though the victim is past all medical treatment. Madeleine submits calmly to arrest. She makes no comment at that time or at any subsequent time. She is initially remanded into custody at Downview Prison, but following a successful bail application made two weeks ago is now living under strict restrictions in her sister's house in Beaconsfield.

By the looks of it, I can expect statements from the cleaner, the police and ambulance staff, a pathologist, and a neighbor who says he heard shouts and screams coming from the Smiths' house on the night it's presumed Edwin Smith died. No doubt the prosecution will get round to providing them at some point soon. I think back to what I was doing that Sunday night three weeks ago.

We'd gotten back from a partially successful weekend away to the seaside — Matilda had fun on the beach, at least, though Carl and I squabbled and slept, untouching, in a bed more designed for a dirty weekend than dirty looks over broken promises. It's easier not to remember it, and I drag my thoughts back to the case.

Patrick has included a note about Madeleine's movements that weekend. She says that their fourteen-year-old son, James, was home for the weekend from boarding school, and that she and Edwin had dropped him off at London Bridge to get the train back to school in time for Sunday-evening chapel. His name is also included in the list of prosecution witnesses, although they have yet to serve his statement.

Madeleine has given a brief statement to her solicitors about her background. She's originally from Surrey, traveled extensively through her childhood with her diplomat family. She's a trained accountant but hasn't worked for years. She became a mother at the age of thirty. She and Edwin had been together for nearly twenty years, were happy, and she has no comment to make about the night in question. No comment at all.

When I arrive at the station, I see Patrick

before he sees me. He's leaning against the wall, looking at his phone, and at the sight of him something jolts in my chest and I stumble, my bag catching on my ankle. He looks up and smiles, a proper smile that reaches his eyes, and I laugh, so relieved to see someone who looks pleased to see me that I forget for a moment that I've finished with him. He touches my cheek when I reach him and I'm ready to catch him up on my thoughts about the case, but then his phone rings and he turns away from me to take the call. We don't talk much on the train on the way to meet Madeleine, though every now and again he looks up between emails and pats my leg. I force myself to shift away from him, reminding myself firmly that it's over between us and that while he might be being lovely now, he wasn't on Friday and so many other times besides. I know he's no good.

Beaconsfield is a pretty commuter town, dotted with boutiques and gastropubs. We take a taxi from the station to the house where our client is staying and wait at the closed electric gates to the property. The house is big, dwarfing its garden, and surrounded by equally big houses, all recently built and shiny.

A woman sticks her head out the door of

the house and looks at us for a moment. Apparently reassured by what she sees, she retreats inside and the gates open slowly. We walk through and crunch over gravel to the front door. It opens abruptly. Patrick moves forward and shakes the woman's hand.

"Good to see you again, Francine. Alison, this is Francine, Madeleine's sister," he says. He stands to one side and I shake hands with her, her fingers tight and bony on mine. She gestures us into the house to meet Madeleine, who is sitting in the living room, her legs tucked up under her on a sofa. She stands to greet us.

She's a thin woman, tall, her hair thick and smooth but with highlights outgrown by an inch or so. Tendons are prominent on her neck and a pulse beating blue on her temple. Francine is thin, too, though sleeker than Madeleine, a gloss to her hair and skin. She's tense, shifting from foot to foot, her fingers pulling at the edges of her cardigan. Looking up at them I feel smaller and stockier than usual, a workhorse to their thoroughbred elegance. They're both dressed in shades of beige, taupe trousers and smooth oatmeal knitwear, clearly cashmere. Madeleine is subtly jeweled, diamonds at her ears and encircling her fingers, an encrusted eternity ring hanging loosely on the fourth finger of her left hand. I twist the white gold bands round my ring finger, hiding the small solitaire diamond on my engagement ring on the inside so that it digs into my hand.

"I don't want to think about the prison. It was a nightmare." Madeleine picks at the skin around her nails.

"We got you out as soon as we could." Patrick's voice is gentle. There is a fragility to Madeleine that demands soft voices and careful language. It's not a tone I've heard from him before.

"Can I offer anyone a cup of tea?" Francine says.

I nod. "Milk, no sugar. Thank you." The task might calm her down, smooth the tension that prickles around her, so we can begin to draw out Madeleine.

As Francine bustles out of the room, Madeleine uncurls her legs a little.

"There was so much shouting. I tried to sleep, but I don't know how anyone could sleep through all that . . . It was hell. I could sleep at the police station, but not there. Five nights of it . . ."

She pauses and smiles up at her sister, who has returned with mugs of tea on a tray laden with milk, sugar, and three different kinds of cookies.

"Can I get you anything else?" Francine asks.

"No, this is great," I reply. We all chime in with thanks.

"I'm fine, Francine. Why don't you leave us alone to have a chat?" Madeleine smiles at her sister and Francine finally leaves, closing the door behind her.

"Let's make a start." Patrick pushes the tea tray to one side and deposits the files from his bag onto the coffee table. I reach into my bag and pull out my brief and my notebook. "Let me introduce you properly to Alison Wood, who will be representing you in this case."

I nod at Madeleine.

"Alison has been practicing for over fifteen years. She's done a lot of complicated cases, both at the Crown Court and in the Appeal Court, too." Patrick gestures at me as he speaks. It doesn't feel like me he's describing. "She's going to be great at working out what's best for your case. We'll make sure we look after you."

Madeleine looks at her hands. "I don't think there's anything to be done, though. I did it, and that's all there is to it."

"Hold your horses. We don't need to have that kind of conversation yet, let's just go through the preliminaries first." At last he sounds like the Patrick I know, abrupt, abrasive in tone. And I'm glad he's stopped her — there's nothing worse than a client who talks too soon about the offense. They need to wait for us to ask the right questions. "Alison, why don't you talk Madeleine through what's going to happen next."

"Right. Okay, Madeleine, this is where we are now. The case has been transferred from the magistrates' court to the Old Bailey, and the next court appearance will be the plea and trial preparation hearing, the PTPH. That's when you'll enter a plea to the indictment."

"That's not for a few weeks, though. Is it?"

"No, not until mid-November. Four weeks away. We've got very little by way of evidence from the prosecution at the moment, but they'll serve more soon. I hope." I watch Madeleine as I speak but she isn't making eye contact with me, instead still looking down at her hands. Her fingernails are bitten to the quick, the only crack in her perfectly groomed facade. She nods once and I continue.

"We need to go through all the evidence before that hearing. As I said, you will need to enter a plea at that stage, and if it's not guilty, then a date will be set for the trial."

"And if it's guilty?"

"Then the matter will be adjourned immediately for sentence."

"So that's what I want to do." She looks up at this point, meets and holds my gaze. She looks determined, unblinking. Too much so. I wonder what she's trying to hide.

"Madeleine, I would strongly advise you to wait until we have gone through all the evidence before you make any decision as to the next step to take. At this stage holding a firm view is not necessarily the right way to go."

She has a stubborn set to her jaw but at least she's listening. "I know what I did."

"Well, I don't. And there are legal aspects of this to consider too. So please, can we take it a step at a time?" Out of the corner of my eye, I see Patrick nodding his agreement.

Madeleine gets to her feet and paces to the window, paces back again. For one moment I think she's going to sit down next to me on the overstuffed leather sofa, but she turns away at the last second and walks again to the window. "You shouldn't have bothered getting me bail. I should be locked up."

Patrick pauses for a moment before replying. "You don't have any previous convictions. You've never been in any trouble before. The court accepted that there's no one who is at risk from you. And it's much better from the point of view of preparing your defense."

Madeleine sighs but doesn't argue. She moves back to the sofa and sits down.

I clear my throat. "Every conversation that you have with us, your lawyers, is privileged. That means that it's entirely confidential, and no one can make us tell them what you've said. There are some difficulties, though, if you tell us something in conference, and then want to say something different in front of the court during the trial. We can't lie about what you've said. It causes us professional embarrassment, which could mean that we can't continue to represent you. Does that make sense?"

"Yes, it does," Madeleine says.

I take up my pen and notebook. "So could you tell me what happened that weekend? Let's start with the Saturday."

"James was home for the weekend. I made us cheese on toast and some salad for lunch, and we went out for a meal that night, to a steak restaurant on Clapham Common. James went on to a party in Balham thrown by a school friend, and Edwin and I took a taxi home." She stops to draw breath. I note down the last bit, nod at her to continue.

"We watched a film and then we went to bed."

"What film?" I ask.

"Does it matter?" She shrugs. "*Goodfellas.* Edwin loves those sorts of film."

Then her head jerks as she realizes what she's said. "Loved." She puts her head in her hands for a moment, breathes in, out. "We went to bed after it finished. James came in around midnight, I think. I didn't hear him come in, though — I was exhausted."

I open my mouth to comment on a child his age being allowed to wander round London on his own at midnight, and stop myself. For all I know it's perfectly normal. "Does he go to many late parties?"

"When they happen. It's hard to say. Sometimes he does, sometimes he doesn't. I find it hard to keep track."

I think about Matilda. No chance will I let her go to parties on her own like that in the future. No chance at all.

Madeleine continues. "We got up late on Sunday. I made roast chicken. Then we took James to London Bridge and dropped him off. After we came home, Edwin said he wanted to talk to me. He told me he was leaving me."

My hand swerves across the page. This isn't what I'd expected. I open my mouth to ask a question but she keeps on talking.

"I drank most of a bottle of gin and then I blacked out. I came to when our cleaner started screaming. When I looked up I saw Edwin, dead, and the knife at my feet." Her voice is so quiet now I can barely hear it. "I didn't mean to do it. I don't remember doing it. I'm sorry . . ."

Madeleine is pale but as she reaches the end there's a dull flush on her cheeks.

"Tell me a bit about James," I say. Softly, softly — I figure this will be an easier way in before I address her relationship with Edwin.

Her flush subsides and her face relaxes. "What do you want to know?"

"What he's like? How does he like school, for example? How long has he been boarding?"

"This is his second year. He went there just before he turned thirteen. He says he loves it."

"Do you find it hard, having him away?"

"It was to start with. But you get used to it. It would be such a waste of his time, having to travel to and from school every day.

He'd have been coming home so late, you know. He does so much sport . . . It wasn't that I didn't want him around. Edwin thought . . ." Madeleine's voice trails off.

"Edwin thought what?" I speak quietly, trying not to scare her off.

"Edwin thought it would be very good for him, that he'd learn to stand on his own feet. And Edwin thought that maybe I did too much for James and that he needed to learn how to look after himself a bit more."

"Did you agree with Edwin?"

Madeleine pulls her shoulders back at the question, her chin jutting forward. "Of course I agreed with him. He was quite right. He knows about boys . . . Knew."

"Okay. You said James loves it. What is it he particularly enjoys?"

"Well, the sport, definitely. And there's a lot of routine. James likes routine. He was always happiest when we were all in order, when I was being calm and dinner was ready in time, that kind of thing."

I take a note. "Were there times you weren't calm?"

"No one's calm all the time. And things could get a bit on top of me . . ." Madeleine's hands claw tightly at each other. "That was another reason why Edwin thought it was better for James to board. It would give me more time to get everything done, so that we could really enjoy it when we were all together."

I note down her answer. "How did you feel about that?"

"Again, Edwin was probably right. I'm always so busy — it's really hard to keep everything together." Her voice is shaky.

"What are you busy at? What do you do?" I keep my voice neutral.

"Between the gym and Pilates and all the fundraising for the gallery . . . I don't want to let myself go. Edwin wouldn't . . ." Again her voice trails off.

I pull at the waistband of my skirt, uncomfortably aware of the way it's digging into my side. Not enough time for Pilates, that's clearly the problem with my own marriage.

I read through my notes again. Time to go in harder. "Madeleine, what can you tell me about your relationship with Edwin prior to the weekend of his death?"

"What about our relationship?"

"How you got on with each other. Did you spend a lot of time with each other? Did he travel a lot? That kind of thing."

"Of course he traveled. He was in New York every week."

"Every week? That seems a lot," I said.

"Maybe you don't know many people in

the City? It's perfectly normal for that kind of job." She's drawn herself up to her full height, her voice cold.

I pull the collar closer on my Hobbs suit against the chill. It might not be couture but at least I paid for it myself. It's the first flash of steel I've seen from Madeleine, and an image comes into my mind of her standing, knife in hand, over the lifeless body of her husband. Then she sighs and slumps her shoulders and the image leaves me.

"What did you do when he was away?" I ask.

"The same. I've already told you. I've been arranging a dinner for the gallery — it's been a lot of work," Madeleine replies.

"Which gallery?"

"The Fitzherbert in Chelsea. They don't get nearly so much funding from the government now so they really rely on private donors. It's very important work." Madeleine was flushed again.

"Not interested in people charities then?" I say, unable to resist.

Patrick interrupts again. "I'm not sure I see the relevance of this."

I smile at him, at Madeleine. "Just trying to get a full picture, that's all. Madeleine, prior to this weekend, would you say that you and Edwin had a good relationship?"

"I thought so. That's why I was so shocked when he said he wanted a divorce." Madeleine looks at her hands again, twisting round and round in her lap.

"Why do you think he did?"

"I just don't know." Her hands go back over her face, her head hunching down between her shoulders. She starts to sob.

I want to ask whether Edwin was having an affair but she keeps weeping, the sobs become louder and more visceral, great tearing sounds from her gut.

"And now he's dead and I'm never going to know if he meant it or if I could have made it all right. It's all my fault it's all my fault it's all . . ."

Even Patrick looks uncomfortable, edging from side to side in his chair. I think he's going to put an arm round her but instead he starts straightening the papers from the file, rearranging Post-it notes and keeping his head firmly down. Madeleine's sister comes rushing in, without knocking.

"You need to leave now. It's too much for her," Francine says.

"We do have a few more questions . . ." I say it as more of a comment than a question, pretty sure that she'll make us leave.

"I don't care. You can ask them another time. She's had enough for now."

I put my notebook back in my handbag and get to my feet. Patrick does the same.

He coughs. "We're going to have to come back soon — next week. It's important for Madeleine's defense that we get the full picture of what happened. And what came before."

"Fine. That's fine. Just not today. This is enough for now. It's going to take me hours to calm her down, and I just don't have time . . ." Francine lays a hand on Madeleine's shoulder and shakes her gently. "Madeleine, shhhh. The children will be back home soon."

Patrick and I leave them to it. We call a minicab from outside the house and travel to the station in silence, catching the London train with only a couple of moments to spare.

5

"I'm going to get a drink. Do you want one? Gin?"

I nod and Patrick walks off to find the buffet car. I feel drained, Madeleine's sobs still ringing in my head. We only spent an hour and a half with her but it feels like much longer. Tilly will be finishing school now, running out to greet Carl, who'll be standing chatting to the other parents. Maybe they'll go to a café for hot chocolate. Or maybe one of her friends will suggest a play date and Carl will take her there and sit and drink tea with the mum while the girls play dress-up. I can almost smell Matilda's hair for a moment, silky against my face, her head warm against mine. My heart lurches with a jolt of fear as she disappears from me, but Patrick returns with the gins and I take a long drink, exorcising my dread with spirits. It's been a difficult afternoon, that's all. Patrick leans forward, pushes his hand hard up between my legs and whispers into my ear. "There's a toilet just there. No one else is in this carriage."

I know I should argue, remind him that I've finished the relationship. I don't. I look at him for a moment, the heat from his hand insistent in me. Pouring the rest of my drink into my mouth, I swallow fast and follow him, grabbing my handbag at the last minute.

He locks the toilet door and turns to me. I hold my breath, waiting for him to kiss me, pull my face in towards his, maybe touch my cheek with some tenderness like he did earlier today. My nerves are jangling, strung tense by Madeleine's emotion, but this'll be the way to calm down. We face each other for a moment, eyes locked, and this — yes — *this* is the moment that he kisses me, and pushes his hand down past my tight waistband into my underwear and the day unwinds . . .

I sigh and he pushes me gently down to my knees and unzips his fly. Nothing like a quid pro quo. Trying to avoid a puddle of piss, I shift on my knees over towards him and take hold of him, balancing my other hand against the sink unit beside me on which he's leaning. He grasps my head and pulls me closer, and I shut my eyes.

After Patrick finishes, I swallow and then rinse my mouth with water, spitting it out against the mirror. I'm tired, and I can see my mascara is blurred in the corners of my eyes and any lipstick long smeared off. My sense of tired disquiet has come back as the afterglow fades. I see this dissatisfaction mirrored in the face of the woman waiting outside the train loo, toddler in hand, tutting quietly as Patrick and I return past her to our seats. I forget my handbag in the rush of it all and she calls to me, holding it out with a stiff arm as if to minimize any potential contact between us.

While I retrieve my bag, head hung so as not to catch the woman's eye, Patrick sits back down and goes straight on to his BlackBerry, each key click furthering the distance between us. I look out the window, trying to ignore the scent of stale urine that's emanating from something near me. I was sure I'd avoided the piss on the floor. Finally I pick up my bag, sniff one corner. Then I touch a finger to it, pull it away. It's damp. I've protected my knees, but not the Mulberry bag I bought myself with the fees from my first big trial. Patrick sees what I'm doing and grimaces in disgust before returning to his emails.

My phone rings as I transfer the final

items from the stained handbag to the wheelie bag. My heart sinks the moment I see the name of Matilda's school appear on the screen, and I straighten my shoulders before answering, pulling myself away mentally from Patrick to the responsibilities of home. The teacher barely waits for my hello before telling me that I'm late to pick up Matilda.

"Carl was collecting her today. That was the arrangement." I try to keep calm, to emulate the businesslike tone of the teacher on the other end.

"Not according to him. He thought you were picking Matilda up."

"He told me his last client was at two." Closer to panic.

"To be honest, it doesn't matter who told who what. It's five past four and Matilda still hasn't been collected. We can put her into late club until quarter to five, but we need to know what arrangements are going to be made to collect her."

I look out the train window. We're approaching Marylebone, at least, but I still have to make my way from the station all the way up to Highgate.

"Can't you get hold of my husband?"

"His phone is switched off."

"I'll be there as fast as I can. I'm on a

train right now."

"We'll see you at four forty-five." Not a question, a statement as the call ends.

My heart rate's beginning to rise, a tightening of panic in my throat. Poor Tilly, left waiting like this. I was sure . . . But there's no point, I just have to get there. I pull a mirror out of my handbag and check my face, ensuring that no sign of Patrick still adheres.

Patrick eventually looks up from his screen. "What's happened?"

"I was sure Matilda was being picked up. She hasn't been, though. And I'm going to be late."

"Ah, well, I'm sure they'll get over it." He looks back down, clearly without any interest in the subject. I'm about to say more about it but bite my tongue — what's the point? He suddenly glances up again.

"Does that mean that we can't have a proper discussion of the case when we get back?"

"Well, yes, I'm afraid it does. I have to go and pick her up."

"Isn't there anybody else?" He sounds impatient.

"No, there isn't. They can't get hold of her dad so it's up to me."

"Have you tried calling him?" Patrick is

completely engaged for the first time since we've sat back down.

I shake my head, call Carl's number. It goes straight to voicemail.

"It's off. The school said that too. There's no point — he never answers when he's with a client." I return to salvaging what I can from the piss-stained bag.

"We need to discuss the case. That's more important than babysitting. He should be doing it. You need to chase him. Call him again."

I dial Carl for a second time. The call goes straight to voicemail. "I told you. And it's not babysitting, Patrick. It's looking after my daughter. I have to collect her." I finish with the handbag, roll it up, and push it into the overhead rack. If someone else wants it, they're welcome to it. The train approaches the station and I pull on my coat, walking over to the door in preparation for our arrival at Paddington. "I'll call you later."

He doesn't argue further. His face twists and he puts his hand out, touches mine. I pull my hand away, now too preoccupied with Matilda to welcome his touch.

"We'll have to impose a financial penalty. It's going to be a twenty-pound fine." The teacher — Mrs. Adams, I'm almost sure her name is Mrs. Adams — writes in a notebook and shuts it sharply, her red-painted nails clicking against the hard cover. I bite my lip, hyperconscious that if I hadn't been trying so hard to keep my name in Patrick's little black book maybe my name wouldn't now be included in this one.

"I'm sorry. I had an important meeting out of town, and I was sure my husband was going to make it in time," I apologize.

"He told us yesterday that you would be collecting her. Matilda was very excited that you were going to be in school to pick her up." She doesn't say "for once." She doesn't have to. I try to ignore it.

"I must have got confused about arrangements. I'm sorry. Anyway, I'm here now. It's just one of those things. Come on, Matilda, let's go home." I reach over to take her school bag from her.

"I'll need the twenty pounds now, please." The teacher moves so that she's standing between Matilda and me, a solid barrier of dun-colored knitwear planting itself firmly in my daughter's path. I desperately hope a more personal appeal will work.

"Mrs. Adams, I really am sorry about the delay. I'm afraid I don't have twenty pounds on me. I used my last cash getting a taxi up here from the station. You said I needed to be here and I made it just in time. We'll bring it in tomorrow morning. I'd really appreciate that, Mrs. —"

"It's Ms. Not Mrs." The interruption is abrupt.

"Ms. Adams, then. Sorry. Tomorrow. Come on, Matilda." I move sideways and hold my hand out to her. The barrier moves again, surprisingly nimbly for something of that breadth.

"Anderson. My name is Anderson. I am responsible for after-school care and for enforcing punctuality. The fine will be thirty pounds if you pay it tomorrow." Her chin is up, her color raised. It looks as if this is the most fun she's had all day.

I look at my watch. This exchange has taken ten minutes — will I be charged for that too? "I will bring in twenty pounds tomorrow, first thing. In cash. In an envelope. With your name on it, Ms. Anderson. And I apologize for any inconvenience that has been caused. But now I am going to take my daughter home."

I move fast and pull Matilda out from the gap between Ms. Anderson and the wall. She scoots through, head down, just as the teacher shunts sideways to try to stop her. I stand and look at the woman for a moment, and she meets my gaze straight on before I pull Matilda round and wheel her and my trolley bag out of the building. Ms. Anderson is muttering something about tomorrow under her breath but I've had enough. I walk as fast as I can out of the school building and through the gates before the woman is able to throw a force field out and bounce me back again into her hostile glare, only stopping when we've gotten well round the corner.

I pull Matilda in close and hug her. "Sorry, darling. I thought we'd never get out of there."

"She was so cross," Matilda says into my shoulder, part thrilled, part horrified.

"I know, I'm so sorry. Let's go and get some sweets. We need something for the shock." Matilda laughs and we go into the next shop we see and I buy her two packs of Millions and a Chupa Chups.

We walk slowly down the hill towards Archway, the skyline of London blurring before me, the Shard sharp through a haze that I don't want to acknowledge is tears. At least Matilda's happy, eating her sweets. I wipe my eyes with my sleeve. I've had enough of maneuvering the wheelie bag and I fight the urge to throw it into the nearest bin, stuff it in and push it down between burger wrappers and bags of dog shit until I can't see it anymore, my latter-day ball and chain, the mark of every barrister trailing round the criminal courts of the southeast. I brush my sleeve once more across my face, tears finally subsiding.

"I'll make sure I don't do it again," I say, kneeling down beside her.

Matilda thinks about it for a minute and smiles. "You didn't do it on purpose though. So that's okay."

I smile back and she hugs me. I stand up and we walk the rest of the way without speaking, the squeak of the wheels of my bag and Matilda's crunching the soundtrack to the journey.

"I can't even get angry with you anymore. This has to stop. You have to be more organized." Carl doesn't raise his voice. He doesn't have to.

"I must have got confused. I thought you said . . ."

"You know I always have a client late on Tuesdays." He shakes his head, turns back to the tomato sauce on the stove.

"I must have got it wrong." There isn't anything else I could say.

"Yes, you must have done. And then you go and fill her up with sweets. She'll never eat supper now."

I wait to see if Carl has anything else to say, but he just pours water from the boiling kettle into a saucepan and adds two handfuls of pasta. As he starts to grate Parmesan I back quietly out of the kitchen. The silence lies heavier on me than any reproach. I have to do better.

6

Two weeks later and we're well into October and a trial at Basildon Crown Court in which I'm defending a midranking footballer on charges of unlawful sexual activity with a child. It's fair to say that the trial has not been an unmitigated success, his demeanor in the dock poor, and even as his representative, I can't feel sorry that he's been convicted. After he's sentenced to five years I go down to see him in the cells.

As I wait at the custody suite door, I check my phone. Spam, spam, various court developments, Patrick. *Patrick.* I open the email fast, heart pounding. I've only seen him once in the last week, late on the Thursday afternoon in his flat. He'd texted to see if I was free and asked me round. The light was falling as I arrived and I watched it turn dark outside the slatted blinds of his bedroom, lying quietly beside him as Bob Dylan told me not to think twice. And it was all right, close, together.

Next conference booked with Madeleine Smith on Wednesday, meeting 2 discuss after.

Sort out ur childcare.

I grimace at my phone. It's as if that afternoon never happened, as we go back into our usual sniping. He breathed into my hair, our heartbeats slowing together until they were in time. We kissed as we both came. An afternoon in a million, he'd called it. Perfection. I didn't even want to exhale in case I blew it all away. But as I dressed to go he turned away, looking at his phone, and barely lifted his head to say goodbye though I tried to kiss him.

"Miss. Miss! Who are you looking for?" A muffled shout from the entry phone to the custody suite brings me back to now.

"Peter Royle."

"Right."

The meeting is as unpleasant as I knew it would be, Royle furious about his five-year sentence, cigarette sticking out of his mouth. Some sporting types keep fit in jail but I'll guess not Royle, he's too much of a spoiled brat for that. Adulated on the pitch as the star striker for Basildon United and admired off pitch on the odd occasions he deigned to turn up to work as a car mechanic, he's singularly ill-equipped to deal with the reality that just because a fifteen-year-old girl is up for it doesn't mean it's legal to do anything with her, let alone get off with her repeatedly and push his luck towards a shag, until after one particularly persistent attempt at getting her to give him a blowjob she told her mum, who reported him to the police. I tell him that, on the face of it, there are limited if any grounds for appeal against either his conviction or his sentence but that I will go through it all thoroughly and advise soon. He makes no move to take my hand when I try to shake his, and all in all I'm glad to get on the train back to London.

It shunts along through the east of the city, industrial sites giving way to rows of identical houses, the gardens running down onto the tracks. The banks of the railway line are littered with detritus; empty cans, discarded clothing, old plastic bags like witches' knickers in the stunted trees. I wonder if anyone ever climbs over the fences to fuck on the grass as the trains pass, escaping their daily existence for a moment of quick ecstasy to the rhythm of the

22:08 from Basildon to Fenchurch Street station. That's one from the Monopoly board, I remember. At least I've gotten out of jail free. No such luck for Peter Royle. I search myself for any feeling of compassion for him but no, not a thing. He's exactly where he deserves to be and I hope it brings some comfort to his victim and her family.

It'll be good to get back to Madeleine's case again. I close my eyes and lean back against the scratchy upholstery of the train seat. Thoughts of Patrick dance through my mind, Carl's face glowering behind, their images swirling together as I fall into a fitful sleep, waking with a jolt as we arrive at Fenchurch Street.

Patrick and I meet at Marylebone two days later and take the train up together. He isn't in a talkative mood and after a couple of attempts to get conversation off the ground, I leave him alone.

"We need to find out more about the relationship with the husband," he says as we wait for the heavy iron gates to swing open.

"The journalists have given up now," Francine says as she lets us in through the front door. "I thought they'd never give up, but then she never leaves the house, so they couldn't get anything." She gestures at Madeleine, who stands awkwardly in the doorway between the hall and the kitchen. "I'll leave you to it. But don't go upsetting her like last time. She isn't strong."

That I agree with. Francine a vibrant original and Madeleine a pale, washed-out copy. If she shrinks any more she'll disappear, washed out from view the way her husband's blood will now be scrubbed from their bedroom carpet.

We sit in Francine's kitchen, a room far tidier than my kitchen ever is, jars and tea towels coordinated in a muted *eau de Nil.* Madeleine's hair is better groomed than the last time we met, the roots now disguised with honey and caramel streaks of blond. I push my hair back from my face, shoving it behind my ears. Patrick sits at the end of the table, blue notebooks open in front of both of us.

"The plea and trial preparation hearing will be happening in a month," I say. "Normally you would be expected to put in your plea, but in this case —"

"I want to plead guilty." Madeleine's face is contorted as she interrupts me, the words forced out but so quietly I have to strain to hear her. "I just want this over and done with."

"I take your point, Madeleine, but we need to make sure we've covered all of the options first." My voice sounds raucous compared to her whisper.

"There are two options, guilty or not guilty, and I'm going to plead guilty. I did it, I stabbed him, and that's all there is to it." The volume of her voice rises and she thumps her hand on the table.

"There is a third option at this stage, which is not to enter a plea at all. There are a lot of aspects to this that I think we need to explore. And we only have a prosecution case summary at the moment. You could lose some of your discount —"

"What does that mean?" Madeleine looks at me intently.

"You get a shorter custodial sentence if you plead guilty at the first opportunity, but in this case, I'd advise patience until we have more information," I say.

"I'm going to get life anyway. It doesn't matter."

"It does matter — there are different levels of life imprisonment. And even if you plead guilty, we will need all the information we can gather in order to mitigate properly. I think that you should enter no plea at the

PTPH."

"The what?" she asks.

"The hearing I mentioned, the plea and trial preparation hearing. I suggest you make no indication of plea, and then we will get more of the prosecution papers, the witness statements, the forensic evidence. We can also explore the background to all of this more with you."

Madeleine nods. "I suppose that makes sense. I still think I'll have to plead guilty in the end."

"Let's see how we go. Now, we started talking about your relationship with Edwin last time." I try to sound calm, not startle her. "It's important that we understand the dynamics between the two of you before we can advise further."

"What does it matter now? He's dead and I killed him." She's speaking through her hands. Francine opens the door of the kitchen and walks in to stand beside Madeleine. She looks over at me as if to ask if she can stay and I nod. Perhaps her presence will help to calm Madeleine.

"It's important to get a clear picture," I continue. "It's my job to defend you, to make sure that you're given the best advice possible. I can only do that if you tell me everything."

Madeleine takes a deep, shuddering breath and straightens up. Francine sits beside her, facing me, and puts her hand on Madeleine's arm.

"Would you like Francine to stay with you while we talk?"

Madeleine shakes her head, pauses, then nods.

"You told us before that the last thing you remember in conversation with your husband was that he told you he wanted to leave you. Is that right?"

Another nod.

"And the impression I got from what you said was that this had come out of the blue for you?"

"Yes. I knew we had ups and downs, but I never thought we'd split up. I never thought he'd let me go." Madeleine has stopped crying now, but still speaks very quietly.

"Perhaps we should go back a bit, to the beginning of your relationship. Where did you meet him?"

Madeleine smiles, looking off over my shoulder into a distance farther than I can reach. "He was so beautiful. I was too, if you can believe that. They called us the golden couple. Everyone wanted to be friends with us, to see if some of the magic would rub off. That's what they said, anyway. Remember that, Francine? Those first few years?"

Francine nods. "Yes, of course. You were both so happy." Her tone is anything but happy. I look at her but her expression is neutral, not showing any trace of the bitterness that's crept into her voice.

"Yes, so happy. We met at college. I was the year above him, actually, but it didn't matter. I was so pleased to meet someone like him. It happened like a flash, the first day he walked into the bar. We just connected. I was living in a shared flat off campus and he moved in within days and after that we were inseparable."

"It sounds very romantic." I scribble away in my notebook. Did anyone ever describe Carl and me as a golden couple? I don't think so. But we were happy, once. In our twenties, before it all became so complicated, when weekends could be spent in bed and no one turned their nose up at cheap wine, just happy that there was booze to be drunk. We met in bars round Waterloo after work, a Cuban the favorite for a long while until we visited Havana and saw the real deal. That was the holiday we decided to fuck every day until the night we fell asleep on the beach and I was so eaten by mosquitoes that every touch was painful and we had to give up. Still, we laughed. We can't even smile at each other now.

"He couldn't stop doing things for me. He bought me presents, told me he loved me all the time. We moved into a little flat, just him and me. That was all we needed. It was a wonderful time." Madeleine is still smiling.

"You changed course, though. Remember?" Francine interrupts. Madeleine makes a face, twisting her mouth in an emotion that's hard to read.

"Yes, well, I should never have been doing law. It was all too much for me. I didn't want to spend all my time in the library."

"So what did you change to?" I can see her point. I remember the lawyers at college, strange mole-like creatures who emerged blinking each morning from spending all night poring over volumes of case reports. I did a law conversion course after a history degree — I argued that it gave me depth but secretly worried that other people understood the subject far better than I did.

"I switched over to an accountancy course. Still a lot of work, but less library-based. And Edwin thought it would be more useful. A good skill to have."

"As opposed to law?" I couldn't help sounding surprised.

"Well, he didn't think I had what it took to be a good lawyer. Too quiet, he said. And I don't like confrontation. Never have."

"Did you enjoy accountancy?"

"It was okay. I did have to work but it was better. I was at home more. We spent all our time with each other when he wasn't working."

"What subject did he do?"

"Economics. He was always determined to get a job in finance. Most of us didn't have much of an idea about the future but Edwin was very clear. It was one of the most attractive things about him." Madeleine is smiling again. I look over at Francine but her face is blank.

"How did you get on with him, Francine?" She looks taken aback by my question and pauses for a moment before replying.

"Fine. It was fine. My husband and I were living in Singapore at that stage, so we didn't see that much of them. Maddie wrote, of course, and later there were emails. She sent pictures. Lots of pictures. We got to know him like that. And we got to see how well they were doing." I take another note.

"Do you still have those photos?"

"I do." Francine sounds surprised by the question.

"Do you think we could have a look at them?" I said.

"What do they have to do with anything?" Madeleine says, her voice impatient. I turn to her.

"It might help me to get an idea about the two of you, when you were younger. When did you get married?"

"Nineteen years ago. It would have been twenty years ago this year." Suddenly Madeleine looks distressed, the reality of her situation smashing into the bubble of memory in which she's temporarily been encased. She lowers her head. I write some notes, give her a moment before continuing.

"You were married for some years before you had your son?"

"Yes. I wanted to have children immediately and we tried but it didn't work out for a couple of years. Then Edwin got on board and I had James. I was so happy."

"What do you mean, Edwin got on board?"

"He really hadn't thought it was a sensible thing to do. He had his career to think about and he wanted me to work for a while too. But he didn't want to have a row. He knew I wouldn't agree to taking the pill, because I was being so bloody-minded, so he dealt with it himself." Her tone is almost sing-song. Francine is looking uncomfortable, shifting in her chair, her lips compressed.

"How did he deal with it himself, Madeleine? What did he do?"

"He got hold of the pill from a doctor friend of his. He'd bring me up a cup of tea every morning, and mix it up in there. I've always had a sweet tooth, I like a bit of sugar in my tea, and so I never noticed any difference in the taste. It was absolutely for the best, though. It would have been awful to have had a baby earlier and spoiled everything."

I gape at her. "That's administering a noxious substance. It's illegal. A criminal act —"

She interrupts me. "It wasn't like that. It wasn't like that at all. People always make things sound so nasty, but he was just looking out for me. For us. I wasn't making the right decision so he did it for me."

I write a few more notes but can't focus, I'm so shocked. I know what it's like not to get pregnant when you want to, the roller coaster of the hope of trying each month and the pain when each period starts. We had Matilda easily enough, but were never lucky enough to have a second. I've packed it all away but the feelings can leak up sometimes. And to think those feelings in Madeleine were caused simply by this horrendous action of her husband . . . My hand tightens on my pen. Patrick clears his throat. I jump. I almost forgot he was there.

"I think we need to go through the legal defenses to murder, don't you agree, Alison?" His voice is controlled but I can tell by the tension round his mouth that he is as horrified as I am by Madeleine's revelation.

"I just need a minute, I'm going to . . ." Madeleine's sentence trails off and she gets up and leaves the room. Francine half rises to go with her, then sits back down again. She shakes her head.

"I knew things could be bad. I didn't know about this, though. So even then . . ." she mutters, almost to herself.

"Even then what?" I try to keep the urgency out of my voice, sensing an opportunity now that Francine is opening up.

"I thought they were so happy. At the start, I felt so jealous of them. But now . . . I'll try and find those photos for you." Francine's voice keeps disappearing and it looks as if she might cry. I'm about to ask her more when I hear my phone beep and reach into my handbag, an old one I'm using in place of the ruined Mulberry. I look at the phone. It's a message from an undisclosed number:

I know what ur doing u fucking slag

I blink and open it, hoping for more clues as to the sender. Nothing. I don't understand. I look up from my phone to Patrick, back to my phone again. But Madeleine comes back into the room and I refocus. I turn my phone off, hands shaking, heart pounding, and bury it down at the bottom of my bag.

Madeleine's words echo through my mind while the stark letters of the text message dance in front of my eyes. Patrick gestures impatiently for me to start talking again once she settles herself at the table but my words come out in incoherent jumps. Eventually he takes over.

"Right, Madeleine, I just want to talk through the basics of the offense with which you're charged. Essentially, a murder is committed when a person of sound mind and discretion unlawfully kills any human. And what that means is that if you aren't mentally ill, or weren't acting in self-defense or suffering from a loss of control, you're guilty," he paused, "of murder."

She nods. I start to pull myself together.

The legal terms are soothing, calling me back into a world whose rules I understand. Patrick clears his throat and speaks again.

"It's a bit more complicated than that, to be more accurate. There are a number of full defenses, but I don't think in this case they apply, or that the evidence is there to support them. In the absence of any defensive injuries or signs of a fight, I don't think we could possibly argue self-defense." Madeleine makes a noise as if to argue but Patrick holds up his hand and keeps speaking. "So that leaves us with the question of whether you are of sound mind and discretion; that is, not mentally ill." Francine then tries to interrupt but Patrick plows on. "Or it leaves us with what are called the partial defenses that would reduce this to voluntary manslaughter, namely diminished responsibility or loss of control. I think we can assume this wasn't a suicide pact gone wrong." Madeleine opens her mouth but no sound comes out. "Do you agree, Alison?"

"Yes, I agree." My barrister's wig is back on my head. "And I think that what we need to do, Madeleine, is to arrange a meeting with a psychiatrist, because it would be extremely helpful to have an idea of where you are now mentally and, if possible, how you were at the time of the offense. Even if it's just to rule out that line of inquiry."

"I don't want to be mad. I really don't think I'm mad." Her words are quiet but drop into the room like stones into water.

"We're not suggesting that for a moment. We do need to explore every angle, though," I say.

"What about loss of control? What does that mean for this?" Francine asks.

"It can mean various things. But I don't want to go into it until we've had a full account from Madeleine as to the whole history of her relationship with Edwin, and a minute-by-minute account of what happened that weekend. I agree though that the first thing we need to have is an independent psychiatric assessment."

"There was a therapist I was seeing for a while. I only went twice, though, and then Edwin found out." I still have to strain to hear Madeleine.

"What happened when Edwin found out?" I ask.

"He said I shouldn't bother, that it was a waste of money. I didn't need to talk to anyone, and if I did, I could always talk to him."

"How did you feel about that?" I say.

"I didn't mind. I didn't really like the

therapist, and it was difficult going through it all."

"Why did you decide to go in the first place?"

"I wanted to talk about my drinking, see if there was a way to control it." Madeleine stops talking and sighs, looking out the window behind me.

"When was this?" I draw an arrow from the bottom of my notes up to the top of the page and hold my pen in readiness. I wouldn't have thought of her as a drinker, too uptight for that.

"About five years ago." She focuses back on me, turning her gaze away from the view of the wall of the house next door that she seems to find so enthralling.

"Why didn't you like the therapist?" Patrick interrupts as I'm about to ask her my next question.

"He told me if I ever came in drunk to a session that he wouldn't be able to talk to me. I was cross — that wasn't the point. It wasn't that I drank all the time or anything — it wasn't like that. I just drank too much sometimes. I didn't feel like he was listening to me at all. And there was something a bit creepy about him."

I write down her answer, nodding to myself.

"What was creepy about him?" I say.

"Just . . . he sat a little bit close to me, I thought. Held on to my hand for slightly too long when he shook it. Nothing I could put my finger on, but I didn't feel comfortable."

I nod again. "You said Edwin 'found out' you were seeing the therapist. What did you mean?"

"He saw a receipt in my bag. I thought I'd thrown it away, but I forgot." Her mouth twists.

"What happened when he found it?" I keep my voice even.

"He wanted to know what it was for, and how I'd had fifty pounds to spend. I didn't want him thinking it was anything bad, so I told him. I said it was for him, because my drinking made him so unhappy. He understood in the end."

"What did you tell him about the money?" I ask.

"I said I'd saved it out of my allowance. He was cross at first, but when he understood I'd done it for him he was okay."

The pill, bag searching, housekeeping money, questioning over receipts. I'm trying to make sense of everything she's telling us, trying not to think about my own home life.

"You've explained a bit about your drinking, that it wasn't an ongoing issue, but rather one of moderation. How long was this a problem for, though?" I ask.

"Since I was a student, I suppose, on and off. More recently, I found some of the dinners very stressful," Madeleine replies.

"Dinners?"

"The work dinners. Edwin always wanted me to host. Or be the perfect guest. I found it difficult. He didn't like that. There was one time I was sick . . ." Her voice trails off. I look up at her — she's pale, one hand shading her eyes.

"Are you all right?"

"Yes. This is difficult, that's all. I've got an awful headache."

"We've got a lot to go through — let's leave it for now. In the meantime, would you be happy to talk to a psychiatrist? It would be very helpful to see what they think." As I speak I draw question marks beside my notes, then turn to a new page.

"I don't think it'll make any difference, but if you want me to, I will."

Madeleine's voice is the clearest it's been throughout the whole interview and I write in firm letters at the top of the page, CLIENT AGREES TO PSYCHIATRIC REPORT. The atmosphere in the room lightens. Patrick straightens himself up from the table, piling up his papers and placing them back in his briefcase. Francine rises and mutters something half-audible about photographs, then walks out of the kitchen. I put my notebook and pen in my bag, touching my hand against my phone. The text message comes back into my mind. But I haven't finished with Madeleine yet.

"We'll arrange it for as soon as possible," I say, running through a list of experts in my mind.

"Thank you." She stands and reaches her hand across the table to shake mine. Her grip is firmer this time than it was before. She looks revived and I make a mental note to try to work out why, what has happened in this interview to leave her happier than the last. Is it because we've kept the questioning away from the day of the incident itself? It will be only a temporary reprieve.

Francine comes back into the room holding a large brown envelope that's full to bursting. She holds it out to me. "Here are the photographs I have of Edwin and Madeleine."

I take it from her, nodding my thanks. "Do you mind if I take it away? I promise I'll be very careful with it." Both Francine and Madeleine nod. I put it securely in my bag and zip it up. This time I'll be more careful than to let it get stained with urine.

Francine calls a minicab for us and when it arrives, walks with us to meet it.

"You're being very kind to look after Madeleine like this," Patrick said.

"It's not easy . . ." As Francine says this, the electric gate starts to close and she walks back inside her house. Patrick and I get into the cab back to the station.

7

The train is late. I pace from one side of the platform to the other, debating whether a muffin and a latte will make me feel better or worse. Patrick goes straight to the kiosk and buys a black coffee, pouring something into it from a hip flask that he takes from his briefcase. He doesn't offer me anything and something in his expression makes me reluctant to either question what he's doing or ask if I can join him, even when he lights up a cigarette in direct contravention of the No Smoking signs on the wall. My head's jangling, part hoping that he'll touch me, drag me into whatever corner he wants and push me face-first against the wall and force himself inside me. My mind flits to the text. I take my phone out of my bag, turn it back on, and read the message again.

I know what ur doing u fucking slag

It can't mean this. No one knows about this. We've been so careful. It must be a mistake that it's been sent to me.

"What did you make of it?" Patrick comes up beside me, making me jump.

"Make of what?" I push my phone deep into my jacket pocket, reluctant to discuss the text. If I don't mention it, maybe it'll go away.

"The conference. Obviously. What else would I be talking about?"

I shrug. Patrick's voice is clear but now I notice that his eyes are bloodshot, rimmed with red.

"You're looking tired. Too many late nights?" I say.

"What? I was asking what you thought about the conference." He looks away from me, down the platform.

"I think there's something there, in the relationship. That's what this is about."

"She stabbed her husband to death. So glad to have the benefit of your great legal insight." His voice is scathing. I'm not going to let him rile me. I shrug. He pulls out his pack of cigarettes again and this time I reach out for one and take it and the lighter from his hand. I light the cigarette and inhale deeply before I continue talking about the case.

"Yes, of course she stabbed him. There's no other explanation for what happened. But there's a lot she isn't saying. This business about the pill, him giving it to her without her knowing. That's not normal behavior."

"Sounds like a bloody good idea to me. Save a lot of trouble."

"Seriously? What trouble has a woman's fertility caused you?" I'm surprised by his vehemence.

"None of your business. There's a lot you don't know about me. Not that you'd ever bother to ask. And for fuck's sake start buying your own fags."

Ignoring the final dig I snap back, "You said no questions. Right at the start of this." I'm indignant and don't care if it shows. I remember the conversation very clearly. We stood outside a pub on Kingsway, one autumn evening about a year ago, both hammered. His philandering was legendary, a broken marriage somewhere in his background and several broken hearts, but that wasn't enough to stop me. When he looked at me there was a jolt in my chest and I knew he could really see me and how much he wanted me. I bit his ear and in turn he took me by the throat and pushed me against the wall and hissed, "No biting, no questions. We fuck, that's it." I'm not going to break the rules now.

He throws the remnants of his drink onto the train track and turns back towards me. "Of course, no questions. How could I forget?" he says. Then he takes a deep breath, seemingly to calm himself down. "Yes, I agree. There's an aspect of control in the relationship, from what she's said so far."

I nod. "So maybe there's more, something worse in his behavior she's not telling us about yet . . . If there aren't psychiatric issues, that's the only feasible defense, if this were a loss of control in the context of domestic violence. On the bare facts it doesn't look good." My voice trails off as I think again about the stab injuries found on Edwin's body and the bloodstains on Madeleine's clothes.

Before Patrick can reply the train pulls into the platform. We climb on in silence and sit opposite each other. I'm ready for his move, tip of my tongue at my lips in anticipation, remembering the way I gagged as he pushed his erection into my mouth. *Open your throat,* advice I've gleaned for years from magazines and porn, *just relax.* Easy to say when talking about downing a pint but opening my throat while trying to breathe through a nose of pubic hair and simultaneously keeping my balance on a urine-sodden train floor? Not so easy. Then why am I so keen for a repeat performance? Why am I sitting on the edge of my seat waiting for him to lean forward and touch me? Christ, it's an empty compartment, we could even do it right here, right now. Who's to see? The words of the text message jeer in my head — *I know what ur doing* — but I shut them down. No one knows, no one has seen. I'm sure of it.

I put my hand on his knee, move it higher up his thigh. He pushes it off so hard it feels like a slap. I sit back as if burned.

"What are you doing?"

"I thought . . ."

"You thought wrong. Just think about the case. That's what matters."

"Aren't we going to discuss this when we get back into town?" I don't want to talk about it on the train.

"I'm not going to have time — I'm going out for dinner tonight. I'll arrange a time for the beginning of next week."

"Who are you going out for dinner with?" My voice is casual but he's not deceived.

"It's really none of your business," he says.

I lean my head against the glass, looking out at the passing houses. In one garden, as the train slows, I see a couple kissing. I wonder if they can see me, if they wonder who I am, why the woman with her face slumped against the window is wiping away tears. When we reach Marylebone I wait until Patrick gets off the train before I turn from the window and gather together my things.

The Bakerloo line runs fast. I'm at Embankment before I know it, wheeling my bag up Essex Street, past Cairn's Wine Bar, past the Royal Courts of Justice, coming to a halt in the clerks' room. Mark the clerk hands me the brief for the following day, a bulky pile of papers tied roughly together with pink tape, loose documents and photographs about to fall out from either side.

"Why's it in such a mess?" I'm not impressed.

"It's a return from out of chambers. Twenty-seven King's Bench Way. Their stuff is always in a mess."

"Great. So pleased." I look at the back sheet. The Crown Court at Wood Green. At least it's local. Relatively.

"It's a fixed trial, miss. Five, six days," Mark says.

"Okay." I undo the pink tape and look at the indictment. Seven counts of attempted grievous bodily harm, one count of dangerous driving. I nod. "Okay." It's going to take me most of the night to prepare it. "Thanks." I back out of the room, clutching the papers to my chest.

I dump my bag and coat beside my desk and lay the brief out in front of me. Before I look any further at it or at the photographs Francine has given me, I phone Carl. I know he's at swimming with Matilda.

"Hello? I can't really hear you." Carl's voice is faint.

"Hi, it's me. How is she getting on?" I shout.

"Fine. She's doing well." Suddenly the line clears, the last words loud in my ear.

"I bet. Look, I'm afraid I've been given a trial last minute. It's going to take a while to prepare. I'll be home soon but I'm going to need to work tonight."

A long silence. Then, "Right. I promised Matilda we'd go for pizza after as she's done so well."

I look at my watch. Five o'clock. I've got hours. How long can it take to eat a pizza? "Shall I meet you up there? I'll work afterwards."

Another long silence. "You'll be preoccupied. I know what you're like. Don't worry about it. Stay in chambers and get the work done. We'll be fine." He sounds matter-of-fact.

"I'll need to eat. Seriously, I can come now and meet you there, put Matilda to bed before getting on with it." I don't mean to sound pleading but something throbs in my voice. I desperately want to see her.

"Honestly, it's fine. Come back when you've finished. Remember, I've got the men's group meeting at the house tonight so you can't come back too early."

I start to speak but Carl cuts off the call. I look at my phone, unsure what to do. Maybe they'll go with one of Matilda's friends from the swimming class. I've never been, I don't know, the parents could be anyone. Right now Carl could be smiling into the eyes of another mother, blond hair damp from the laps she's swum while her daughter tumble-turns her way into the squad with Matilda, slim and muscled from the butterfly strokes I could never in a million years master. Right now he'll be laughing and telling her not to worry, his wife won't ever bother coming to the pool, too busy working or whatever, let's take the children and maybe we can even have a glass of wine to celebrate . . .

I shake my head clear, stunned by the

vividness of the scene I've created. Carl won't have eyes for anyone else — he's with Matilda and he wouldn't want to upset her. And anyway, he won't be dallying. He'll be tidying up the living room, bringing through chairs from the kitchen so that there'll be room for everyone in his men's group, a couple of boxes of tissues on the side tables in case anyone gets emotional. That's my guess, anyway — Carl won't ever tell me what happens. Strictly confidential, he says. The group has to have complete trust in him. I always nod, too conscious of my own lies to want to push it.

I open the brief for the trial tomorrow and spend some time reading through it. It's not as bad as I first feared. Dangerous driving and attempted murder — the defendant lost his temper with a group of teenagers who'd been shouting at him in a supermarket car park, got into his car, and drove it up onto the sidewalk at them. He didn't hit anyone and his car stalled in any event. There are about twenty witnesses to what happened, which explains why the trial is in for a week. It speaks for itself, really.

But even though I'm prosecuting, I feel sorry for the defendant as I read his police interview. He has learning and physical disabilities and a specially adapted car. Reading between the lines it looks as if his life is regularly made hellish by these youths and I can't blame him for losing it. Not that it's my job to say so. I make some notes for my opening speech and hope that he'll be adequately represented. I check out who the solicitors are for the defense and sigh. I know the firm well. Harrow-based and full of shysters — they've never provided me with a full brief when I've acted for them; a name on a Post-it note if I'm lucky. They do as little preparation as they can get away with, and instruct the cheapest counsel they can find. After some more reading, I draw a line mentally under the trial — with any luck it'll crack. They'll offer a plea to something, I'll haggle it up to a more serious offense, and we'll be wrapped up by the end of the day.

I finish my preparation. I tidy the brief into a pile and tie it back up neatly with pink tape. It's in a far better state than when it was given to me. By now it's after seven. I text Carl to ask whether they've had a nice pizza and then sit looking at the screen of my phone for a moment before texting Patrick.

Are you OK?

He was strange this afternoon. I haven't seen him drink from a hip flask before. Or turn down the offer of sex. Maybe he's realized now how fruitless this is and has decided to call it off with me. Maybe this dinner is a better offer, a younger, fitter version of me but without the husband and child. And maybe it would be good, the end of the affair, no more guilt, no more self-loathing. No more distraction away from my family. Maybe I'd have time for friends again too.

My phone beeps with a message and I jump for it. Carl. Pizza fine. Matilda in shower. All OK. I send back a thumbs-up emoji. No point trying to beat words out of the laconic. Then I switch off my phone and take the photographs of Madeleine and Edwin Smith out of my bag.

There are about forty photos. I try to put them into some kind of chronological order, using their apparent ages and Edwin's hairline as a guide. I remember Madeleine told us that she and Edwin met at university and these pictures stand out, her young and pretty in a pair of striped dungarees while he stands behind her smiling in a plainer sweater. They follow a typical trail of holidays: what looks like backpacking in Europe, posed against the Colosseum and the Trevi

Fountain, the pyramids of the Louvre and Gaudi's lizards. Now it's farther afield, a backdrop of paddy fields and a volcano — Indonesia, possibly? — and now Petra.

We went there too, Carl and me, laughing at the camel that couldn't stand under the weight of an obese tourist. The thought of it now makes me cringe, its legs wobbling as the owner yelled at it to get up, get up. Long dead now, I expect, as dead as the force that drove Carl and me to join hands as we walked up the long path to the Monastery at the top of the hill. Dead, too, as the man with friendly eyes and a shy smile who looks at me out of the photographs I have spread across my desk.

Perhaps we were in Jordan at the same time? It's impossible to tell. I look at the backs of the photographs to see if there's any clue as to what year any of them were taken. Nothing. Apart from one on which is scrawled in blue pen, *She said yes.* I turn it over. No longer dressed in student clothes, Madeleine is radiant in a blue fitted dress. She sits at a restaurant table, smiling, Edwin for once beside her rather than behind her, holding her close with an arm round her. A waiter must have taken the photo for them. There are champagne flutes on the table — perhaps Edwin hid the ring in one of the glasses and waited for her to find it? Or maybe he carried the box in his pocket, patting his trousers every now and again to see if it was still there, hoping she wouldn't see or ask what he was doing.

Did Madeleine expect the proposal? Was she happy? She's smiling in the photo. Edwin's arm is close round her, elbow at her neck — was she comfortable? Is that a shadow of strain I can sense in her eyes, a tiny restraint even in the joy of the moment? The writing on the back is confident, firm. *She said yes.* Shouldn't there be an exclamation mark, punctuation to fit the occasion?

We didn't have a camera with us the night that Carl proposed. There wasn't champagne either. We were discussing whether we could afford to move anywhere nicer than the place in Bow in which we were living at the time and when I said we should think about buying somewhere he said, "In that case we should get married." I nodded, and then he said, "Actually, I think we should anyway." Nothing more was said until he told me a couple of weeks later that he'd booked the registry office for a fortnight's time — I didn't see why not. His mother came, and my best friend, Evie, and I'm sure I must have looked radiant at some point, even if there isn't a photograph of it staring at me from my desk. On the upside, I'm not on bail for Carl's murder, so maybe things could be worse.

In so many of the shots Edwin and Madeleine look entirely normal, like anybody else. Like Carl and me. There's nothing to indicate that fifteen or so years later she'll end up stabbing him to death.

Here's a wedding shot, arum lilies in a neat bouquet. Here's Madeleine pregnant, standing sideways against a doorway framed with wisteria. Here she is holding the baby, Edwin standing next to her, again holding her close. In every single photo she's smiling, happy. I'm wasting my time. There's nothing to be found in these photographs to give me any clue as to why she killed him. What they present to the world is perfect, impregnable. It would be as much use to look through photos of Carl and me to try to spot when we started to break. I sigh and switch on my phone.

It beeps immediately, a message from Patrick.

Drinking in Cairn's. Come if u want.

I text back. Thought you were having dinner.

He replies. I was.

I check the time — his dinner's been short. Not a date, then. My shoulders unknot. I've been looking at the photographs for the best part of an hour and haven't yet found anything — I might as well stop work now. I put them back into the envelope and put it in my desk drawer. I pack the papers for the next day's trial into my bag and turn off the light. No one else is in chambers by now, the building empty of noise. It isn't that late, not even nine yet, but it could be midnight. Shadows from the branches of the trees outside the clerks' room play across the wall as I set the alarm and leave the building locked.

8

I walk into the bar and look for Patrick. Instead of sitting at a table on his own, as I expected, I'm surprised to see him at a long table surrounded by all the usual crowd from chambers, even though it's a Wednesday night. I slide into a seat between Sankar and Robert.

"Any wine going spare?"

Neither of them reply. It's noisy, music blaring from the overhead speakers, and as I settle into the corner I watch Patrick. This is his domain, his element. He's the brightest flame at the center of the fire. He's telling a story that's making the people closest to him laugh and the people farther away from him strain to hear what he's saying. Alexia is on the periphery, smiling. It's not the quiet drink with him I anticipated, but I'll have to deal with it. He asked me to come — the thought gives me a small flicker of his warmth. I bash Robert's arm and he turns, a look of surprise on his face at seeing me there.

"Any wine going spare?"

"You need a drink."

We speak simultaneously. I laugh. He reaches over to the table and slops red wine into a glass beside him. I pause only briefly to wonder if it's clean before deciding I don't care and downing it. Robert refills my glass.

"Long day?" he says.

"Yep. I've only just finished work. How about you?"

"I've been here since about four. My wife's going to kill me. I only came in for a couple . . ." His voice is slurred.

"Don't we all." I finish off half of the new glass he's poured, put the rest down on the table. Tendrils of calm stretch through my mind, the dim light of the bar taking on a golden hue. It's fine, I'm allowed to be here. Carl doesn't want me home, he's busy counseling his men. Matilda will be fine, replete with pizza and no doubt nearly asleep. I've done my work and I deserve a drink. I take another large swig and look over at Patrick again. He's sitting next to Mark the clerk and, now I'm looking more closely, I see on his other side a pretty woman I don't know. She seems to find him particularly amusing and the calm I feel diminishes, a chill at my fingertips.

"Who's that?" I nudge Robert.

"Who's what?"

"Her. The woman next to Patrick." I keep my voice casual.

"I don't know, some woman. She came in with him."

"When did he get here?"

"I have no idea — a bit after me." Robert turns round and looks me straight in the eye. "Jealous, are we?"

"Don't be ridiculous." I finish my glass of wine and reach for the bottle but it's empty. "I'll go and buy some more."

I squeeze past the group and make my way to the bar. The place is rammed, everyone treating Wednesday as if it's a Friday night. I avoid looking at Patrick as I walk past him, though I can see out of the corner of my eye that the woman next to him has her hand on his arm. I put my chin up and keep going.

It takes a good ten minutes to get served, it's so busy. I order two bottles of Rioja, not wanting to go through the wait for a second time. Robert is sitting in my space by the time I get back but moves again to make room for me. I pour drinks for him and Sankar, waving the bottle at the people on the other side of the table but they're all on white. I don't try to catch Patrick's eye.

I drink and Sankar tells me about his case that day. "You'd have thought she'd have realized he was sticking a carrot up her arse every night — Rohypnol's powerful stuff." I drink some more. Time ticks on, first ten, then half ten, my hunger and tiredness subsiding as the wine takes a firmer hold. I look at my phone. Nothing. Robert and I sneak outside for one of his cigarettes.

On the way back in, making sure no one can see, I text Patrick. Fancy a fuck? He doesn't even twitch. His phone must be off. Why would he ignore me when he asked me to come to the pub? He's still engrossed in conversation with the woman next to him. Sankar doesn't know who she is either, and I don't want to ask anyone else, sinking further and further into my glass. We finish the two bottles and Robert fights his way up to the bar for more. It's thinning out by now. What was a group of nearly twenty people is now about ten in number. I smile and chat to the girls on the other side of the table, the ones drinking white. Alexia, and another pupil whose name I can never remember. They're talking to a tenant from chambers called Pauline who always seems rather disapproving when she speaks to me.

Tonight, less so — she's flushed with wine and we chat about my murder case.

"It's so odd, looking at other people's photographs. We always think we're so unique, and yet we're all just doing the same things, going to the same places, eating the same foods . . ." I'm rambling now, forgetting halfway through what point I want to make.

"I know exactly what you mean. It's like Facebook. All interchangeable." Pauline nods.

"I mean, one minute you're there having your photograph taken in front of the Parthenon, holding hands; the next you're stabbing him to death with a kitchen knife. It could be any of us, really, if you think about it."

"That's so right," Pauline keeps nodding and I nod, too, impressed at our profundity.

"What do you think of him?" she says, changing the subject so suddenly I don't register immediately what she's said. I look at her blankly. She's pointing over at Patrick.

"What about him?" I say.

"I mean, he's a good solicitor," she says, moving her head close to mine in a conspiratorial way. "But I've heard some rumors . . ."

"Rumors?" I say, trying to keep my voice neutral.

"Just, something about someone he shouldn't have tried it on with. But I don't know . . ." She trails off.

I'm feeling more sober by the second, my senses on full alert. I don't know what she's getting at — could she be referring to me? Is she the one who sent the text? "I've never heard anything like that," I say, "and spreading that kind of thing can be very damaging."

She backs off, face full of contrition. "Hey, I'm not trying to make trouble here. I was just saying . . . I'm sure there's nothing in it, though."

I nod.

"I'm going to get a drink," she says. "Can I get you anything?"

"I'm fine, thanks. Going to go soon, I think," I say, and watch her as she makes her way up to the bar.

The next moment I jump as someone shrieks and a glass smashes. I spill the red wine in my glass all down my shirt instead of drinking it. I glance up, looking for the source of the commotion. I work it out quickly. Patrick is wearing even more red wine than I am, his face dripping with the stuff. The woman I don't know is standing over him, brandishing the bottom of a wineglass, shards of glass still adhering to the stem. There's broken glass on the table and on the floor. She's shouting something but I can't make out the words. I jump to my feet but before I can move over to their side of the table, Pauline has run back and is standing in front of the woman with her hands extended. For a moment I think she's going to stab at Pauline but instead she stays entirely still before dropping the glass to the floor. Pauline puts her hands on the woman's shoulders but she resists the embrace, shaking Pauline off before picking a black handbag up off the floor and stalking out of the bar.

Patrick is wiping the wine from his face with a white napkin. His shirt is soaked — her glass must have been full.

"What was that all about?" I shout but he doesn't react. I shout again, more loudly. "What the fuck just happened there?"

My shout coincides with a lull in the music, falling into a silence. What people there are still left in the bar stare over at us, their attention attracted by my yells if not by the original scene. Patrick mops at his shirt, folds the napkin, and puts it on the table before finally looking up and at me. He says something but the music has started again and I can't hear him.

"What?"

"She didn't like my shirt." He smiles.

"For fuck's sake." I'm too angry to continue. I get up and retrieve my own bag. I can't deal with whatever it is that's going on. Pauline stands and looks at me, a quizzical expression on her face. I can't deal with that right now either. Without saying goodbye to anyone, I also stalk out of the bar, exiting through the back door so that I don't have to walk past Patrick. I've had enough. The only reason I can see behind his invite is to humiliate me by brandishing another woman in front of me, and I'm not playing anymore.

I see a taxi with its light on as I turn into the Strand and I hail it, grateful to be escaping. I'm drunk but not too much, focusing clearly on the street signs as we drive up to Archway. I get my phone out of my bag and text Robert to say sorry that I walked out, that I've got a trial starting the next day. He won't care. He probably didn't notice. As far as Patrick is concerned, I'll deal with it in the morning. He'll explain or he won't. I shut my eyes and lean against the window. I don't understand what's happening.

When I arrive back I'm surprised to find

the men's group is still in progress — it normally finishes by nine at the latest. As I walk through the front door it sounds as if they're watching something on television, but when I slam the door shut the noise stops. Carl rushes out of the living room.

"You're back earlier than I expected. We've just had a breakthrough with something."

"Early start tomorrow." I keep my head down, hoping he won't notice I'm drunk.

"Get to bed then. We'll be finished soon."

He retreats into the living room, shutting the door quickly behind him so that I can't see who's in there. I want to shout, *Whose house is this? Who pays the fucking mortgage?* But I don't. The anger subsides and I stomp upstairs. I undress in the dark of our bedroom, a glint of orange light coming through the curtains that never quite block the streetlight outside. The skin on my chest is sticky from the spilled wine and so I shower, only washing my body, keeping my hair out of the water. I pull on a nightie and brush my teeth, moving the brush carefully along each quarter of my mouth for the required thirty seconds.

When I'm satisfied I no longer stink of wine and fags I put on my dressing gown and go through into Matilda's room. She's fast asleep, hugging Pink Elephant close. I kiss her forehead and pull the duvet a little farther up over her, covering her arm, before sitting down on the floor beside her and watching her sleep. She sighs and rolls over, her face towards me. My throat constricts. This, this is who I'm betraying. Carl matters. Tilly matters even more. She's not the one who's rejected me, pushed me away so many times. She deserves better from me, a mother without a split heart. I love her more than I can say, but not enough to turn away from Patrick. Or at least, not so far. I touch her cheek, breathing a silent promise that I'm going to try harder, become the person she deserves. I almost believe it's true.

Then I return to our room and get into bed, putting my phone on to charge on my bedside table. I pick it up to turn on the alarm — by now I'm so tired it'll take an earthquake to wake me in the morning.

Two messages. One from Patrick.

At ur chambers. Where the fuck RU?

I rub my finger slowly across the words before I delete it, newly resolute.

Then I look at the other message, sender unknown.

I'm watching u u fucking slag. I know what ur doing.

The letters of the text dance in front of me. Does someone know about Patrick and me? It can only mean that. But I don't know who it can be. I try to swallow the panic down, delete the text. It's not there anymore. It didn't happen. It's another mistake, the sender targeting me by accident, a digit wrong in the number. I set the alarm for half past six and roll onto my side, eyes shut. I'm not tired, though. My mind's racing. Much as I want to pretend the texts aren't happening, I can't escape from it. That's two now, and I need to recognize the truth, acknowledge the danger. Someone is onto me. They know what I'm doing, and they don't like it. I curl up, drawing my knees up to my chest, feet tucked in under the duvet. I'm cold, fear seeping into my bones.

Later I hear the voices of the men leaving the house, a chorus of good-nights and the gentle shutting of the door. Later still I hear Carl come up to our room, his steps quiet, his movements gentle. I don't stir, breathing deep and regular. Soon he snores.

It's a long time before I sleep and then I

dream that I'm stabbing repeatedly up my thighs with the broken stem of a wineglass until I reach the place between my legs and fuck myself with it. I wake shuddering in the dark. I lean into Carl's warmth, one arm around him. Asleep, he doesn't pull away as he does when we're awake, the conflict ceased between us, if only for now. He's my known known, father of my child. We've traveled the world together, made a home. It's time to make it work again, for Matilda, for us. I fall asleep with my head against his shoulder.

Carl's space is empty, the pillow cold when the alarm wakes me at half past six. I'm going to suggest a weekend away. We'll get his mother to look after Matilda and we'll go away to a nice hotel for the night. We'll eat nice food and drink nice wine and maybe, just maybe, we'll kiss and hold hands. Maybe, just maybe, we'll make love like we used to. Patrick's face creeps into my mind but I banish it. I don't want that anymore, the guilt of it. There's nothing about it that makes it worthwhile, so fraught with shame. He's not even reliable, there's always the uncertainty of not knowing whether he's thinking about me or anyone but . . .

The texts have been a wake-up call. I

might think we've tried to be careful but maybe we haven't been that subtle, discreet enough — I guess anyone from chambers could have seen us kissing in the alleys behind Fleet Street or standing together in the bar that little bit too close. It could be anyone texting me and I won't be dragged into this drama anymore. I can still hear the smash of glass and the scream from the night before — I don't even want to know why the woman was so angry with Patrick or what he's done.

"Coffee?" Carl has come back into the bedroom, mug in hand, which he places on my bedside table.

"Thank you. That's lovely." I mean it. He hasn't brought me coffee in bed for a couple of years at least. He always used to, the aroma seeping through the house a comforting start to the day. I'll take this as a good omen. "I've been thinking, shall we try to go away for the night soon? We could ask your mother to look after Matilda."

Carl looks surprised. "What's brought this on?"

"It would be nice to spend some time together. On our own."

"I don't like the idea of leaving Matilda . . ." His voice is reluctant.

"I know you haven't wanted to before, but

Tilly was younger then. But now surely, with your mum? She'd be all right for one night," I say.

"I don't know. It might be too much for Mum."

"I'm sure she'd love to. There's no need for her to do much. Matilda's a big girl. They don't even need to leave the house if that would make you feel better. I'll make sure there's food in, all of that." I stretch my hand out to him. He looks at it for a moment and then takes it in his. His grasp is loose, impersonal. But it's a start. I have to get him to change his mind about leaving Matilda with other people — I've never wanted to push it before, but it's time.

"I'll talk to her," Carl says. "We can see. I guess one night would be okay."

"It really would, I'm sure of it. It would be good for them to bond more. Your mum's always saying she'd like to see more of Tilly." Carl raises one eyebrow but I plow on regardless. "She did say that to me once, a few years ago. Look, we need to bond, too. Tilly needs us to be happy, together. Don't you think?"

"We can try," he says.

"It's what you'd advise a client to do, I'm sure. Spend time together, talk."

He nods, takes firmer hold of my hand. I

wonder if I should reach to him and kiss him but Matilda walks in and jumps on the bed.

"You didn't wake me up!" Her hair sticks up at the back and she's still warm with sleep. I pull her to me for a hug. She lets me hold her for a moment, then moves away and hugs Carl. He sits down on the side of the bed with her in his arms and I can see exactly how we should be as a family. It's going to happen. I'm going to make sure of it. I shower and dress for work with a lighter heart than I've had for months. When I go down to the kitchen, Carl has made scrambled eggs, not just for Matilda but for me as well, and we sit together and eat at the table. I pull my wheelie bag out the door with a flourish, ready to take whatever Wood Green Crown Court has to throw at me.

9

Another week passes. The trial at Wood Green is effective, youth after youth appearing in the witness box to insist how threatened they'd felt by the defendant's dangerous driving. The defendant is barely audible as he gives evidence, his barrister not much better. As I feared, he's represented by someone who looks as if she's left bar school only months before. I tone it down as much as I can and in the end he receives a suspended sentence. Judgment almost worthy of Solomon, I think but don't say to the judge as I make my application for prosecution costs at the conclusion of the trial.

Patrick texts me a couple of times but only in relation to Madeleine's case — the date of the PTPH is coming closer, the prosecution are still being slow with disclosure. He makes no reference to the events in Cairn's and neither do I — I'm not going to give him the satisfaction. I'm not interested in his power games. We don't mention our relationship. Our former relationship, that is.

I spend that Friday night at home with my family, with Carl and Matilda. I only have a small amount of preparation to do for a trial of an indecent assault on a child that's due to start at the beginning of next week. I make sure to get up early, so as not to spoil the weekend with it. We go to Hampstead Heath and watch Matilda climb the oak trees near the gate into Kenwood. Carl doesn't say if he's talked to his mother about looking after Matilda for a night but I don't want to push it — I know he'll come round to the idea in his own time. He can see that I mean it, that I'm trying.

I'm careful not to argue with him, even when he tells Matilda to come down from the lowest of branches. He's only looking after her. She's not old enough yet. We collect orange and brown leaves from the ground and I put them in my coat pocket.

"I'll make lunch," I say as we go home.

"Are you sure?" Carl says. "It'll be easier if I do it."

"I want to," I say. "Tilly, what would you like for lunch?"

"Hummus and pita bread. And some carrots. Is there any ham?" she says.

"I'm sure that can be arranged," I say. "Nice and easy." I don't remind her about her short-lived flirtation with vegetarianism, simply relieved it passed so quickly.

Carl sighs. "We don't have any ham in. If you ever did the supermarket shop . . ."

I'm determined not to have a row. "Then pita and hummus it is, Tilly. Okay?"

"Okay!"

After she's had her food she asks if she can have an orange. I pass one over to her, and a table knife. "Make a nick in it," I say, "and peel from there. It'll make it easier."

She starts to cut at the orange but she doesn't have hold of it properly and the knife slips. She cries out. I reach her fast but not before Carl, who's sprinted in from the front room.

"How could you be so stupid as to give her a knife?" He's holding her arm and brandishing her finger at me. I look closely. There's a tiny scratch, a small drop of blood forming at one end.

"It's stinging," she cries.

"That'll be the juice," I say. "Come here and let's hold it under the tap. You're being very brave."

Carl seems reluctant to let her go but eventually she comes over to me and I hug her and we wash her hand before I wrap it in a bit of paper towel.

"Shall I cut up the rest for you?"

"Yes, please."

We sit back at the table together and I finish peeling the orange. One bit of pith has a trace of blood on it and I stare at it, heavy in my mind as to whether it was wrong to let her cut the fruit on her own. It was only a table knife, after all. It was the serrated bit that caught her finger.

"Really, Alison, you have to think more about these things," Carl says.

I take the peel and throw it away.

Sunday is better, a bit. I cook a roast without any issue. Matilda clears her plate, but Carl leaves most of his and scrapes it noisily into the bin.

"You just have to practice with cooking, that's all," he says, and pats me on the shoulder before eating a protein bar from the cupboard. I want to defend myself, point out that at least I'm trying, but I swallow it down. I can see I need to do more to convince him that I've changed and I know I will, in time. I nod.

Later in the evening I take the leaves from my coat pocket and I put them in a fan shape on the pinboard in the kitchen, a reminder of the trip to the Heath. It can get better, I'm nearly sure.

There are no more anonymous texts.

While I'm on my way to court on Monday morning Patrick texts me.

I miss u.

I don't reply and he doesn't text again, but despite myself I feel a small knot of tension release in me, a worry gone I was refusing to acknowledge was there in the first place. And the words remain in my mind, behind the thought of the weekend with Carl and Matilda.

The trial collapses within two days — the main prosecution witness crumples under the gentlest of cross-examinations from me. Her memories of dates, times, and places are all confused, muddled through the decades since she alleged the abuse happened. The case doesn't even get as far as the jury. Mindful of my success in my earlier trial, I make an application of no case to answer at the end of the prosecution and again it's successful. My client is grateful, an exhausted man in his sixties, a retired piano teacher against whom the prosecution have failed miserably, whose life has been almost destroyed by the allegations. I hardly had to try to get it kicked out — the CPS ought to be ashamed of themselves for bringing such a weak case to court.

I hear the complainant's sobs as I leave the court building but keep my head down. I have to do my job, defend my clients to the best of my ability. If what she alleged is true, it's a terrible situation, but the evidence has to be strong enough to convince a jury beyond reasonable doubt . . . It should never have gotten to this point. I say goodbye to my client outside the building. He shakes my hand. His wife hovers at his side, small and anxious. She keeps looking behind her nervously and I hurry them away from the building before the complainant comes out.

The clerks have left a message on my phone telling me that there's been a delivery of papers in relation to the Madeleine Smith case, so I make my way up to chambers, anxious to see what else the prosecution might have served in advance of the PTPH. I still don't know how Madeleine is going to plead — I don't want her to plead guilty, at least not yet. It seems to me there are a lot of aspects of her relationship with Edwin that require further exploration. As I'm thinking it through my phone rings. Patrick's office. I raise my chin, preparing myself to talk to him. I needn't have bothered steeling myself though; it's his senior associate, Chloe.

"Hi, Alison. You've got the papers through okay? We need to arrange another conference with Madeleine. Any chance you could see her tomorrow?"

"Yes, sure. My trial's finished," I say.

"Great. And Patrick was wondering if he could pop round to chambers shortly, have a quick chat about it in advance of the conference," she says.

"I haven't read the papers yet." I'm trying to stall.

"I think he's quite keen. You can go through them together," she says in a voice that doesn't invite disagreement. We get on fine, Chloe and me, but I do what she tells me — Patrick's more senior, but she's the powerhouse of the operation, with an encyclopedic knowledge of all the firm's cases.

"Okay, no problem then. I'll be here."

"Great, I'll let Patrick know," she says, and cuts off the call.

I text Carl.

Conference in the murder. Back by 8:30 xx.

An extra kiss for luck. He wasn't expecting me to be home early because of the trial so it should be all right. I'm glad I haven't told him it has finished already. Then I check myself — why am I thinking about lying to him?

The pathologist's report has been sent through, fleshing out the details of the wounds that finished off Edwin Smith. I read through it. There are fifteen in total, varying in depth. The report includes photographs. I look for some time at the slash on the neck, smiling beneath the mouth. The sheets beneath him are soaked in blood. The prosecution summary, of which I already have a copy, states that the clothes taken from Madeleine Smith were visibly covered in blood and I check through the new bundle to see if it includes any forensic evidence relating to this. Nothing yet. I turn back to the pathologist's report. No defensive injuries. The wounds are all to the neck and torso. The body was found lying on its back and that's how it's been photographed, an aerial shot and then all the close-ups of the injuries. A diagram has also been attached, a crude outline of a man's body, with short lines showing the locations of the injuries.

I sift through the bundle again and find a

photograph of the knife alleged to have been used in the attack. A Global. I look at it, trying to see through the dried blood whether there's any indication of wear to the blade. Mine has become blunt through years of use and dishwashing. The sharper the blade, of course, the less force needed to push it in and out of Edwin's body.

Putting the knife photograph at the back of the pile, I turn to the toxicology analysis in the report. Alcohol levels four times the legal limit for drinking. No further toxicology analysis is available at this stage — I know it usually takes longer. I'm surprised they've been able to provide as much as this, really. The levels of alcohol are enough in any event to explain the lack of defensive injuries. Edwin could well have been out cold.

Other than the pathologist's report and the photograph of the weapon, nothing else of substance has been provided. There's an interview summary showing that Madeleine made no comment in interview, but not a full transcript of the questions asked. Not yet. I check the dates — it should all be served by the end of November, if not before the PTPH.

"We don't really need much more from

them. The judge may well say we've been given enough to get her to enter a plea," I say to Patrick once he's arrived and settled himself down in the conference room. I try not to look at him too intently, aware though of every movement of his hands, his arms.

"Yes. But she hasn't given us a defense. Not yet." Patrick has the photographs spread out in front of him, big cuts and little ones.

"Given what she's told us about him giving her the pill without her knowledge, and the whole allowance money control thing, we're agreed there's a strong possibility of an abusive relationship. Yes?"

"Yes, of course. But that's not enough in itself to bring it down from murder. We need more for loss of control," Patrick says.

"It will all depend on whether she opens up to us. Right now we've got nothing. No evidence of any qualifying trigger, nothing. Just a bottle of gin and a blackout. Though you have to admit her account doesn't make sense. Not fully," I say.

"You're right. She's very closed. Perhaps you should talk to her on your own? I wondered if she might be more relaxed without anyone else there. Woman to woman."

I shift in my seat, uncomfortable at the suggestion. "Is that really appropriate?"

"I don't see why not. You're good at getting people to talk," he says, I glance at him. He's looking at the photographs, not at me. I turn my head quickly.

"Well, if you think I should, I will. We need to try to get some more out of her before the next hearing. It would be preferable if she could enter a plea." I'm trying not to react to his last comments. There's a warmth in his voice that I can feel reflected in the flush creeping up my cheeks.

"I'll arrange it. I spoke to our psychiatrist, too. He'll have the preliminary report together for tomorrow. If we arrange the con for the afternoon, does that give you a chance to read it in the morning? You're free tomorrow, aren't you?" he says.

"Yes. That would be good. And you're right, she might be less hysterical if it's just me."

"I'll get Chloe to set it up."

Patrick nods and picks up his phone, typing a message. I start to speak but he interrupts, "Alison, I'd like to take you home and cook you dinner. Is there any chance you could do that?"

"I don't think that's such a good idea." It's not what I'm thinking, though. Seeing him again has only reminded me how much I still want to kiss him. I try to tamp down the feeling but for a moment I hear, clear as a bell, the scrape of fork against china as Carl throws away the food I cooked the night before last.

Patrick tries again. "I'd really like to. I know it's been a difficult couple of weeks. We haven't talked, and I, well, I've missed you. Please let me cook for you?" He reaches out his hand to me, palm upwards. "Please?"

I try to hold on to the thought of Carl and Matilda waiting at home. I try even harder to keep hold of the dancing image of the letters on my phone, the anonymous person who knows about us and hates it. Hates me. It all dissolves, dust to dust. "Yes. Please. I'd like that too."

We hail a taxi on Fleet Street. Patrick leaves chambers before me, meeting me under the arch at the top of the exit from Temple. No one was there to see anyway. He holds my hand in the taxi, fingers curled around mine. I lean into him. He turns and kisses the top of my head.

"Off anywhere nice?" asks the taxi driver. I know he thinks we're a couple.

"Just home for dinner," Patrick says. "Quiet night in."

I don't say anything. The taxi has cut round St. Clement Danes and is heading back along the Strand, past the Royal Courts of Justice, past Chancery Lane. Fetter Lane's a chance for me to tell Patrick to get out, I'm going home — I let it pass. I could tell him to get out at Ludgate Circus, ask the cab to go left up Farringdon Street towards Islington. I don't. We take a right and head south over the river to Patrick's top-floor flat near Tower Bridge. I've been here before but only once, the afternoon some weeks ago when we watched the light fade through the blinds. He pays for the cab and opens the door for me. I pull my bag out and follow, walking quietly through the entrance to the building and up in the lift. I touch my fingers to his lips and he smiles.

"We're here," he says as the lift arrives at the top floor.

He opens the front door and I dump my coat and bag inside. He pours me a glass of red wine and I walk over to the long windows that give a view of the river. The lights from a thousand windows are bright in the dusk of the evening. It's only half past seven but it's nearly fully dark. I drink half the glass of wine in one gulp.

"What are you cooking?" I walk back over to the kitchen, open plan to the living room.

Patrick has taken off his jacket and is chopping something on a wooden board. I look at the knife more closely — not a Global. One with a wooden handle. Probably Japanese. The kitchen is sleek and shiny, pots lined up in order of size on the shelf behind him.

"Lamb and harissa kebabs. Some couscous," he says.

"Nice." I'm impressed. "I didn't know you could cook."

"You know now." He starts chopping again, his knife moving swiftly through the onion.

"Looks like you were planning this. Or did you get ditched at the last minute?" I regret the comment as soon as I've said it and wash my mouth out with the rest of the red wine.

"Don't, Alison. Just don't. Anyway, have you texted home to say you'll be late?" He takes another onion and cuts it in half, his knife banging hard onto the board.

I raise my hand. Touché.

"I find it hard to believe you're not married," I say.

"At my age, you mean? I'm not fifty yet, there's still time."

"I didn't mean —"

He laughs. "Don't worry, I know what you

mean. I was, once. In my early twenties. We got carried away. Then she went off with someone else. But it was for the best."

His voice is light but I look at him closely to see if there's any trace of hurt underneath.

"You think?" I say.

"Definitely. I prefer it this way. Marriage doesn't look that great from where I'm standing. This, on the other hand . . ." He smiles at me.

There's cigarettes on the counter, and an ashtray. I gesture at them to ask if I can have one.

"Do you even buy any?" he says, but nods assent.

"It means I don't smoke too much," I say. "I can't smoke at home."

"I guess not." He switches on the extractor fan as if I've reminded him to mitigate the smell. It's a moment of indulgence, sitting in a warm kitchen with wine and fag. I can't remember the last time I smoked indoors.

When I've finished I put down my empty glass on the island beside the stove. I go over to the white leather sofa and pull out my phone from my bag. It's only 8:15 — I'm not late yet. But I know I'm going to be . . .

This conference is going to run over — sorry. I'll try not to disturb you when I come in xx

Then I put my phone back in my bag. None of this is happening, it's not real. And if it's not real, I'm not real, and nothing I do is real. The wine takes hold in my brain, a warm floating, and I let go of the rest of the anchors, turning back to Patrick and pouring myself another glass.

The lamb is tender and the wine mellow and Patrick's hands on me gentle, so gentle as I respond to his lightest touch, the two of us moving as one. He sighs into my hair and pulls me close.

"Why can't it be like this all the time?" I say.

"You know why. Can't you just enjoy it, stop worrying?"

"I suppose." I shut my eyes.

This time he's put on some Schubert, piano sonatas, and the sound soothes me gradually towards sleep. A loud beep breaks through the calm. Patrick lets go of me and reaches for his phone and at the same time I reach for mine. He starts tapping his screen and I activate mine, seeing a text from Carl.

Mum says no problem for looking after Matilda in November. I'll book a hotel. See you later xx

Reality dumps a bucket of cold water over me. I pull away further from Patrick and sit up.

"I'm going to have to go. It's after eleven," I say.

"Fair enough. That was Chloe, by the way. The conference is set with Madeleine for tomorrow afternoon. You're still all right for that?"

"Yes, that's fine." I get up and go to the shower, washing myself quickly. I dress while Patrick lies in bed watching me. Before I leave I sit beside him on the bed, hand on his chest. I lean over and kiss him.

"This was a good night."

"It was. You see, it can be good. If you just let it." He sits up and pulls me into a hug. I subside into him and then stand up.

"I'll call you after the conference."

"Good luck with it." He waves one hand and turns his attention back to his phone.

I find a cab easily outside his flat, even though it's started to rain, and sit in silence looking out the window. Patrick, Carl, Patrick, Carl, the names chiming in turn with the windscreen wipers. It's as much of a mess as ever but I can't stop the smile that reaches across my face or the warm feeling inside that's for once loosened the tight knot under my ribs. I am going to let it be good. At least for tonight.

As the cab drives up towards Archway I check my phone. Patrick has texted.

Good night darling. Sleep well. That was a lovely night.

I run my finger over the screen, smiling. The nicest text he's ever sent me — I hug the thought to me. The phone screen dims, then lights up again. Another text. Without a sender number.

Stay the fuck away from him.

My hands are shaking as I delete both texts. This isn't going away — I'm going to have to tell Patrick. I turn off my phone, the hostile eye into my world.

The house is dark as I let myself in and tiptoe up the stairs. Carl is asleep. He shifts over as I get into bed, his back warm against me. I lie awake wondering if someone is lying next to Patrick, or if they are standing outside, watching.

But are they watching him, or me?

10

I wake when Carl brings me coffee. Twice in a week — it's a record, for the last couple of years at least. I'm groggy, pulled from the depths of a slumber that only came around four or five. Carl sits on the side of the bed next to me.

"How was your meeting? Is the murder going well?" he says.

"It's all fine. Sorry I was late," I reply, trying not to show surprise at his interest.

"It's no problem. Matilda was fine. I did some work. I saw details for a weekend conference on sex addiction and the internet — it might be interesting."

"Sure, yes. That's what your group meeting is about, isn't it?" I take another drink of coffee. He's not the only one who cares.

"Amongst other things. Anyway, I told you I talked to my mother? She's fine with that weekend in November. Just for one night but we can go somewhere nice."

"Where are you thinking?" I say.

"Brighton, maybe? Somewhere on the coast? I'll have a look."

"Great." Matilda runs through at this point and again the three of us are together on the bed, a family triptych. I hug her and Carl joins in, and for a moment it's all there is until I cough and the spell is broken. Carl walks downstairs, Matilda goes to her room to get dressed, and I shower and wash what's left of Patrick off me. I shampoo my hair and stand under the warm water rinsing it off for a long time until Carl thumps on the door and I dry myself quickly and let him have the bathroom.

Dressed, I go downstairs and make another coffee. Matilda is by now sitting at the kitchen table eating a bowl of cereal. I kiss her on the top of the head and wander into the living room. It's tidy, the books in their usual order on the shelves and the magazines that Carl persists in keeping piled up neatly underneath the television. Something feels wrong though, a note chiming a little off key. I stand in the doorway, looking around. Then it hits me.

"Was someone smoking in here?" I call out.

"What?" Carl's still upstairs.

I walk out to the bottom of the stairs.

"Was someone smoking in the house last night? It smells."

"No, it doesn't." He comes downstairs, wrapped in a towel.

"It does. Look, in here. In the living room." I stand there sniffing. It really does, I'm sure of it. There's a staleness that reminds me of my student flat, when everyone smoked with abandon. A staleness I smelled in Patrick's flat, truth be told, despite his attempts to air the place. I think for a moment of the luxury of being able to light up in his flat — I haven't smoked a cigarette inside my house for the best part of ten years. Though I don't miss the smell. Carl comes into the room, sniffs as well.

"It definitely doesn't. You're imagining things."

"I'm sure it does, though." Now I'm beginning to wonder.

Carl walks over to me and smells my jacket. "It's you. Your suit stinks. It's all that time you spend in the cells. And in the pub."

I pull my collar up to my nose and inhale. All I can smell is perfume and a hint of fried food. But if he says it smells . . . I was wearing it when I was smoking last night. I leave the room and return to the kitchen, standing in the doorway and breathing in.

"It smells a bit in here too," I say.

"I told you, it's your suit. You always smell of smoke." Carl stands right behind me and pulls at my jacket to emphasize his point.

"Mummy, please don't smoke, it's yuck and you'll die, they told us at school." Matilda's face crumples and she looks as if she's going to cry. I go over to her and try to hug her but she pulls away from me. "You smell of smoke, Mummy, I don't want to smell it."

"Alison, leave her." Carl pushes me to one side and picks Matilda up. He holds her close, turning to face me over her shoulder. He looks at me with disappointment. "I wish you'd think more."

"I do think —" I start to say.

He interrupts, "I just worry about Matilda being exposed to secondhand smoke."

"I'm not. I don't think my clothes smell. It's the house . . ." My words trail off.

"It's clearly not the house. No one's allowed to smoke in the house. Just get your suit dry-cleaned and tell your clients they can't smoke in front of you. Think about Matilda."

I shrug, nod. Maybe he's right. Maybe it's me. I could swear that it's the house, but I can't swear it's not me. The smoke from all the cigarettes I've ever smoked and my clients have ever smoked must follow me in a miasma to which I've become so used I don't notice it anymore. I retreat upstairs to get my stuff together.

I'm ready to leave by the time Carl and Matilda come upstairs for her to clean her teeth. I stick my head round the door and say goodbye. Matilda is too busy scrubbing to notice at first, but then sees me. I blow her a kiss and she blows one back.

I leave the house fast, looking around to see if anyone is there, watching. It's bright sunlight and the sense of menace I felt the night before has faded. I check over my shoulder once or twice but the street seems so normal that my fears subside even further. Once I'm on the bus I face the inevitable and turn my phone back on. It beeps, and texts start to arrive. I open the first, one from Chloe:

> Madeleine in London today. Conference in office at 12 pm. OK? C

I'm about to reply when I see there are two more messages waiting for me. Both from the anonymous source.

> I know ur still at it u fucking bitch.

The second, a list of emojis. A man and a

woman standing holding hands, an angry face, a yellow woman with her arms crossed in front of her and a skull.

Even though my hands are still shaking from the first message, menacing in its implication that someone knows what Patrick and I are doing and when, looking at the emojis I can't help but laugh. It's like *Scooby-Doo* when they pull the mask off the scary monster. I'm dealing with a teenager here, surely. No self-respecting stalker is going to use emojis. I feel a certain relief and check my emails instead. There's nothing untoward, one from the clerks confirming the arrival of the psychiatric report on Madeleine into chambers. It's time to think about the case.

It keeps nagging, though. It is a skull. Just because it's laughable doesn't mean it's a joke. I text Patrick.

I've been sent some anonymous messages — I think someone knows about this.

I sit holding my phone in my hand waiting for him to reply until the bus arrives in Fleet Street.

He still hasn't replied by the time I've walked into chambers. I greet the clerks and take the new papers in Madeleine's case through to my desk. I check my phone again — nothing. I sit down at my desk and start to read. When I'm halfway through the psychiatric report there's a beep and I see a message from Patrick.

What kind of anonymous messages?

I forward them to him, with an additional message from me:

What do you think?

He replies immediately.

OK it's a bit odd but try not to get paranoid.

I reply.

It sounds like they know what's going on. And I think it's a woman. They used a woman emoji.

He replies.

Try not to worry. Let's talk about it later. Going into court.

Maybe I am overreacting. Someone's trying to mess with my head but it could be anyone, it doesn't have to be anything to do with Patrick. He's right, I am being paranoid. I've got years' worth of clients who might be trying to have a go. It could be anything. I put my phone down and open the files in front of me, try to concentrate on some work.

I read through the papers but the words aren't going in. I can't focus, my mind jumping from one explanation to the next. It must be something to do with him. Surely? Maybe he's shagging someone else as well and maybe they're getting off on laughing at me about it, and he's telling her everything and then she's saying *oh I know what would be funny silly cow going home to her husband like that* and then she's sending them and he knows all about it . . . That can't be right. He wouldn't do that to me, making out like he cares and being so nice to me and all the time laughing at me. I walk up and down the room, trying to calm myself, but now the thought's in my head it won't go. I know he's in court but I need to ask him, must speak to him.

I retrieve my phone and try to call him but it goes straight to voicemail. "I need to ask, Patrick. Are you sleeping with someone else? I don't know what else to think." I hang up. Moments later I regret it but it's too late, it's done. I can't retrieve it, can't delete it. My agitation grows.

I'm about to call again when I'm interrupted by Mark, who knocks on the door and sticks his head round the side. I compose my face to normal.

"Yes?"

"Message from Chloe at Saunders & Co, miss. Double-checking you know you're not going to Beaconsfield this afternoon. The client'll be in the office," he says, not giving any indication as to whether he's heard my outburst.

"She texted earlier. I must have forgotten to reply," I say, affecting calm. "At twelve, is that right?"

"That's what she said." He leaves, shutting the door behind him. I force my mind back to Madeleine's case, looking at the papers in front of me.

Diminished responsibility is out as a defense, that much is clear from the psychiatrist's report, though he describes Madeleine as extremely unforthcoming. Very guarded. Her childhood is reported as normal, no major traumatic events, and her adolescence and early motherhood all fine. One brief spell of depression and anxiety immediately after her son was born, but a short course of antianxiety medication sorted that out. I check the drug — it turns out to be the same one that I was on for a while in my twenties. I remember taking myself off it cold turkey, as I no longer trusted the doctor who was prescribing it to me. As the drug withdrew from my system my brain had moments when it felt as if it was crackling, the nerves exposed harshly against a dark screen. But I also remember the way that a weight lifted from me as the pills began to kick in at the start. The psychiatrist has discussed with Madeleine whether she feels that any medication would be of assistance now but she's said no.

And despite what she said to us in the second conference, it doesn't seem that she's admitting to any issues with alcohol, though the psychiatrist has noted that Madeleine said she had drunk so much that she has no recollection of the events of that night or of stabbing Edwin — I still wonder if she'll stick to that story if I question her more about it.

A witness statement has also been provided by the cleaning lady, an Ilma Cooper, the first witness on the scene. It adds some flesh to the bones already provided in the prosecution summary. She was surprised on her arrival by the behavior of the family dog, a cream Labradoodle. The dog was normally placid, she says in her statement, but on this morning could be heard barking as Cooper opened the door. There was a smell when she entered and she saw that the dog had crapped on the hall floor, which was unusual. It was in a panic and wouldn't settle to be petted, instead running up and down the stairs in an anxious manner. Cooper removed her coat and then went straight up to the second-floor landing, unnerved by the dog's behavior. The door of the master suite was open, and she entered to find the scene of the crime, the body of Edwin on the bed and Madeleine on the floor beside it.

She remarks on the strong smell of alcohol around Madeleine and that there was a half-empty bottle of Hendrick's gin on the floor next to her. None of the cheap stuff for my client. We've got Gordon's at home but I make a mental note to get some Hendrick's in, try it with cucumber, a finer route to oblivion. Cooper says that Madeleine was at first unresponsive, sitting on the floor beside the bed with her knees held tightly to her chest. After a few attempts to get Madeleine to speak to her, Cooper shook her gently by the shoulder and at that point Madeleine focused on her. Cooper said she needed to call an ambulance and the police, and Madeleine acquiesced without saying anything to her. Cooper called 999 on her mobile from the bedroom and when the police arrived she let them in, leaving Madeleine sitting upstairs in the same position. She watched Madeleine being taken away by the police and said that she had been completely calm, eerily so.

I think about how I might react if I'd just killed Carl — shocked? In denial that it had just happened? Had she really been drunk beforehand, or did she do it and drink afterwards? I know she isn't trying to defend herself on the basis of intoxication — not that that route would be available to her in any event — but still, it's an interesting situation. They have a row, he's out cold, she stabs him while he's sleeping . . . It's hard to make a connection between this Madeleine and the one I've met in Beaconsfield. Nervy, yes, emotional, definitely, but the epitome of poise, groomed and chic. Not the kind of woman to lose control.

I look again at the statement, at the last paragraph, where Cooper describes Madeleine's appearance after she has come downstairs with the police officers.

She always wears beiges, creams, those sorts of colors. So it really showed when she stood up and came downstairs. All the blood. Up the edges of her sleeves, like when you get wet from the washing-up, and over the front of her jumper. There was so much blood. It was the same with the dog. That dog always shows the muck, it's not a practical color. Washing her is one of my jobs, every week. I didn't notice when I first came in because of the barking and running round, but afterwards I saw. Her muzzle was all stained brownish red, all up her face. I had to wash her immediately, it made me feel so funny. I thought I was going to be sick. It took three goes with the shampoo to get it all out.

The dog, the blood, the smell of shit in the hall. I can picture the dog in the bath, standing while Cooper scrubbed and scrubbed at it, the fur stuck close to its skin and the water draining away, rust-stained until it finally ran clear. I clasp my hands together, feeling the blood pumping through the veins, a slow, regular beat. Then I shake my head clear. There's only so much reality I can bear before I have to push the horror back, return to a cool analysis of the case. I'm not here to smell the stench of death,

I'm here to reduce the mess to its component parts, file it under a subsection of a statute here and a common law defense there.

The phone rings. It's the clerks reminding me to leave. I fold the papers back together and put them on the shelf beside my desk, hoping that the image of the bloodstained dog will soon stop following at my heels.

11

I try to call Patrick as I walk up to the office, but again it goes through to his voicemail. I leave another message. "Sorry, I know it wasn't helpful leaving a voicemail like that. I'm really freaked out about this, though, and I need to talk to you." At least no other message has arrived. Chancery Lane is busy with people going for lunch, carrying takeout bags from Pret and Eat and looking intently at their phones as they go. I blend into their number, dark suit, black pumps, a sense of purpose to my day.

Chloe's in the front office when I arrive, waving at me in greeting. She gestures to Patrick's office.

"I've put her in there," she says. Her voice is lowered and I have to stand close to hear her. "I think she's quite nervous." There's a pause. "I suppose one would be." Chloe isn't someone who appears ever to be affected by nerves.

"Thanks," I say. "I'll go through."

Madeleine is immaculate, her hair in perfect waves past her shoulders. She's wearing a jacket on this occasion, not knitwear, cream again with some sort of beige weave through it. Tweed or something. The cuffs skim her hands and I try not to stare, try not to imagine them soaked in blood.

She's sitting on the client side of Patrick's desk. I walk past her to the chair on the other side. The room's dim, the blinds half-shut as usual. I've never been here when it's fully light, regardless of time of day. I sit down and pull out the papers, turning on the lamp that's on the desk. Its light is yellow and ineffective.

"Do you think we could get something to eat?" she says. "I'm suddenly really hungry. I don't want to hold you up, but maybe we could talk about it over lunch?"

It's not what I expected. My initial instinct is to say no, but I look at her more closely and see how uncomfortable she seems. She's perched on the edge of the chair, her legs tightly crossed, her hands scratching at each other. I remember the purpose of this exercise, to talk to her on my own, get her more at ease with me so she can give me the information I need to defend her properly.

"I don't see why not, if we can find somewhere quiet enough," I say. "There's a wine bar along the way that shouldn't be too busy now."

We leave Patrick's room. I stick my head round into Chloe's office. "We're going to go and get some lunch."

She raises an eyebrow so I walk in closer to her desk. Lowering my voice, I say, "You're right, she's very nervous. Some food and a less formal environment may calm her down."

Chloe nods. "You may have a point." She looks back at the papers she's reading. "Anyway, good to see you."

We head for Jasper's, a basement wine bar not far up High Holborn. As I hoped, it isn't too full. I ask if we can have a table in the corner and they seat us there, Madeleine on the banquette, me with my back to the room.

"Would you like some water for the table? Still or sparkling?" the waiter says.

"Sparkling?" Madeleine says, looking at me for agreement. I nod.

"And will you be having wine?"

I open my mouth to say no, water is fine,

but Madeleine speaks again, "I'd quite like a glass. What do you think?" She looks at me. I shouldn't, this is work, but on the other hand, the purpose of the exercise is to make her feel more relaxed.

"A small one," I say.

She turns to the waiter. "Two small glasses of sauvignon blanc, please."

I push the knife and fork away from the place in front of me, and replace them with one of my blue notebooks. I take the cap off my pen and write *Madeleine Smith Conference Wednesday 29 October,* underlining the words. I'm opening my mouth to ask the first question when the waiter returns with the wine, putting it down clumsily so that it slops over the side of the glass and onto the paper, smudging the ink. I dab at it with my napkin, annoyed that the page is spoiled.

"Cheers." Madeleine holds her glass up to me. I grimace, and after a moment, hold my glass up and clink it against hers. This feels wildly inappropriate.

"Cheers."

She takes a long drink then sighs, smiling. She looks around the room. "Thank you for agreeing to come out instead of being in the office. This is a lot nicer. It's almost like being normal again. I haven't been out since it all happened . . ."

I'm struck that *it all happened* refers to the bloodstained scene about which I've just been reading. I look at Madeleine closely, searching for a trace of emotion, but she's reading through the menu intently. Anyone looking at us would think we were two friends meeting for lunch, not an alleged murderer and her barrister. "It must all be very difficult," I say with as neutral a tone as possible, trying not to think about how odd this situation is.

"It really is." She takes a sip of wine. "Now, what are we going to eat?"

I look at the menu. I'm not bothered what I eat, keen to get the conference under way. "We do have quite a lot we need to talk about," I say in an attempt to prompt her.

She doesn't even look up from the menu, entranced. I skim it again. Steak. I'll have a steak. My minds stutters for a moment, wondering who is paying for this, but then I take another sip of wine and I realize I don't care.

"What are you going to have?" Madeleine asks.

"Steak, I think. Easy," I reply.

"Same here. Good idea. We should get some red." She turns back to the menu.

I flip over to a new page in my notebook,

one that isn't stained with wine, and write the title on the top line again.

"Madeleine, you know that we're here to talk about what's happening with your case and what your plea is going to be at the hearing."

She nods, still looking at the menu, before gesturing to the waiter.

"A bottle of the Châteauneuf-du-Pape," Madeleine says to him, pointing to the list of reds on the menu in front of her.

He notes it down, an impressed expression on his face. I wonder again who's paying for this lunch, and suppress the thought with a large slug of sauvignon. It gives me a burst of courage — this is my conference, and I have to stop letting Madeleine run it. I'm taking charge.

"Madeleine, I do have to ask a few questions. We need to understand the relationship between you and your husband," I say.

The cheerful expression leaves her face and she presses her hands to her mouth, a flush rising up her face.

"I'm sorry, but we really must. You've said that the last thing you can remember that Sunday night is that he said he wanted to leave you. Is that right?"

She's about to reply when the waiter appears with the red wine that she's ordered.

He goes through the whole performance of showing, telling, pouring and, composed once more, Madeleine takes the fresh glass and swills it round, smelling it before nodding her approval. He pours a glass for me and tops up hers. I'm about to say that I'm not going to drink any more but then another waiter appears with a notepad, asking for our food orders.

"We're both having the steak, please," Madeleine says. "Medium rare. And a green salad. That okay, Alison?"

I smile and nod. Some conference this is turning out to be — despite my best efforts, Madeleine is firmly in the driver's seat. She gestures at the red wine as if to ask what I think of it and defeated, I taste it. It's delicious, much nicer than the sauvignon that I've just drunk. More mellow, less acid on my throat. The tannic fumes are soothing and even though I'm irritated that we're not getting on with the case, she's so thin and nervy it's hard not to feel sorry for her. Her jacket is clearly designer but it's hanging off her, too loose in the shoulders. She was wearing a scarf when I first arrived but this has slipped down and I can see how knotted her neck is. My face looks twice the size of hers, looming moonlike in the mirror behind her. I have another drink.

"I wish we didn't have to talk about it, Alison," she says. "I wish we could just enjoy lunch."

"I know, but I really need instructions from you if I'm going to advise you properly about the conduct of your case. You're facing life for murder, Madeleine," I say, leaning across the table towards her. "There might be something we can do to make that a lesser sentence, a lesser offense. But you have to tell me what happened."

She covers her face with her hands for a moment, then lowers them, raises her chin. She's about to speak but the waiter serves our steaks. He puts them down on the table, goes away, and then comes back with the salad and two sharp knives. I cut into my steak and watch as blood pools on the plate from it. It's not medium rare, it's practically blue, the flesh dark red and glistening under the lights, the fat exploding yellow under the charred brown surface. I take a mouthful and chew, swallow. Madeleine hasn't even looked at her food. She's finished her glass of red and is topping it up. I'm about to say something, anything, to prompt her to start talking again, but she begins.

"I don't know when it all started to go wrong. I mean, I know what you think, the business with the pill. I could see your face when I was telling you."

"I'm sorry, I didn't mean —" I say.

"Of course not. But as I said at the time, you had to be there to understand. Edwin was always very good at knowing what the best thing was to do. At least at the beginning . . ." she says. She's looking away from me, over my shoulder. I keep cutting, chewing, swallowing. Nothing to disturb her calm.

"He did go too far. He'd make all the decisions for us. For me. And I didn't mind. It was a relief to have someone take over. I loved him so much, I just wanted him to be happy. And I wasn't always good at making him happy. I fucked up a lot." She pauses, drinks again.

"Fucked up in what kind of way?" I ask when she doesn't start speaking again.

"I couldn't cook properly, I wasn't looking after his clients well enough. I didn't present myself well enough. I guess I was too young to understand what was needed, how it was a job for me as well as for him. I was an extension of him and I needed to be better at it, otherwise I was just letting him down."

"Did anything happen when you let him down?" I ask.

"He'd get so angry . . . Again, it was my

fault. I'd push him too far, get the meal wrong, wear the wrong clothes. I'm not surprised he'd get so cross. I would have, in his position," she says.

"Madeleine, when he got angry . . . what did he do?" I'm keeping my voice very calm, level.

She holds up her left hand, palm outstretched towards me. I look at it for some moments before realizing what it is she's showing me. The little finger is bent like a claw.

"I can't straighten anymore it. Not since . . ." Her voice fades off.

"Not since?" I say, quietly.

"I burned the meat. It was a dinner for one of his main clients and her wife. He told me they were very particular, used to eating in all the best places . . . I said we should get a caterer but he wanted them to have a proper English home experience . . ."

"And?"

"I fucked it up. Got too drunk." She looks at her glass and laughs. Drinks deeply from it. "The meat burned, I was a bit sick. We got a takeaway — I thought everything was all right. I thought they saw the joke. But after they left . . . I'd had so much to drink it didn't hurt so much that night. But the following day . . ."

"What did he do, Madeleine?" I say.

She pauses, takes a deep breath. "He took my hand and bent my finger back and back until it snapped."

I'm holding my hands together, my steak forgotten. "Did you go to hospital?" It's an effort to keep my voice neutral.

"No, he wouldn't let me. I think it must have broken in a couple of places, that's why it's crooked now. I tried strapping it up but it wouldn't go straight. You see why I don't like to talk about it?" she says.

"Yes. I can see why. Look, I've read the psychiatrist report, but it makes no mention of any of this. It talks about your relationship having been typical, a normal one."

"He didn't ask anything about this sort of thing. And I didn't want to bring it up cold," she says.

"I do understand how difficult this is for you, but we're going to have to know all of it, Madeleine. All of it . . . You'll have to speak to the psychiatrist again, give him all these details."

"Not him. I didn't like him," Madeleine says.

"Okay. We'll find someone else. You must talk to them whether you like them or not, though. It's too important. This could turn it from murder to manslaughter. And that would make a huge difference to the outcome."

Something shifts in the air, the resistance I'd sensed earlier fading to a ripple, then gone. Madeleine sighs as if she's been waiting for this to happen, as if I've taken a weight off her. I feel relief too, a sense of vindication that however unorthodox, coming to this restaurant, having a drink with her, has worked. I've found the key that's going to unlock the case.

"Do we have time?" she says.

"We have time. Don't worry about that. We definitely have time. Let's eat lunch and then you sit and tell me everything. I'll write it all down, and then we'll know where we are."

"All right. I'll stop being difficult." She laughs, again without humor, and starts to eat her food, slicing the meat with precision.

We finish the bottle of wine but don't order another, switching to coffee for the rest of the afternoon. By the end of the session I've filled pages upon pages in my notebook, and I know exactly what we need to do next. When the bill arrives I pay it without hesitation — I've had the breakthrough I need. I walk Madeleine to Holborn Tube station and walk down Kingsway, my mind spinning with everything I've been told.

Patrick calls me back around five.

"What was that message all about?"

"I left another one saying sorry," I reply.

"I know, but I don't understand what this is all about."

"I'm just trying to work out what these texts are about. They could relate to you and me," I say.

"It could be anything, one of your old clients, someone to do with your husband. You can't assume it's to do with me."

"It might be. They always arrive after I've seen you," I say.

"That could just be coincidence. Do try and be calmer about it."

"What do you think I should do?"

"There isn't much you can do. Wait and see if anything else happens. You haven't directly been threatened. If you are, take it to the police."

He's right. I'm about to say so but he starts again.

"And honestly, it's none of your business whether I'm shagging someone else or not — you're the one who's married, not me. Surely I don't have to point that out."

"Right. Yes. Yes, of course." I can't argue

with that. "I'm sorry. It was a stupid thing to say. I'm just a bit freaked out."

"Okay. Was it a productive conference with Madeleine? Chloe says you went to Jasper's — I hope you kept it sober."

He's joking. He's got to be joking. Are we going to have a row about this? There's a dull throb behind my right eye, a reminder of the wine that we drank.

"I was perfectly sober, thank you," I say, striving for a dignified tone. "It was a conference, even if we chose to have it in a wine bar. She gave a lot of instructions."

"Let's hope you weren't too pissed to remember the half of them," Patrick says.

It's like talking to Carl. I take a deep breath. And another. "I'll type the notes up for you. Then you'll see." I hang up.

Once I've finished typing up the notes and my conclusion, I email it to Patrick. I have given him a plan of action, a list of the witnesses he needs to track down and of the evidence that we're going to need. I keep my tone professional, businesslike, treating him like any other instructing solicitor. It's a good piece of work, summarizing both her statement and the legal analysis required to back up my point. Once the email has gone through I log out and turn my computer off. It's time to go home.

It's dark as I wheel my bag through Fountain Court. The streetlights are lit and there's a hint of fog in the air. It's got that Dickensian feel that gets the tourists so wild for the Temple. I wheel past a group of them, led by a guide. She's telling them the history of the buildings and I want to stop, join them, pretend I know nothing about the reality of what happens behind these walls. I want them to be as romantic as they look, to imagine that the insides match the outsides with fireplaces and dimly lit candelabras, not filing cabinets and badly placed plasterboard. They probably see barristers as romantic too, sweeping gowns and horsehair wigs, fighting for the causes of justice and righteousness. I think that way too, sometimes, despite the reality; the mundanity of crisscrossing the southeast from magistrates' court to magistrates' court, the momentary glory of a win in the Appeal Court soon lost in the frustration of being last on the list on a Friday at Wood Green. But still, there's nothing like the thrill of knowing a jury's on my side, convinced by the arguments I'm putting forward.

I go through Devereux Court past the Freeman's Arms, past all the duffers with red noses telling war stories about the time they got someone off with their brilliant advocacy. I can see them through the windows, surrounded by nodding pupils. I was like that once, ready to suck up any old nonsense for the sake of getting ahead, being noticed by them and maybe getting some work to do that might make solicitors like me or the clerks more likely to push briefs my way. I drank my way through Monday to Friday, nodding and smiling and laughing in all the right places.

Robert from chambers is standing outside Cairn's having a fag. I stop beside him and steal a drag before remembering the row of the morning, Matilda's heartfelt pleas for me not to smoke. Damn. I wave goodbye to Robert and trail up to the corner shop opposite the Royal Courts of Justice. It's still open and I buy mints and water, swilling my mouth out and sucking the mints down by the handful. I can't deal with any more rows tonight.

"Alison. Alison!" Someone's calling my name. I keep walking. The volume of the shouts grows and then he's standing in front of me. "I saw you passing — I was in Cairn's. I need to talk to you."

"I've got to go home, Patrick."

"Are you okay?" He's right up in front of me now.

"I'm fine," I say.

"Sorry if you thought I was suggesting you can't do your job properly," he says.

"We had a drink," I say. "But we didn't get drunk."

"Of course not. I was the one who suggested getting Madeleine to open up a bit, after all. And look, do you want me to go with you to the police with the text messages? I can see why it's frightening."

I can imagine the police reaction. They don't even investigate burglaries anymore. What on earth would they do with four cartoon emojis from an anonymous number? There's nothing concrete enough.

"I don't think it's worth it. Not at the moment. I don't like it, though," I say.

"Of course you don't. But look, seriously, you can't go getting upset about me seeing other people. It's not fair. We can't work like that," he says, his face earnest.

"I don't mean to. It's hard, though."

"I know. But those times that you're with your family, it's hard for me. You can't tell me that I shouldn't be with other people. Be fair."

I sigh. I can't argue. "But please, not in my face. Like that night in Cairn's."

"Okay, fair enough. Not in your face," he says. "I'll take care of it."

"And what if I get another text?"

"Delete it and forget about it, if you don't want to go to the police. As long they stay at this level there's nothing to worry about." His voice is reassuring and I want to fall into it. Something holds me back from it, though, a sense of a shadow lurking over my shoulder.

"But what if . . ."

"Stop with all the what-ifs, the speculations. There's enough to worry about without adding to it," he says. "Now, are we going to go and get a drink, or what? I've got some food at home if you fancy dinner?"

He reaches his hand out to me and I'm about to take it but then my phone beeps.

> I've booked a hotel in Brighton. Winter beaches! We liked it last time, so I thought it might work. See you in a bit — there's a chicken in the oven xx ps Matilda says hi.

Carl. And a photo attached, a selfie of the two of them smiling at me, heads together in front of the camera. I turn the screen off quickly, not wanting Patrick to see them.

"I have to go home," I say. "I promised. They're cooking me supper."

His face closes. "How lovely. Family time. Don't let me keep you, then."

"Patrick. I have to go. What are you going

to do?" I don't mean to ask but the words slip out.

"I'm going to go and have a drink."

"I can join you for one. If that's any good," I offer.

"I'm not some charity case. Just go home." He turns away and walks back down Essex Street.

I open my mouth to call after him, close it. Turning away from Essex Street, I take the crosswalk in front of the Royal Courts of Justice. I'm ready to wait for a bus, part of me wondering if he'll appear again out of the dark, but the number 4 arrives almost immediately and I climb on.

I text Carl.

On the bus xx

Nothing from Patrick. Nothing from anyone else. It's time to go home.

Kisses from both Carl and Matilda when I open the front door. The air is fragrant with the scent of roasted chicken. Carl mixes me a gin and tonic and Matilda tells me all about her day and how her best friend was being mean but "I told her how I feel about it, Mummy, and she's stopped." She sits on my knee while I read her a story about a boy who turned into a cat for a day and Carl sits beside us listening, a half smile on his face. He touches my arm, then leans over to kiss me again on the cheek.

"It's good to have you home, Alison."

"I haven't been gone that long," I say, laughing.

"I know. Just nice to have you home. Isn't it, Tilly! We like it when Mummy's at home." He pulls Matilda off my knee onto his. I resist the urge to hold on tight to her. Instead I lean over into him. The triptych from the morning is reformed.

We eat together at the kitchen table, the meat tender. Together we talk to Matilda while she has a bath, and together we put her to bed, singing nursery rhymes to her and holding her hand until she closes her eyes. We go back downstairs and Carl pours us both another glass of wine from the bottle he opened when we ate the chicken. We sit down on the sofa in the living room.

"So you thought Brighton?" I say.

"Yes. Close enough, lots to do. And a winter beach just for you." He opens his laptop that's on the sofa beside him and clicks through some windows until he finds the one he's looking for. He passes the laptop to me. "This is the hotel I liked."

It looks good, sea view, white sheets and

waffle robes in the bedrooms. I smile at him, touched at the thought he's put into it. I move the cursor over to the menu so I can see exactly where it is but as I do so Carl snatches the computer away from me and slams it shut.

"What did you do that for?"

"Maybe I'm planning another surprise," he says, leaning forward and kissing me, my face in his hands. His tongue moves into my mouth. For a moment I can't even explain, I feel strongly that I want to bite it, thrust it out and push him away from me. It's almost as if he's a stranger. And then the smell of him overcomes me, the Carl-ness of him, and that urge passes, another one replacing it.

"What about Matilda?" I say eventually.

He doesn't reply, but leans over me to push the door shut. He kisses me again, holding my face, before his hands move down, down . . .

Matilda doesn't disturb us. We all sleep well that night.

12

Over the next week, communication with Patrick is brief and to the point. He's tracking down the witnesses, taking their statements and weighing up their evidential strength. Madeleine has an appointment to see the new psychiatrist just a couple of days before the plea hearing. I know of her professionally, this shrink. She's good. Fast. The report will be turned round in time. Besides, I've nearly got enough for a defense case statement, even now. Unless my plans fall apart, Madeleine will be pleading not guilty to murder when she comes before the judge in the Old Bailey, and we'll be getting our case in order to offer a plea to manslaughter on the basis of loss of control. If the prosecution accept it, the judge will have complete sentencing discretion. In other words, not a life sentence. It's not great but it's the best I can do.

And with that under control, I'm able to

concentrate on my other cases, the usual juggling act of travel and last-minute instructions, missing papers and crashed court computer systems. There's a change of plea in a robbery and he goes down for five years — not a bad result, really. The following day I have a PTPH for what's going to be a very difficult rape trial I'm prosecuting, one of the awful he said/she said variety, where CCTV evidence will be provided that follows the pair all the way to the door of the hotel. Shame it didn't film through the keyhole. It's hard enough to get a conviction for rape without multiple images of the woman snogging the man in various doorways around Borough Market and into the Premier Inn near Tower Bridge — I know the jury aren't going to like it, the waters being muddied like that.

I hate this sort of case. It's clear from the victim's statement that what started as a bit of drunken fun turned into something utterly terrifying, the trauma showing through the formality of the statement. The defendant had a smirk on his face throughout the hearing that made me want to punch him, the kind of entitlement that made me believe entirely that he knew what he wanted and he went for it, regardless of no meaning no. I hope the medical report of her injuries will help to convince the jury that what happened was not consensual. However rough the sex I've had, I've never needed stitches. From the defense case statement it's clear he's going to say that they were both so out of it they didn't notice that she'd been hurt — I intend to argue that if the jury don't accept that the victim clearly said no and is now regretting it and lying to cover it up, they should accept that if she was too drunk to notice a massive anal tear, she was too drunk to consent to sexual activity. One way or the other, I want to pot the fucker.

That weekend goes fast. Carl's away at a conference, not the sex addiction one he talked about before but a different one, dealing more specifically with internet pornography addiction. A place became available at the last minute. I take photographs of Matilda playing on the swings and drinking a hot chocolate at the café in the park and send them to him, an innocence to inoculate him against the horrors he'll be hearing about. His mother calls and we have a chat about what she needs to do with Matilda the following weekend when she's looking after her.

"I'll make sure the fridge is full. I'll leave you a meal plan, save you having to think about that," I say.

"No need, I'm sure I can manage to cook for the two of us. Do you want me to take her to any activities? Does she have anything at the weekends? I find it so hard to keep up with all your arrangements," she says.

"She can miss things for one weekend. Let's keep this simple." Carl won't like it but I don't think it's on, making his mum drag Matilda to swimming.

"Thanks. I think that would be easier."

"Definitely. I prefer to avoid swimming myself," I say, laughing.

"Yes. Carl told me." She doesn't laugh back and I get off the phone quickly. It'll be better if Carl talks to her and makes sure she's comfortable with all the plans.

The Monday slips fast into Tuesday and beyond, a five-day trial at the Crown Court in Harrow, another multihanded robbery. Patrick sends me some more updates. I'm cautiously optimistic about the prospects for Madeleine's case — we're getting more information than I'd hoped.

The jury are so fast to convict on the Friday that even with sentence (four years, could be worse) and a postsentence conversation with the client I'm out by three. Robert and Sankar have both texted to suggest drinks but I'm happy to say no. I'm going home. I want to spend the Friday in with

Matilda.

Between pizza and a film about a panda with fantastical skills in martial arts she's happy, and frankly so am I. I've gotten through a whole week without speaking to Patrick about anything other than work. I'm not washing another man off me when I shower, thoughts of him aren't distracting me from my family. I've got my integrity back. That's not the only reward either. My phone has stayed silent for the whole week, no threats or accusations from the anonymous accuser. Whatever Patrick says, I know it's someone connected with him. And they've achieved their goal, however indirectly. I'm keeping away from him, no problem. This week.

Once Matilda is in bed, I pack for the night away. Carl is out on an emergency session with one of his clients who's called in a state, meeting him at the therapy room he rents in an alternative remedies clinic in Tufnell Park. Poor Carl, he has to keep his professional certificates on the wall at home — the day he can hang them up at work, knowing that he isn't sharing the room with any other therapists, that's when he'll know he's made it. I can sympathize with that. Getting my own desk in chambers was a massive deal, getting my name up on the board outside chambers as a full tenant — I still remember the thrill it gave me when I first saw it there.

I look at the dresses hanging up in my wardrobe and pull one out, a wrap dress I've always liked. Carl's never been that keen on it — something about the length — but I think it suits me. I fold it and put it into the bag I've laid on the bed. But the thought of my excitement when I got tenancy comes back. I've got that. Carl hasn't. He's had to deal with redundancy, with being a stay-at-home parent while I've gotten on with my career. He may have a client base that's growing, and I can see that the men's group is a big achievement in terms of his therapy practice, but he still has to share a space with an aromatherapist and a Reiki healer. All his professional accomplishments are only advertised on our kitchen wall.

I pull the wrap dress out of the bag and hang it back up again. Then I take out the dress he bought me a couple of Christmases ago, the time we screamed at each other for hours after we'd finished dinner. "When would I ever wear something like that?" I cried. "You don't know me at all." Its shortness and redness were an affront to my child-bearing body, every flaw only to be magnified by its unforgiving vermilion.

"It'll suit you. You need to try something new," he said, astonished by my level of rage. "Don't tell me what to do," I shouted and collapsed into tears for the rest of the night.

I finger the material and hold it up against myself. The tags are still on, as untouched as when I unwrapped it. It's not as bad as I remembered it. It's the kind of dress Patrick might like to see me in, I think absently. But it shouldn't be about Patrick. I'm thinking about Carl. This is the sort of thoughtful gesture I'd like him to make to me, to show appreciation of something I'd done or given him. I undress and pull the dress on, grimacing at the tightness of it. It's definitely not as bad as I thought, cut well enough that the right places have emphasis, and the wrong ones a gloss of red silk that distracts from what's beneath. I shimmy in the mirror — it's all right. I take it off and pack it in the bag, pulling on some pajamas.

It's nearly ten by now and I text Carl to see if he'll be back soon.

Not long. Sorry about this. Bit of an emergency situation. Don't wait up for me xx.

I text back.

OK. Night night xx.

As long as he's finished by tomorrow, that's all I care about. I read for a while, a thriller about a toxic marriage in which everything is breaking down, and I smile. That's not us, not anymore. We're off on a weekend break. I'm smiling as I fall asleep, the book slipping to the floor as my grip loosens.

"I'd rather we drove," Carl says the following morning as we lie in bed.

"Why? The train is much quicker." I can't be bothered with all the sitting in traffic that driving will entail.

"I'd prefer it. More quality time with you." He leans over and kisses me.

"I don't call sitting in traffic quality time. It's annoying."

"There might not be traffic. We can take turns," he says.

"I suppose so." I really can't be bothered, but this weekend is about making an effort.

"It'll be fine. I'm sure I'm not too tired to drive," he says.

"What time did you actually get in?"

"After one. He was in an awful way. One of those near suicide situations, you know. I couldn't leave him." Carl's face is troubled.

I don't know, and I'm glad not to. It sounds awful, though, and I say so.

"It is awful, Alison. It is. I don't think I'll ever get used to it," he says.

"I hope you don't have to. At least you were able to help."

"If I did help. You just don't know. I'm very worried about him."

"You've done all you can, and I'm sure you did a brilliant job. Remember, you need time off too," I say, growing alarmed that our weekend might be canceled.

He sighs. "He has my number. And he was a bit better by the time the session ended."

"Good. I'm sure he'll be all right," I say.

Instead of replying he rolls over in bed and hugs me. We lie for a moment together, until I remember his mother's imminent arrival. We get up and shower, give Matilda breakfast. I don't argue about driving anymore. Once his mother arrives I kiss her and go into the living room so that Carl can brief her. It's not that we don't get on, exactly, but I think such things are better coming from Carl. I sit on the sofa and wait until they come through. Matilda is running behind them and jumps on her granny's knee.

"Careful, darling. Not too hard." She's smiling but I can't see it reach her eyes.

"Sorry, Granny." Matilda jumps off and runs to Carl, who swings her round and sits her down beside him.

"So, Matilda, you're going to be a very good girl for Granny. You're going to eat everything she gives you and go to sleep exactly when she tells you, yes?" he says.

She nods, biting her lip. Then it bursts out, "How long are you going for?"

"We've told you, just one night." He's reassuring.

"Will I be able to talk to you?" she says.

"If you want. You can call anytime. Just ask Granny."

We leave shortly after. It doesn't seem fair to string it out. Carl's mother is getting increasingly edgy, straightening the sofa cushions and pulling at the curtains until they're perfectly aligned. As I walk out of the living room, she's arranging the ornaments on the mantelpiece in order of size, large to small. Matilda comes to the door with us and hugs us both. I try not to time the hugs, hoping it's my imagination that she's clinging on to Carl that much longer than to me. It's good for her, that's what I tell myself. She should spend time with other members of her family. And I've never found Carl's mother that bad. Some of the stories he tells about her are a little . . .

concerning, but if he's happy for her to have Matilda, so am I.

"They'll be fine. Won't they?" I say as I indicate and pull the car out into the road.

"Let's hope so. Don't tell me you're having second thoughts?" Carl says.

"Not at all. Just . . ."

"This was your idea." His voice is sharp.

"I know it was my idea. But . . ."

"No, let's not do this. They'll both be fine. I turned out all right — she can't be that bad a mother," he says, more softly this time.

I don't reply. The traffic's heavy going up towards the North Circular and I need to concentrate. Once we're through the worst of it, I turn to ask him about the conference from last weekend, but I see he's stuck a scarf against the car window as a pillow and is already asleep. I'm glad, in part — better he catches up on his sleep — but I begin to grow more irritated the longer the journey goes on. I don't want to disturb him, hoping that he'll wake up himself in time to swap over with me, but he doesn't stir, even though with traffic it takes well over three hours to get there.

"You should have woken me up," he says as he gets out of the car.

"I thought it would be good for you to

rest," I say, smiling, hoping that my act of generosity will reap its reward. But he walks forward into the hotel without thanking me or making further acknowledgment of it. I trail behind, carrying my bag.

"I want a drink." I go straight to the mini-bar as soon as we've checked into our room. "Christ, it's just got water in it. That's a fucking joke." I slam through it again to see if I've missed something but no. Sparkling water. Still water. And one can of Fanta. "Kill me now."

"Calm down. You don't need a drink. It's only two o'clock. Much too early." Carl's voice is quiet and soothing, as if he were talking to a fractious Matilda. I resist the urge to punch him.

"I may not *need* a drink, but I want one. That was a fucking awful drive. It's okay for you, you were asleep the whole time," I say, my voice rising.

"I asked the hotel if they'd take the alcohol out of the room. We don't need to drink to have a good time."

"Did you actually just say that? You sanctimonious prick."

"I'm going to run you a nice hot bath and make you a cup of tea and then you'll feel much better." He stands up and goes into the bathroom. I hear water rushing from the taps and a floral scent fills the air. He comes back into the bedroom and busies himself at the kettle. I'm speechless. For a while.

"You asked them to take the alcohol out of the room? Seriously?" I'm trying to keep calm.

"Yes, I did. Come on, Alison, you know what happens. And I don't want to spoil this. I don't want you knocking back spirits midafternoon. We can have a chilled-out afternoon and have a drink this evening with dinner."

He walks over to me and holds out his hand. After a moment I take it, my hand stiff, and let him pull me up and into an embrace. Any other time I'd kill him for this, but I'm not going to let it spoil the weekend. Even if something in me holds back a little from him.

After the bath and cup of tea, I have a nap. I know the Lanes are out there and the Royal Pavilion but I feel poleaxed with exhaustion, the drive and the past week catching up with me. Carl is dozing in bed, still tired even after his long sleep in the car. I climb in beside him and lean on his chest and drift off, waking after the light has faded, my head thick with sleep. He's awake now, holding out a glass of water to me, which I drink, surprisingly thirsty. He smiles at me.

"It's nearly time for dinner. We'd better get ready."

I throw the covers off and get up. The sea view has been entirely wasted on me today, although it's nice to see the lights on the pier. Maybe it'll be sunny in the morning. We'll walk down over the shingle, our feet crunching on the stones as the seagulls cry overhead. I've read about the people who swim off the pier — there's some club of endurance nuts who go in every day come rain or shine. If we're awake early enough maybe we'll see them. I try to imagine how it must feel to swim in the deep, with no way of knowing what lies beneath, the cold and waves pulling you down.

I shower and then dress while Carl has his shower. The more I look at myself in the dress he gave me, the more I like it. It isn't me, but that's part of it. It's almost transgressive, to see myself as he sees me, not the mother of his child but someone who's not afraid to flash a bit of tits and arse, wrapped up in red silk. I've brought lingerie to go under it, black push-up bra, black underwear as usual but small, much smaller than I'd usually wear, even garters and stockings. The full fishing tackle. If he wants a cliché he can have it, all wrapped up in his Christmas cracker of a dress. I don't look like me, but I look good.

He doesn't register me immediately when he comes out of the bathroom. I'm standing at the mirror on the bedroom wall, circling my eyes in black kohl. I look at myself to check I've got the flicks even on each side and catch his eye in the mirror.

"Are you wearing that?" I can almost hear the mirror crack from side to side.

"I thought you'd like it. You did give it to me," I say, turning to him.

"I didn't think you liked it," he says. He has a towel wrapped round his middle and he pulls it off and starts drying his head with it.

"I changed my mind. Don't you like it?" There's something solid in my chest, an obstruction past which I can't breathe.

"It's okay. You were probably right, though, I can't choose clothes for you. Did you bring anything else?" He sits down on the bed and starts to put on his socks.

I don't want to cry. I've done the Amy Winehouse flicks, for god's sake. But it's close. "Is it really that bad?"

"Nah, it's fine. Maybe you'd be more

comfortable in something else, that's all. But if you don't have anything else with you . . . It's fine." Both socks on, he walks over to his bag and takes out a pair of underwear, puts them on. Jeans next, and a blue shirt. Brings out the blue in his eyes, that's what he always says with a wink when I suggest he wear a different color.

He comes over and stands next to me. Our reflections look into the room, a clean-cut man with a twinkle and me done up like a dog's dinner. I pull at the dress, trying to make it cling less to me. He puts his arm round me and squeezes. "You might look like a bit of a skank, Alison, but you're my skank." He leans over and kisses me on the cheek. "Right, let's hit the town. You wanted a drink?"

He's out the door before I've shut my mouth, slack-jawed at the sting of his words. But how the evening goes now is up to me. Either I'm oversensitive, tell him what a shit he's being, or I grow a sense of humor and stop being so pathetic. He mightn't like it now but he chose the sodding dress and actually I think I look quite good, regardless of what he says. I grab my coat and join him outside the room. He locks the door and we go down the stairs together.

■ ■ ■ ■

Up the hill and round the corner and through the Lanes we go. He's booked a tapas place — "really good review in the *Guardian,* Alison." And when we find it, it is nice, the chairs almost comfortable enough and the tables almost far enough apart. I'm the only person in the room in a dress but I'll style it out, rubbing my finger surreptitiously across my teeth to ensure none of my red lipstick has migrated there. The waiter comes over and I ask for a gin and tonic. He asks if I have any preference of gin and remembering Madeleine I request Hendrick's. Carl takes a while over the cocktail menu, asking the waiter if he has any recommendations and even after he's been told them, *umm*-ing and *ahh*-ing over the comparative merits of a Dark and Stormy or an Old Fashioned. I'm starting to feel both emotions pretty strongly when he goes for a dirty Martini — maybe it's a message as to how the evening will turn out. He is being a twat at the moment but we might both relax with a drink.

"Do you know what you want to eat?" he says.

I look at the menu and it's all good.

"Don't mind. Order what you like."

He nods and when the waiter returns, he reels off a list of food. I don't listen, enjoying the sensation of gin hitting my throat and loosening my shoulders. When Carl's finished with the food I ask for another gin and open the wine list to choose a bottle.

"White or red?" I ask.

"White. I think. Do they have it by the glass?" Carl says.

"I'm ordering a bottle. That's fine, we'll go white." I look down the list, see a sauvignon but resist the temptation. Farther on there's a white Rioja and I gesture the waiter over again and point it out to him. He serves it at the same time that the first of the dishes start to arrive. Carl's ordered lots — ham croquetas and patatas bravas and a tortilla and something with octopus tentacles and another croquetas and, the most sublime, a chunk of goat cheese drizzled in honey. Neither of us has stopped to talk, inhaling the food. I've barely stopped to drink either, but when we've finally gotten through everything I lean back and take a deep swig.

"That's better. I was starving."

"We got through it all. I was afraid I'd ordered too much," he says.

"I think that was just right." I finish my glass and top it up and push the bottle towards him so he can fill up his own glass. "What's the plan for later?"

He looks at his watch. "It's already pretty late. We could have a drink at the hotel?"

I make a face. "I thought we could go dancing?"

"You know I hate dancing." His tone is final.

"I guess." I have another drink and then stand up to go to the loo. I'm steady on my feet, my head clear. That's one advantage of eating all that food, it keeps you sober. "Back in a minute."

We stay in the restaurant for a while longer, finishing off the bottle of wine and an after-dinner cocktail. I call it that, though I have another gin and tonic. Carl again discusses his choice with the waiter before ordering an Armagnac. I take a sip and shudder at the taste — too strong for me.

It's nearly half eleven when we leave the restaurant. Outside it's dark and crisp and clear. Brighton is preparing itself for winter, if not there already. I can see stars in the sky that aren't visible in London, not obscured here by the orange haze to which I've become accustomed. As we walk I stumble, my heel catching on a paving stone, and I take hold of Carl's arm to steady me. He seems resistant at first but then relaxes into me. At the top of the hill down towards the hotel, we stop for a moment and he kisses me.

"I'm sorry I was being a shit earlier. I thought you looked beautiful tonight," he says when he breaks off the kiss.

My mind's hazy — the evening's blurring into a fog, only the odd detail jumping out at me. The croquetas, I remember those particularly. They were really good. And Carl says he was being a shit — was he? I don't remember how. If he says he was, he must have been, but I didn't notice. I'm liking being held by him and the way it feels when he kisses me. I put my arms up round his neck and pull his head back towards me and we kiss for longer, the warmth between us growing. I don't know whether it's being away in a different place, if the dirty-weekend vibe of Brighton has gotten to me, but I'm feeling distinctly up for it. This is more like a night with Patrick.

"Let's go back to the hotel," I say, tugging at his hand. He follows. I stumble again and feel his arms hard around me as he stops my fall. We kiss at the bottom of the road, kiss again outside the entrance to the hotel. "One more drink," he says, and we kiss in the bar.

Then black.

■ ■ ■ ■

He's sitting on the chair watching me. I'm lying across the bed, half-dressed. It's morning, the light cool in the room. His stubble is dark against his chin and the shadows are dark under his eyes. I feel something sticky underneath me and put my hand down into it, bring it up to my face. My fingers are red. I roll over and look sideways, down. There's a big red stain under where I've been sleeping. I'm still in my lingerie, underwear still on, garters and bra. I'm gripped by a certain fear and look again at Carl.

"What happened?"

"You know what happened."

"I don't have any idea. I remember getting to the bar and then it's blank," I say, that fear leaving me and another rising up, totally unknown.

"This is why I didn't want us to drink," he says, his voice tired. I realize now he's still wearing the clothes he had on last night.

"Did you sleep on that chair?"

"Alison, I haven't slept. I've gone round and round in my head trying to see where I've gone wrong, what I've done to make you so unhappy that you always get so drunk." I think he's going to stand up and maybe come over to me but he shifts his weight in the chair and settles back down.

"I didn't think I'd drunk that much," I say, mentally calculating. A couple of gins, half a bottle of wine, maybe another gin, tops. Surely not enough for a blackout. "I'm sorry, I really was trying not to."

"You should have tried harder. I can't deal with it when you're in that state. You can't even look after yourself." He gestures at me. "I could only just get you onto the bed, and take your dress off so you'd be more comfortable. You were so out of it you didn't even know your period had started. Look at yourself."

I am looking. I can see. And I know it's a bit grim. This is the man, though, who I sent out to buy me all the essentials after Matilda was born — nipple cream, piles cream, super-duper fit-a-barge-size maternity pads. I shat myself in front of him as I gave birth. Since when was he so repulsed by me?

"How did we get to this?" I say, sitting up and bringing my knees under my chin. My head spins with the movement and I swallow back some sick.

"You drank too much. That's how," he says, his voice dismissive.

"I didn't mean now. I meant overall . . ." The urge to vomit becomes stronger.

"You —" he starts to say but I don't hear any more as there's a ringing in my ears and lights dancing in front of my eyes as the acid pushes up my throat and into my mouth. I'm jumping up and running but the dress that's on the floor by the bed gets caught round my feet and the sick is pushing out and pushing out and then it's all over the room and down me and splattered all around me, a mix of wine and bits of last night's tapas. Carl gets up and sidesteps the mess, his face twisted.

"I can't even . . ." he starts. He shakes his head, looks at me, away from me, back at me again. "Alison, I'm not dealing with this. You sort it out — actions have consequences, and this isn't just going to go away. I'm leaving now. I'll book the room for another night so you can get it all cleaned up, but I'm going home. Don't come back until you're fit to be around Matilda."

I'd argue, beg him to stay, but I feel too awful, the acid eating away at my esophagus. I stay on the floor where I am, soaked in puke, too abject even to apologize. He shuts the door as he leaves and as he does, another wave of nausea engulfs me. I make it to the loo in time, and retch for a long while until I vomit a thin, yellow thread of bile. It's only then I can manage to stand up and return to bed, where I lie dozing until the smell becomes too overwhelming and the sun is low in the sky.

13

I'm back from Brighton and putting it all out of my mind, the shame of the staff seeing the state of the room and my hasty retreat, the only upside that as he booked it they don't know my name, only Carl's. Every evening this week I want to sit down with him to try to sort out where it all went wrong, but every evening he uses his courtesy as a shield, deflecting any comment I make. He's deft at avoidance, working late or retiring early. I'm ready to give up. And as the days go past, I put thoughts of it farther from my mind. It's Madeleine's PTPH on Thursday and the statements I've requested are rolling in, rich with details and possibilities of defense. Carl may not be talking but at least the potential witnesses are.

I'm surprised it didn't happen earlier. She had to put up with so much. I saw her

> injuries, sometimes, bruises on her face and arms. I was most shocked in the summer of 2015 when I saw that she had three cigarette burns on her hand. She never told me how they happened, but it didn't look accidental.

That's her friend Maud, a parent from James's prep school and a florist. Not just any florist either, one with a Mayfair address and a nice sideline in evening classes. I've thought before about signing up for one.

> And there was one time I saw the way he spoke to her. A horrible tone of voice, really angry. James, their son, was often ill and Edwin could be very impatient about it. I think he thought Madeleine mollycoddled him. But he was shouting at Madeleine about having brought James home early — "I can't believe you did that. I won't tolerate this anymore." His voice frightened me.

So far, so much in support of Madeleine's account of her marriage. What she outlined to me should fit neatly into the loss of control line of defense to murder, bringing it down to manslaughter, as I told her. We need to establish that there was a pattern of violence towards Madeleine, and that on top of that Edwin's behavior that night was the final straw, that what he did to her and said to her would be enough to send anyone over the edge. And from what she's told me, it definitely would.

Next statement, from her doctor.

> Madeleine Smith has been my patient at my general practice clinic in Wigmore Street since 2006. I have treated her regularly over the years for a series of injuries, mostly minor, but some necessitating hospital treatment. I have refreshed my memory from the notes, copies of which are attached to my statement as my exhibit 1. However, there are two occasions which stand out for me, and for which I have required no reminder. The first was in the summer of 2007. Madeleine's son James was three, also a patient of mine. He had been very ill with vomiting and diarrhea, and was so dehydrated that he needed to be hospitalized and put onto an intravenous drip for rehydration. The following morning Madeleine came in to see me with a serious scald over her right thigh. She told me that she had been so upset the night before, as a result of James's hospitalization, that

she had accidentally poured a kettle of boiling water over her leg. There was something in her manner that seemed odd, but I put it down to her natural concern for her son at that stage. The second was more recent, in 2015. She was very upset when she arrived for her appointment. Once she stopped crying she showed me her left hand, on which she had sustained three burns as if cigarettes had been extinguished on the back of her hand. I asked her how it had happened and she refused to answer, but burst again into tears and told me that her husband was sending their son James away to boarding school and that she was very unhappy about the decision. I treated the burns and tried to persuade her to talk more about them. What disturbed me further was that the little finger on her left hand was crooked, as if it had been broken and the bones had been unable to knit properly. I asked her both about how she had sustained the burns, and if she could tell me what had happened to her finger before. She left without answering any of my questions, and I have not seen her since. Full details of these incidents are also included in the medical file here attached.

I read the medical notes that are attached, a litany of burns and cuts and bruises. The chronology indicates about two or three incidents a year, with a spike in 2007 and also in 2015, as the doctor's remarks indicate. The two he describes are probably the most serious, though on another occasion he had to stitch up a cut on her left arm (in the notes, "I'm so clumsy"). Those sorts of remarks pepper the notes. At no point did it seem that the doctor tried hard to get a fuller explanation out of her, though it seems at one stage he had thought about it: *It was my view that if I pushed her too much she would just stop seeing me. At least this way there was a full record of all the injuries so that if she ever did make a complaint, it would all be documented* were the final remarks in his statement.

This is all helpful to her case. Extremely helpful, if not totally conclusive. To me, though, the statement that hits the money is from Peter Harrison, a French tutor who taught James at the family house during school holidays. His statement relates in general to the atmosphere he sensed at the house — *When Edwin was away for work it felt calmer, somehow, but if he was there, both Madeleine and James were always on edge* — and specifically to one occasion some six months ago, in which he was sitting in the kitchen with James, teaching him at the table.

> James pulled up his jumper to take it off and as he did, his T-shirt came up with it. I saw his chest. I was really shocked. His ribs were covered in bruises, dark and light purple. He saw me looking and said, "Rugby." I didn't question further, though I wish I had. The thing is, schools don't normally play rugby in the summer term. It would have been cricket.

I pause for a moment after reading this. Even though I'm prepared for it by what Madeleine has told me, it still twists in my chest.

The summary of the new psychiatric report has arrived and it's also as helpful as we hoped. The full report will be ready in about a fortnight and I'm looking forward to it. So far, everything is backing up Madeleine's defense. I have a good feeling about this.

I've robed up by the time I meet Madeleine and Patrick in the Old Bailey, standing outside Court 7. Her sister, Francine, is there as well, but hovering at a distance.

The horsehair wig is itchy on my scalp and the gown drags down my shoulders. Normally I don't notice the sensation but as I catch sight of Patrick every part of me becomes super-sensitive, a flush rising under my skin and an itch on the back of my hands. I compensate with the formality of my tone as I explain the process of today's hearing to Madeleine.

"You'll have to go into the dock, I'm afraid. They'll ask your name and address, and after that the clerk of the court will read out the indictment to you and ask if you intend to plead guilty or not guilty," I say.

"And you really think I should plead not guilty?" she says, leaning forward towards me.

"On the basis of the statement you've given me, yes. It would be very remiss of me to advise you to do anything else. When we've got the rest of the evidence we'll address the possibility of entering a plea to manslaughter, as I explained before. I'll mention it now, but it won't go any further today." I turn towards Patrick, making eye contact with him for the first time since I arrived at the door of court, ignoring the jolt in my stomach as our eyes meet.

"She's right. We've gone through it all pretty thoroughly. And we've got statements from the people you told us about, all of which support aspects of your account," he says.

"Only aspects?" Madeleine says. "No more than that?"

"No one else was there on the night in question. So we only have your account of what happened. But the other evidence serves to corroborate what you're saying," I say.

Madeleine starts laughing. I smile inadvertently, not knowing quite what has triggered it, but my smile soon dies. She doesn't stop. A hysterical tone begins to take over. Patrick takes hold of her by the arm and shakes her very gently.

"Madeleine, calm down. You need to calm down now," he says.

She takes a deep, shuddering breath. "I'm sorry. I was just thinking, Edwin was there, of course. But he can't tell us anything. Not anymore . . ." Now she's crying.

I move towards her to try to comfort her but I catch the eye of my opponent as he strides along the corridor towards court. Jeremy Flynn — the sort of barrister every defendant wants representing them. Tall, reassuringly public school, a three-piece suit fitting him so well it must have been tailored for him — he's straight out of Central Casting. Not that smart, but he looks the part so much it convinces juries every time. I'd been hoping he'd be too busy to take this one on, from the first moment I saw his name on the brief as the prosecutor. No such luck, but maybe by the time of trial he'll have found a more interesting case to do.

"Alison, hello. A word please?" he booms at me.

"Sure." I smile at him and turn to Madeleine and Patrick. "This won't take long. Just preliminaries."

We walk along the corridor to an alcove.

"Am I really to believe this is going to be a not guilty today?" he says, condescension dripping from every word. "Because the last time I looked at the law on murder, it seemed pretty clear-cut that sticking a knife into someone repeatedly is pretty damn illegal. If you'll pardon my pun."

Great, a lecture on law from a dolt with a plum in his mouth. I keep smiling.

"I mean, come on, Allie. What are you trying to do here? Think of the waste of court time and money. Maybe you've got some misguided idea about helping out another woman, but really, you're not doing her any favors. Take it from me, Allie, a word to the wise." He hushes his voice and puts his head to one side. I think he's trying to look sincere.

"You'll receive the defense case statement in due course. And despite the attitude you're showing, I'm putting you on notice that we are actively exploring offering a plea to voluntary manslaughter on the basis of loss of control. In the meantime, I hope you're going to get on and serve me the rest of the papers. I don't have any of the unused material yet," I say, smile stuck to my teeth.

He sighs. "Well, God loves a trier. I can tell you now, though, that you'll be wasting your time. Oh, Allie, such a waste of your talents. When will they stop giving you such weak cases? I suppose they aren't sure you can commit properly to your work, what with everything . . ."

"What do you —" I bite off the sentence. Goddammit, he's nearly got me biting. I'm not going to rise to it. I nod to him, wordlessly, and walk back to Patrick and Madeleine. What Flynn doesn't know is that inside my head I've kicked his wig so hard into his skull that bits of his brain and bone are oozing out over it.

"Anything useful to say for himself?" Patrick asks.

"Nope," I say.

"He's such a cunt," Patrick says, and we

look at each other, once more in perfect sympathy.

We go into court more or less on time, and within twenty minutes it's all over. This may be the most serious crime I've ever represented but now that it's in court it feels like any other trial. The indictment has been read, the plea of not guilty entered. Madeleine's bail conditions have been reviewed and upheld and a timetable has been set for the various exchanges of documentation that need to be made between the prosecution and defense. I will have to prepare a defense case statement within the next couple of weeks, letting the prosecution know in more detail what we propose to put forward as Madeleine's defense. I will also have to serve them with the psychiatric report. They need to serve all their statements and their unused material, which might be of assistance to us if not to them. I'm not expecting any miracles. As I said to Madeleine, it all hinges on whether the jury accepts her account of her and Edwin's marriage, and what she says happened on that night.

She pulls at my gown as we leave the court.

"Are they going to believe me?" she says.

"Who?" I say.

"The jury. Will they believe me?"

"I can't promise that. But we're going to do our best to make sure they do," I say, patting her arm. She doesn't look much comforted but she goes off with Francine without looking back.

"Is our best going to be good enough?" Patrick says, standing close to me.

"I don't know. It all depends on what the son says. Do we know when we might get his statement?"

"Still waiting for the prosecution to confirm whether they're going to call him as a witness. On the face of it, he shouldn't have anything much to say that will be useful for them, so I'm not sure they will. But until we know that, we won't get anywhere," he says, and I nod my agreement. No one would voluntarily put a teenager through giving evidence in the trial of his mother for killing his father, but he might be the witness to make all the difference . . .

"We'll have to wait and see. Shame it's that wanker Flynn, he's not going to be any help. I can try and ask, though. If it looks like I'm really trying to find something else out, there might be a way to do it. Anyway, I'd best get changed," I say, starting to walk away towards the robing room.

"Would you like a coffee?" Patrick asks, a casual tone to his voice. He's looking everywhere but at me.

I pause. Think. "Yes," I say, and turn away to go to the robing room. When I'm finished, he's waiting for me outside and we walk side by side to a café near Ludgate Circus.

We've discussed Madeleine, the rape case, and a big drugs trial that Patrick's starting soon. Silence is one step away, both of us trying hard to prevent it from coming any closer. If we stop talking, pause the noise and let our eyes meet for longer than a millisecond, then who knows what will happen. Maybe I'll lean forward and touch his cheek or maybe he'll take my hand and kiss it, maybe we'll stand up together and leave the café to go straight down to his flat, where we'll fuck without stopping to ask why we ever tried to stop. There's a breathlessness in the back of my throat I try to ignore, taking sips of water every half a minute. He's in the middle of a long anecdote about a gun trial that's going to take place next week in Nottingham when my phone pings. That's when we stop and look at each other, the row we had two weeks before about to fall down between us.

"Aren't you going to look at it?" he says.

I'm hesitant. I don't want to know if it's something nasty. We're almost getting on. But on the other hand, it might be something important. Perhaps something to do with Matilda. I pull out my phone and look at it. It's from Carl.

My mother's asked us to come and stay for a few days. Under the circs I think it's for the best. I'm taking Matilda. We'll be back next week.

I blink, reply.

What about school? It's only Thursday.

Nothing back from him for a moment but I can see the animated dots on my phone that show he's composing something. It comes through.

It won't kill her to miss one day. It'll be good for her to see her Granny.

Anger grabs me. I start to type a reply. Stop. There's no point. Once Carl has made a decision like this I know it's final. I type a different reply instead.

You're right. Hope you have a lovely time.

And that we can sort things out when you get back. I love you both.

He replies. I know you think you do. See you on Sunday night.

I'm winded by it, a jab to the ribs I didn't expect. I look blankly at the screen for a moment and then turn my phone off. There's nothing else to say.

While I'm dealing with this, Patrick has taken a call. I've missed the beginning of it, but once my phone is off I register what he's saying, a clicking sound from the other end of the line filling in the gaps.

"No, nothing like that. . . . A misunderstanding. . . . Well, I'm sorry if she felt that way . . ." His face is tense, his eyes focusing on something on the wall, though when I glance over my shoulder there's nothing there. "Definitely a misunderstanding. . . . Yes, you know nothing like that would . . . No, no, that's not the case. . . . Okay, I'll talk to her, clear this up."

He hangs up without saying goodbye, his jaw clenched.

"Everything all right?" I say.

He looks at me as if from a distance, then his face clears. "Yes, yes, everything's fine. One of my clients is pissed off. I advised her that she'd have to plead guilty, and she's not happy. You know what they're like. Anyway, everything all right with you? Not one of those messages you were getting before?"

"No, it was my husband. I haven't had one of those texts for a while. Since we last talked about it, actually."

"That's good. Sorry I wasn't more . . . helpful." He says the word with care.

"It's all right. It freaked me out, that was all," I say.

"Of course it did. Look, Alison. Can we give it another go? Whatever this is?"

I'm torn for a moment. Then I visualize Carl and Matilda, their faces close together, and very consciously, very carefully pack them up smaller and smaller in my mind, folding them into a little box I tuck right down into the farthest corner. I hold my hand out to Patrick and he takes it.

"Are you working this afternoon?" I say.

"Not anymore," he says, and pulls me in close.

14

"Don't go," Patrick says, holding on to my arm.

"I've got to. I don't want to risk it."

"Risk what? You said they were away." He sits up in bed and takes hold of my other arm too. I pull myself away.

"I think it's better if I go. We can always meet tomorrow."

"I might be busy tomorrow." His tone is sulky.

"That's up to you." I rise from the bed, where I've sat down next to him to kiss him goodbye. I don't want to leave but it's nearly eleven at night. We've been in bed in Patrick's flat since we got there at two o'clock this afternoon, only getting up to pee and, in Patrick's case, to bring through wine and cuts of Ibérico ham from the kitchen every couple of hours. I go over to the mirror and fiddle with my hair, rub away the traces of mascara that are caught in the lines under my eyes.

"I'm only joking. Of course I'm not going to be busy. Why don't you cook me dinner at your house?" he says.

I turn round quickly, startled at the suggestion. He's never shown any interest in my outside life before, keeping me as neatly compartmentalized as I've made my family for today. He doesn't even comment on my stretch marks, the proof of my motherhood.

"Dinner at mine? At my house?" I'm reduced to repetition.

"Yes. I've cooked for you. It's your turn now. And if the house is empty, why not?"

I can think of so many reasons I don't know where to start. Coexistence is one thing, the tracks of him and Carl running parallel. Juxtaposition entirely another. For Patrick to eat from our plates, drink from our cups . . . He'd see the photographs of Matilda, the wedding picture of Carl and me back when we could bear to touch each other. The thought of it brings up goose bumps, the hairs erect on my arm. I turn back to the mirror, faff some more at my face to stall for time.

"I'm not sure it's a good idea," I say in the end, conscious of the weakness of my response.

"It's an excellent idea. You've seen me at

home — I want to see you at home too. I want to get to know you better, Alison. All of you. Christ, I don't even know if you can cook. We've been shagging for over a year and you've never even boiled me an egg," he says, getting out of bed and coming over to put his arms around me.

"I'm not sure egg boiling has got much to do with us," I say.

"What if I want it to?"

His head is next to mine, his chin on my shoulder. He's smiling at me in the mirror, and the temptation is too much. The warmth of his gaze compares so strongly with the contempt I see from Carl that I can't resist it. I'd love to cook for someone who won't spurn my food.

"As long as they really are away. Can I confirm tomorrow?" I say.

He turns me round and hugs me properly. "Yes, of course. Let me know when and where. And I eat anything."

"I'm not that good at cooking — don't get too excited."

"Let me be the judge of that." He kisses me and I kiss him back, until it's clear it's going to lead straight back to bed. I disengage myself.

"I'm going home now. I'll call you in the morning."

"Can't wait." He kisses me once more but this time he lets me go.

The house is empty when I get home. It's the first time I've stayed alone in it since Matilda was born. I dump my coat on the bottom banister and leave my wheelie bag by the front door. I go upstairs to get changed, wander into Matilda's room, and sit on the small bed. She's left Pink Elephant behind, the toy I bought for her the week after she was born. She's been inseparable from it since then. Until now, apparently. Looking more closely, I realize the fur has lost its fluff and the stuffing has gone lumpy. I bring it up to my face and almost gag at the stale smell, like gone-off milk. I'm tempted to put it through the washing machine while Matilda's not there to argue but resist the urge — it's all feeling fragile enough without me robbing her toy of its essence behind her back. I put Pink Elephant back on her pillow.

I shut all the curtains throughout the house and turn off the lights, checking that the back door's locked. This is normally Carl's job. I feel destabilized, freewheeling around the rooms with a sense that my brakes have gone. But the idea of showing Patrick my home is exhilarating. I want him to like it, to read me better through the titles of the books on the shelves. I rearrange a couple, moving the *Twilight* series to the back of a row and pulling forward some Diaz and Pelecanos, *A Dark-Adapted Eye* by Barbara Vine. I look for a while at the wedding photo of Carl and me — it's all right, I don't mind it, though my chin's been seen from better angles.

The one of Carl and me with Matilda smiling between us catches my eye and I take it down from the shelf and gaze at it for a moment. We look so happy, the proud parents, so much younger than today. I do a sweep of the house and remove all the photos of Matilda, piling them up in a cupboard in the living room. I want Patrick to see what I'm like, but not all of me. Not yet. There may be a time for it but we're not there. This is already a big enough step, and who knows where it's leading, if anywhere at all.

By now it's past midnight and I get into bed, sprawled across the middle of the mattress. I sleep soundly without Carl there to avoid, waking only when my alarm goes off at seven.

I text Carl first thing.

Missing you both. How are you? X

He takes a while to reply, but eventually does.

We're fine. Going to the beach today and a castle tomorrow.

The terseness jolts me but on the upside, he's clearly not planning to come home and surprise me. I reply Have fun and put him out of my mind. Not Matilda, though. I think about the way I tidied her out of her own house, and a lump forms in my throat before lodging in my chest. She deserves better than this. I don't have any right to treat her home in this way, to pretend that she doesn't exist. I pick up my phone and call Carl, desperate to speak to her. He doesn't pick up. I try again and again he doesn't pickup. Finally he writes:

We're on the way out. I told you. What do you want?

I want to talk to Matilda.

He replies. There isn't time. And I think it'll only upset her. Stop being so selfish.

I want to call again and insist that he put her on the phone, but it's true, I don't want to upset her. I know she'll be happy hanging out with her dad and grandmother. Best not to make a fuss of her being away — I'm sure they'll be back Sunday and I'll be able to hold her and talk to her about everything she's been doing. I rub my face, hard, and try to put the guilt out of my mind. I've got to go to court and plan a meal.

I think about it on the bus down to Holborn, up the road to the Old Bailey. Lamb. That's what Patrick cooked me before. So it can't be lamb. I'm googling like mad, trying to find something within my skill set that's going to impress him. Seduce, even. The usher calls me three times into court before I realize I'm needed, and the bail application I'm covering for one of my colleagues isn't one of my finest. It's granted, though, and I even remember to call the judge "M'lady." I'm happy to be in the Bailey again today — it's a quick in-and-out, dropping off the papers back to chambers and collecting the papers for my trial next week. I've got the rest of the day to plan dinner and prepare.

I take the Piccadilly line up to Holloway Road station and go to Waitrose. Carl normally deals with the food shopping, whizzing round the aisles like a pro, minimizing the distance between condiments and cornflakes with a carefully planned list.

It takes me three times longer than it would him. I go first to the butcher's counter and look at the different cuts, the oozing blood reminding me of my lunch with Madeleine. It was good food, though, and I use it for inspiration. I pick up two prepackaged steaks and wander back to the vegetables to buy asparagus and strawberries. Sod seasonal, it'll be nice. I return to the cold aisle for frozen chips and, unable to remember if we have mayonnaise in the house, go and pick some of that up too. Finally I return to the cold aisle for chocolate mousse in pots. I can't imagine Patrick wants me to make him dessert, too.

"You shouldn't have made the effort," Patrick says as soon as I open the door.

"I didn't."

"No shit." He's laughing, though, then he leans forward and kisses me. After last weekend I'm not bothering to get myself done up for anyone. Counterproductive. The best sex I ever had as a student was when I wasn't dressed for it, worst old pants and unshaven legs. I should have remembered that before pouring my curves into the dress Carl was so sniffy about. So I'm in tracksuit bottoms and an old T-shirt, no bra, skin showing at the shoulder. To be fair, though, I've spent a bit of time on my face, perfecting a no-makeup-healthy-glow look that uses most of the cosmetics in my possession.

Patrick pushes me through the open door and shuts it firmly behind him. He pulls at the neck of my T-shirt until it tears at the seams. He drops the pieces to the floor. Then he turns me to face the wall and pulls down my bottoms. Pressing hard onto my back with one hand, he undoes his fly with the other. He spits on his hand and rubs himself before guiding himself into me, ignoring my initial gasp of pain. Within moments it's over. He pulls out and turns me round to kiss me.

"I've been thinking about that all day," he says eventually.

I'm out of breath, unsure how I feel about what's just happened. I don't say anything, though, aware now of my underwear round my ankles. I pull them up, and the tracksuit bottoms. I pick up the bits of T-shirt but it's beyond mending.

"I thought you were coming round for dinner," I say.

"I am. And afters. As well as befores."

"I'm going to get a top on," I say, edging away. I stand on something sharp and pick it up; a small piece of Lego I've missed in my clear-up. I look at it, Tilly on my mind. I'm feeling more and more uncomfortable playing the role of mistress in my daughter's home. Patrick's trying to take ownership, insistent.

"Don't. I like you like this." He pulls my tracksuit bottoms down again, but leaves my underwear alone this time.

"The naked chef? Bit clichéd, surely?" I push him off but leave my pants on the floor.

"Nothing wrong with a bit of cliché. Come on, let's have a drink." He hands me a plastic bag of bottles I haven't realized until now he's brought with him.

I take him and the bottles through into the kitchen, conscious of my state of undress but trying to ignore it. Since Matilda was born I've given up on nudity, her presence and the ravages of age combining to make me reluctant to wander round without a protective covering of manky pajamas and a massive fleece I stole off Carl one Christmas. The lights are on in the kitchen and I feel very aware of the neighbors who could be looking in on this floor show. I mean, it's London, we barely speak to anyone, but what if one of them, seeing Carl one morning, were to mention the performance I was putting on for them? Would Carl even care?

I pick up an apron from the stove and put it on.

"Chicken," Patrick says.

"I'm cooking steak. I don't want to burn myself," I say with dignity as I walk over to the kitchen doors and undo the ties on the curtains. We never normally undo them. Dust and dead moths flutter from the folds but at least I'm covered now.

While I'm doing this I can hear Patrick digging round in the drawers. When I turn round he's brandishing a corkscrew and has opened a bottle of wine. I take glasses out of the cabinet and hand them to him and he fills them.

"Cheers," he says, and we clink them together. "What are we having? Apart from steak?"

"Veg and oven chips. Told you I'm not much of a cook."

"I'm sure it'll be lovely." He's got manners, I'll give him that. When he feels like it.

He wanders through to the front room while I turn on the oven and put the chips on a tray. When he returns he's holding the wedding photograph in his hand.

"So this is your husband?"

"Yes. Obviously." There's an edge in the air that wasn't there before. We look at each other for a moment and then he takes the photograph back to the front room. I hear the clunk as he puts it back on the shelf.

"You knew from the start I was married," I say.

"I did. I do."

"You had a go at me for not liking you seeing other people." I don't want to bring up our row, but it needs saying.

He sighs. "Okay, let's not get into all of that again. Sorry to spoil the mood. Let's not think about it now. Out of sight, out of mind, yes?"

Easier for you to say, I think, but I don't argue. I put the chips in the oven and cut the ends off the asparagus.

Wine. Steak. More wine. Overcooked chips pushed to the side. More wine. We lie on the sofa together, feeding each other the chocolate mousse. He pushes me gently onto the floor and now he takes his time, working his way down my body. I try to relax, acutely aware of the mess he might make on the carpet with the mousse he's started smearing all over me, and how I'd explain that to Carl.

"Hey, relax. I thought you'd enjoy this," he says as he raises his head up. His face is smeared in chocolate and all I want to do is laugh. I suppress it and it comes out in a snort. He smiles.

"Exactly," he says, his voice pleased, and then he goes back to what he's doing.

I shut my eyes, wanting to fall into the moment. But the texture of the carpet is digging into my back and the mousse is making my tummy itch. I open my eyes and look around the room, the lights on the TV and DVD player glowing red in the corner. I don't want to push him off and I know it's me who needs to get on with it, not him, but I can't make myself want this. I push at his head.

"I'm not really in the mood for this," I say. "Sorry — can't relax."

He looms over me, grinning. "I'll make you relax. You just need to let me." He starts again but I push once more at his head. He reaches up and grabs my hands, one in each of his. Once he has them secure, he presses my arms down to the floor. He's pulling too hard and it's hurting my hands and my shoulders. I wriggle from side to side to try to free myself but he rests his body across my legs and I can't move. He's pushing at me with his head and his teeth and his tongue and it hurts and I try to move my legs and my hands and I can't and he won't stop.

He raises his head. "I'm going to make

you enjoy this," he says.

"Stop," I cry, and try to twist myself out of the way but it's no good, he keeps licking harder and harder before letting go of my right hand so he can ram his fingers hard inside me. It hurts even more.

"Stop it," I shout, and forgetting about the sofa and the carpet and the chocolate I manage to force myself over and roll away, knocking into the legs of the coffee table. I struggle up to my feet, thigh and shoulder aching from the impact. He stands too, and for a moment I think he's going to grab hold of me again but then he puts his hands up in surrender and backs away.

"Sorry, Alison. Sorry. I thought you'd like it," he says.

"You thought wrong." There's a throw on the back of one of the armchairs and I take it and wrap it around myself. I turn on the light and assess the damage to the room. There's a long smear of brown on the carpet. I sit down heavily on the sofa.

"I'm sorry," I say. "I didn't mean to get so uptight. Maybe it's being here, in the house . . ."

"You've got nothing to apologize for. I should have stopped when you said. I got carried away," he says. He sits down on the sofa beside me and holds out his hand. After a moment I take it, holding it loosely. "But you've never stopped me before."

"I've never wanted to before. Something didn't feel right, though," I say.

"I'm sorry," he says again, and for a while we sit holding hands.

The beep of my phone from the kitchen breaks the silence.

"I'd better see who that is. It might be . . ." I don't finish the sentence but get up and retrieve my phone. It's a message. From an unknown number. Just what we need to top things off tonight.

U rotten slag.

Brilliant. I hold my phone out to him and he takes it, reading the words.

"Fuck's sake. You're not going to take this shit seriously, are you?" he says.

"What do you mean by that? I'm not taking it any way. I'm sick of it," I say.

He looks at the message again and deletes it before turning my phone off and putting it down on the coffee table.

"Please, can we not think about this tonight? Whoever it is, they don't matter. It's meaningless. Buzzing noise."

I sit down on the armchair opposite him, tucking the throw down over my legs. I'm starting to feel cold.

"It's not meaningless. There's something in it. I can't just ignore it."

"You can. If you choose to," he says. "Whoever it is, they're looking for a reaction. Don't give them the satisfaction."

"You sound like someone talking to their child about playground bullies," I say.

"What if I do? I don't want to spoil tonight."

"Who says it isn't spoiled already?" I look at the stained carpet again.

"Again, only if you let it be spoiled. I've said I'm sorry. I got carried away."

"That's not much of an excuse."

"It's the best I've got," he says, and gets up. He kneels on the floor beside me and puts his arms round me and eventually I relax into his embrace. It hangs in the balance for a moment but I can't bear the argument. He did stop what he was doing in the end, and maybe I was being too uptight.

"Let's start the evening again. I'll go and get some more wine."

He goes into the kitchen. I turn my phone back on again. Carl has texted me while it was off, to send a picture of Matilda and his mother baking a cake together. Matilda looks really happy, her hands covered in flour and chocolate round her mouth. A wave of longing for her submerges me and as the ferocity of the feeling ebbs away, I feel bereft, empty of everything good and pure. I'm sitting almost naked in my living room, in the room that Tilly plays in and watches TV in, waiting for a man who doesn't understand no to come back and hassle me again. If I were a friend of mine I would be screaming at me right now, telling me to stop being such a selfish, stupid bitch. The only mess I should be making with chocolate is with my daughter. A lump swells in my chest and my chin tightens, tears leaking from my eyes.

Patrick comes back into the room carrying two glasses of wine. He sits down next to me on the sofa. I get up and move to the chair.

"Fuck's sake, Alison. I've said I'm sorry." He drinks his glass of wine in one.

"It's not that," I say.

"Don't tell me, you're feeling guilty again."

"Look, Patrick, it's complicated," I start to say but he's walked out of the room, coming back in with the bottle of wine in his hand. He tops his glass up, slopping wine over the side onto the carpet to add to the other stains.

I drink my wine. The silence stretches out between us. I feel like I'm looking at us both from a distance, perched somewhere up in the corner of the room, watching two people become strange to each other. Patrick takes a long intake of breath.

"Do you want a fag? I've got some," he says.

"No. I'm fine."

There's a long pause.

"I think I'd better go."

I wrap the blanket around myself more tightly.

"Well?" he says. "Do you want me to stay?"

"Patrick . . ."

"You normally like it rough," he says, his voice sulky.

"I think it's being in the house," I say. "I'm sorry. I didn't mean to spoil the evening."

He reaches over and touches my knee. I try not to shy away.

"It's obviously been too much for you. I'm going to go." He stands. "I'm sorry, Alison. It was a mistake for me to come here. This is your home, your daughter's home — I don't belong here."

I follow him as he walks round the ground floor collecting his clothing. Once he's gathered everything he dresses himself. I stand in the middle of the floor watching him, holding my wrap close around me. I'm trying hard not to cry, a lump growing harder in my throat, my mouth trembling. I want him to leave but I want him to stay too, and if I say one word the dam will burst and I'll start crying in earnest.

Now he's dressed, coat on, shoes laced. Bag in hand, he leans over me and kisses me on the forehead.

"I'll call you."

And with that he's gone. I feel a blast of cold air as he opens and closes the front door. I keep standing where I am. Once the lump in my throat has subsided I pour myself more wine. I turn off the lights downstairs and run myself a bath. My hands are clammy and my feet cold. I lie in the bath for a long time, submerging my head under the water. My ears are full of water and I can't hear anything but the clanging of the pipes as the central heating turns off for the night. By the time I sit up the water's tepid and my fingers are wrinkled blue. Downstairs my phone rings and rings but I get into bed and curl up small, my head wet against the pillow.

I don't think I'll sleep, but it comes easily, waves on waves pressing me down. My phone keeps ringing but the sound weaves itself through my brain like a lullaby. I don't know how many more times it rings that night, but I'm dead to it, Patrick and Carl stalking around my dreams to the rhythm of its call.

15

Carl and Matilda come home on the Sunday. Matilda clings to me like a limpet, showing me the drawings she's done over the weekend. Carl seems indifferent, responding only to direct questions, and even then only tersely. The house is spotless, I've made sure of it, every surface polished to within an inch of its life over the two days I've been alone, photographs of Tilly returned to their rightful spots. I've cooked chicken and macaroni cheese, and she makes short work of both. Carl eats too, shoveling the food into his mouth without looking at it. I'm pretty sure without tasting it either, but at least he doesn't find anything wrong with it.

I bathe Matilda and read her a story after supper. Once Carl finished eating he sat heavily down on the sofa in the living room and opened up his laptop. I asked him if he wanted to help with Matilda and he grunted something indistinguishable at me without turning round. I took that as a no. She cuddles up to me while I brush her hair and dry it, and is asleep before half eight. I'm tempted to go to bed myself, the likely hours of strained silence between Carl and me looming over me. I stand at the top of the stairs and brace myself.

"You had a good weekend, then," I say, sitting down opposite him in the living room. The brown stain on the carpet is now very faint — I spent a long time cleaning it off over Saturday, layer on layer of Vanish to bleach out any trace of everything that happened on Friday night. I try hard not to look at the shadow that remains, though really, given how much attention Carl is paying to me, it doesn't matter.

"Good weekend?" I say again, as he still hasn't replied to my first comment.

"What? Oh, yes. Good to get away for a bit," he says, still looking at his computer. I want to smack it out of his hands.

"The photos you sent were nice." I'm determined not to be put off.

"Yes, yes," he says. Whatever is on his screen must be enthralling.

"Carl, will you look at me?"

"I'm just trying to get some work —" he starts but I interrupt him by taking his laptop out of his hands. He reaches for it but I close it and put it on the shelf behind me.

"Give me back my computer," he says. He looks furious. But at least he's looking at me.

"No. We need to talk."

"We don't need to talk. I want my computer back," he says. He stands up and walks round to the shelf to reach for it but I'm faster than him. I get hold of it and clutch it in my arms. He'll have to fight me for it.

"Don't make me hurt you," he says. Apparently he's serious because he grasps my arms and tries to pry them apart.

"What the hell are you doing?" I push myself back from him, elbowing him off me.

"I want my computer back!" he shouts, right into my face.

"Fine, here's your fucking computer." I twist sideways and put it on the floor, pushing it hard away from me. It slides across the carpet and hits the wall. Carl scoots after it and picks it up with solicitude before sitting back on the sofa with it and turning it on.

I pull up the sleeves of my jumper and see red marks on my arms. "You've bruised me," I say. He doesn't look up.

"Carl, you've fucking hurt my arms. Look at me for fuck's sake." I'm so shocked at the physicality of his response that I don't care how much I annoy him.

Finally he looks at me. "You shouldn't have taken it in the first place."

"We need to talk. You won't talk to me. You've never hurt me before and you're behaving like you just don't care." I don't mean to but I start to cry, my words coming out in an incoherent howl.

"I don't know what there is to say," he says.

"Are we splitting up? Do you want a divorce?" I'm sobbing now.

"Alison, I . . ." Maybe he's about to say something profound but he stops. He's staring at the door. I wait for him to speak, my sobs quietened, and then I see why he's stopped. The door is moving, only gradually, but coming from behind it is a faint sound of crying. He goes over to the door and opens it, and I see Matilda standing there clutching Pink Elephant, her face all scrunched up. Carl picks her up and she collapses onto his shoulder.

"Are you getting a divorce?" she says when she's finally calmed down enough to speak.

"No," we both say together.

"I heard you arguing. I came down and I

heard Mummy say divorce. I hate it when you argue. Please stop it." She starts crying again.

I feel like someone has put their hand through my middle and taken hold of my insides and is twisting them slowly, slowly. There's a pain in my chest, a lump that's spreading tendrils of cold. Carl looks upset too, the indifference in his face displaced by concern for Matilda. He sits down with her on his knee and holds her close.

"Carl, we have to talk. Look at what it's doing to Matilda. To all of us." Now I'm begging but I don't care. Something has to break the impasse.

He sits back in the chair, Matilda leaning against him. There's an expression I can't read on his face — defeat, perhaps. Maybe just exhaustion.

"Okay, we'll talk. Later," he says. He moves Matilda around on his knee until they're face-to-face. "Tilly, sweetie. I'm sorry you heard us arguing, but right now Mummy and Daddy are not getting on very well. It doesn't mean we're going to get a divorce, but we are having some arguments. You know how you argue with your friend Sophie at school?"

He keeps talking to Matilda but I can't hold on to his words. They drift over me until the end.

". . . but we will sort out our problems because we're your mummy and daddy and we love you very much," he says, pulling me back in.

I nod my agreement and go over and kneel beside them. I put my arm round Matilda, trying and failing to avoid also touching Carl. He doesn't flinch from me and I feel that's a start.

"It's very true, darling. We really do love you very much," I say.

We get her fully calmed down and take her up to bed, staying with her until she's asleep, her breathing deep. Carl goes back downstairs first and I slowly follow, hoping that maybe now he'll engage with me.

"That's why it's so important, Carl. Matilda. Not just us. We have to work at this for her. Don't you agree?" I say.

His eyes are hostile. Or maybe just guarded. He's trying to assess my sincerity. I can see his point.

"And I'm sorry about what happened last weekend. When we were away. I really didn't mean to get so drunk — I don't know what happened."

"You never do . . ." His voice is quiet but I can hear the words clearly enough.

"Give me a break, please. I'm trying here.

I really am sorry. I'm going to do my best."

"It's going to take more than that. You've said that so many times before." He leans his head back on the sofa, closing his eyes. He looks defeated.

"Just give me another chance. We have to try and fix this for Matilda's sake," I say.

He sighs and opens his eyes, looking at me fully for the first time since they returned from his mother's. Actually, for the first time since he left me in Brighton. We hold the look for a moment but his gaze drops first.

"I'm tired, Alison. So tired of all the drama. I want things calm and quiet. I want to get on with my work and look after our daughter and not have all of this . . . performance all the time," he says.

"That's what I want too. It's all I've ever wanted," I say.

"I know you think that." His voice is almost kind. "But right now I don't believe it's true. You don't know what you want. And it's killing us."

He can't mean what that could mean because I know there's no way he could know about Patrick but my heart skips a beat and my tongue feels thick and dry. Then a surge of adrenaline hits me.

"It's not just me, you know. You've been off me for at least the last couple of years.

Especially since the summer of last year. You were the one who didn't want to fuck anymore. You've made that clear so many times."

"You see, Alison, this is what I mean. Why are you calling it 'fucking'? With us it ought to be making love. I'm not going to 'fuck' my wife," he says, his head inclined, his expression oozing concern that I can be so dense, so clumsy with language. So uncouth.

"Fucking or making love, whatever you want to call it — you're the one who lost interest two years ago. You know that perfectly well, it was you. You said you were stressed and then that was the end of it. You can't blame me for that."

"Marriage is about more than sex. It's a whole edifice. We're partners in this journey, Alison, and we're traveling together to make the best life for our daughter." He smiles. I think he's about to pat me on the head.

"Will. You. Stop. Calling. Me. Alison? For fuck's sake." I've had enough.

"Don't shout. You'll upset Matilda."

I suppress a scream, punch the arm of the chair hard. It hurts. I nurse my hand and he catches my glance again and for a moment I think we're going to start laughing, the absurdity of our position driving away all the aggression. I mean, it's *us,* it's Carl and me. We've been together for the best part of our adult lives. We've been through everything. But the moment passes and his face hardens.

"We are going to try and make a go of this. Alison. Because of Matilda. But you are going to have to be considerably more grown-up about the whole thing. For better, for worse. Remember?"

Worse. Worser. Worst. I still feel a bubble of laughter in my throat, but it wouldn't be appropriate to release it. Carl's not in a laughing mood. I don't recognize the expression he's schooled his features into, but then I get it — he's Carl the therapist now, brows furrowed with sincerity. I catch the thought and slap it down. He may have started aspects of the rot but it's me who's kept it going. And it's me who is fucking (yes, definitely fucking) someone else. I remind myself that this is for Matilda. I'm going to be a better person for her, a better mother, a better wife.

"I do remember. For better, for worse. We'll make this work, I promise," I say.

This time he doesn't argue. After a moment he holds out his hand to me and I take it. His fingers are cool and although I'm aware that my hands are hot and sweaty he doesn't recoil. He doesn't exactly grasp my hand close either, but it'll do.

I don't sleep much, too aware of Carl avoiding me on the other side of the bed. There's a rickety bridge over the gap between us but it won't withstand much. I get up at six on Monday morning and take myself into chambers early — I can't face another row. I leave a note on the table saying I've had to go to work, with the words *Love You* scrawled at the last moment. I don't know whether the "you" is Matilda or Carl or both but I'll leave it to them to decide. The bus is empty and the streets deserted — it takes no time to get to Fleet Street. I should leave this early more often. The Temple is empty too, only a few lights showing the most dedicated barristers at work.

Walking past the dark buildings I think about my pupillage — the workaholic pupilmaster I had who was always at his desk by seven a.m., and last to leave chambers in the evening. I had another pupilmaster who would often be found sleeping off the night before under his desk, always the first to encourage late-night boozing and clubbing. Fifteen years ago, I was too naive to realize the similarity between them, seeing only the huge disparities in their natures. Now I realize that both were trying to avoid their homes, just as I am now. One would get me drunk with solicitors, one could barely hide his disapproval of me and my drinking, speaking to me with thinly veiled contempt even as he sent out almost verbatim — and unpaid — the paperwork I prepared for him. I developed the skills of hangover management and legal drafting with them — perhaps I also absorbed by osmosis how to fuck up my life. Maybe it's something that goes with the wig and gown, an infinite capacity for bullshit that flies with the defendants but hits a brick wall as soon as it's applied to anyone outside the world of criminal law.

I arrive outside chambers, pushing these thoughts aside. I can try to blame as many outside forces as I like, but my marriage is still fucked. Carl can't look at me and I'm beginning to find his self-professed perfection wearing. He may be better with Matilda than I am but he's had more practice. He plays daddy daycare while I'm out earning the money to pay for the whole shooting match. I'm feeling increasingly angry, the thoughts spinning out of control through my mind. I push through the door into chambers and go to my room — Matilda's there smiling at me from the photograph on my desk. I still haven't bought it a new frame and I'm stabbed by guilt, pulling me out of my loops of rage — the shit mother strikes again. I slump down on the chair, putting my head in my hands.

After a couple of moments I hear a cough at the door. Turning round, I see it's Mark the clerk.

"You're in early," I comment.

"I know. Lots to do this week. Sorting out a new filing system in the clerks' room, so I thought it would make sense to come in a bit early today. How about you, miss?" he says.

"Couldn't sleep so I've come in to do some paperwork. There's always something."

"True. Here's more to add to it." He hands over some papers he's holding. "It came in on Friday."

"I wasn't in." I say, redundantly. He's perfectly well aware of that. I stop talking and look at the paperwork. It's a prosecution statement from James, Madeleine's son. Dated last Thursday.

"When did they serve this?" I ask.

Mark shrugs. "Dunno, miss. It came through with the last delivery, about six on Friday. That's all I can tell you. Look, I need to get on."

"Sure, yes. Thanks very much."

Before reading it I call Patrick to ask when the statement came in and what his view is of James being a witness. I'm not sure if he'll answer as it's still before eight, but he picks up on the third ring.

"Everything all right?"

"Yes, fine. Look, I wanted to ask about —"

"What happened on Friday? I'm sorry, I was being a dick. Maybe I got freaked out being in your house," he says.

I'm startled. It's not what I expected, an apology. A full and frank disclosure of dickery.

"That wasn't what I wanted to talk about. But thank you. I'm sorry you got freaked out," I say.

"It was a lovely evening. I really enjoyed the food. But I was an arse and I'm sorry. Am I forgiven?"

"I, yes, sure. Of course you are." I know he pushed his luck with me, but he did stop in the end. And I wasn't as relaxed with him as usual either. As he said before, normally I like it rough. "Look, it's all right. And actually I wanted to talk to you about James's statement. Are they really planning to call her son to give evidence against her?"

"I don't think they're keen to. I had a

quick chat with the CPS lawyer in the case. But he is relevant to the state of the relationship."

"I guess he must be. Has she been able to see him?" I say before stopping. I riffle through the papers until I find the terms of bail to remind myself. Of course she hasn't been able to — no contact with prosecution witnesses. Whoever they might be.

"Anyway, read the statement. I don't think it's unhelpful," he continues. "I still think we could get this down to manslaughter, with the statement you got out of her."

"I will. Why didn't you mention this on Friday night?"

"Sorry, it went out of my mind completely. I had other things to think about. Remember?"

I do remember. Some of it was even fun. "True."

There's a long pause. I'm about to say something, anything to fill the silence but Patrick gets there first.

"Alison, I know I've said it already, but I'm really sorry. I got too carried away. I should have respected you saying no immediately."

I start to speak but he presses on.

"It won't happen next time."

"Next time?" I say.

"Next time. I want to see a lot more of you, Alison. A lot more. This has made me wake up to myself. I've been thinking about it all weekend. All these years I've played the field, avoided commitment. Maybe it's time I stopped running away. I think about you all the time, you know."

"You do?"

"Yes. I really do. I think we could be something special. Look, we can talk about this properly later? I have to go to court now," he says, and hangs up.

I hold my phone in front of me, looking at it as if it'll reveal more of Patrick's thoughts than he's exposed. *Something special?* My cheeks are warm and for a moment I feel a glow in my chest before reality comes rushing in. Yes, if it weren't for the slight inconvenience of the husband and child I've already got. He's changing the rules of engagement, offering a future that was never meant to be on the table. If I can believe what he's saying, if his words aren't borne out of guilt for having pushed it before. I catch sight of Matilda's photograph again and my heart contracts. It doesn't matter how Patrick feels — Carl and I will have to work it out. Somehow.

I turn to James's statement.

My name is James Arthur Smith and I am fourteen years old. I am in Year 9 and I attend a boarding school called Queens School in Kent. I started there just over a year ago. Before that I was at a school near my home in Clapham. Until I went to boarding school I lived at home with my mother and father, though my father traveled a lot with work.

I spend all the holidays at home now and, in addition to a week at half-term, we can also choose one other weekend to go home during term-time. I went back to school on 5 September, and even though it was so close to the start of term, I decided to come home for the weekend of the 17 September, because a friend of mine from prep school was having a party. I got home late on Friday night. Mum cooked and we had supper at home. Dad was out with work, and didn't get in until late. I had gone to bed, but I could hear them arguing a lot. Dad was shouting and Mum was crying. In the end I went to sleep. I didn't go downstairs to see what was happening as Dad doesn't like it when I do.

On the Saturday I woke up quite late. I had breakfast on my own as both Mum and Dad were out. There was a pile of broken glass on the side in the kitchen, which looked like it had been swept up and left in a heap. I think it was a bottle. I hadn't heard it being broken the night before so I don't know how it happened. I looked around to see if there was any blood anywhere but there wasn't. I wrapped the glass up in newspaper and put it in the bin because I thought it would make them happy if they didn't see it when they got home. I tidied up my breakfast and went upstairs to get dressed and get on with some homework.

Mum and Dad came back at about eleven that morning. I don't know where they had been and I didn't ask them. It's better not to ask questions when there's been a row. I went downstairs and talked to them both. Mum was a bit jumpy and looked like she'd been crying and Dad didn't say much. We had lunch together, though, and it was all right. Mum made cheese on toast because she knows it's my favorite.

We went out for dinner on the Saturday night, to a steak place. They weren't talking to each other, though they both talked to me. I wasn't sure whether Dad was cross but I was careful to say the right things. I drank Coke and they had two bottles of wine. I think Dad had a whisky, too. He normally does. After supper I went on to the party. I took the Tube there as it was just in Balham but I got an Uber home. Mum has set it up on my phone. The party was okay. There was some alcohol but I didn't drink any of it — I don't like how it makes me feel and it just seems to make people angry.

I got home just before eleven, which is my curfew. Mum and Dad were both still up. I think Dad had drunk more as he was swaying when he stood and his face was very red. His eyes were red too, and watery. He was in a really bad mood, though I don't know why. As soon as I came in through the door he came running at me, yelling that I was late even though I knew I was in before my curfew. He pushed me into the door which slammed shut and started punching me in the head and the body. Mum was behind him screaming and pulling at his arm. I doubled over and went down onto the floor, not because he knocked me over, but because I was trying to protect myself. I had my arms wrapped over the top of my head.

He kicked me twice on the legs and then he stopped. I think it was because he was tired, not because he particularly wanted to stop hurting me. His face was very red now, even redder than before. He was making a wheezing noise, his mouth opening and shutting. Finally he said to me, "Just get the fuck out of my sight. I don't want to see you again." I ran upstairs and barricaded myself in my room with a chair under the door handle. I wrapped myself in my duvet and sat on the floor listening to see if he was hurting Mum but I couldn't hear anything and in the end I went to sleep.

I thought about calling the police but it always make things worse in the long run. They've come to the house twice before that I know of when Mum and Dad have had a fight but they've never arrested Dad, and he always found a way to hurt Mum worse later. I can't remember exactly when those times were. Once was three years ago, I think, and the other was last Christmas because Dad didn't like that Mum had thought more about my presents than his.

The next morning Mum woke me up really early by knocking on the door. I was asleep on the floor. When I opened the door she was wearing the same clothes as the night before. They were all creased as if she'd slept in them and she smelled a bit funny. She wasn't speaking. She did a shh sign with her finger to her lips, and came into my room and started packing up my clothes. I took over as she didn't know what I wanted to take. She sat on the bed. I got dressed and then we went downstairs. I could hear Dad snoring as I went past their bedroom. She opened the front door and we stood outside and she gave me fifty pounds and whispered, "I'm okay. Go back to school. I'll call you tonight." I kissed her goodbye and that was the last time I saw her. She didn't call me even though she said she would, and when I tried to call her all I got was her voicemail. My housemaster told me what had happened after school on the Monday.

I did love Dad but I didn't like it when he got angry and when he shouted at me and Mum. I know I wasn't the kind of son he wanted because I was sick a lot and he wanted someone who loves football and rugby and cricket in the summer. I like playing those games, but not that much, and I've never been in an A team or even a B team. He used to call me pathetic and say it was worse than having a girl in the house. That Saturday wasn't the first time he's ever hit me, but it was definitely the worst.

I was happy to go to boarding school because I wanted not to hear their arguments anymore. I've worried a lot about Mum with me not there to look after her but she said it would make her more sad if I stayed at home and saw it all happen.

I haven't seen Mum since Dad died. I know she hasn't been allowed to, and I've been all right staying at school. Everyone is being very kind.

I wish they had stopped being married ages ago. It looked like they hated each other and I don't know why they stayed together. Maybe if they'd had a divorce it would have been better. I never wanted them to be divorced but if they had then Dad might still be alive and Mum might not be in prison.

I put the statement down, its final words running through my head. I look again at Matilda. Carl and I are nowhere near killing each other but there's no escaping the poison in the air between us. Suppressing a feeling of dread, free-falling into an abyss of separation and arguments about custody and finances, I try to list the practical steps I could take. Maybe it's time to be brave, to break the impasse. Our house must be worth something now, the way prices have gone up. We could sell it, split the proceeds. I could get a flat farther out, or rent somewhere. If it's only for me and Matilda it doesn't need to be much, not big. And it can't go on the way it is between Carl and me. The thought of a future with Patrick creeps into my mind but I dismiss it; I have to tackle the situation with Carl first before anything else.

Putting all those thoughts aside I reread James's statement, noting all the relevant details. One more conference with Madeleine and I'll have her defense cracked. I call Patrick later in the afternoon to share my views on the statement and we speak, briefly, his voice warm and pleased to hear me.

16

I arrive at Francine's house the following day at two. For the first time she seems pleased to see me, almost coming forward to kiss me in greeting before remembering this is a professional relationship, not friendship. Madeleine shows no such restraint, leaping to her feet from the sofa in the living room and embracing me warmly. We move through to the kitchen at my suggestion so that I can spread out the statements more easily.

"Have you been given a copy of James's statement?"

"Yes." Madeleine's voice is flat, her initial exuberance has faded.

"For all it's a prosecution statement, in my view it supports the background to your account. I think it's helpful. If they don't call him, which I don't think they're going to, we can call him ourselves." I'm trying to be encouraging.

"It supports me because I'm telling the truth about what happened," she says. For a moment it sounds as if she's having a go at me for needing verification but her face isn't angry.

"Of course, I only mean from the point of view of the case . . ."

"Oh, I know, Alison. Don't worry. It's so awful, though, to read about how he felt about the arguments." She looks down at the table for a while before forcing a smile onto her face. "But it does help, I see that."

"So we've now got a psychiatric report that's more in your favor, testimony from your doctor and your friend, and James's account. There are medical records supporting the history too. It's all coming together," I say, still encouraging in tone.

"But no one saw what happened that night. No one was there on the Sunday. They have to decide if they believe me, right?" she says.

"Yes. But as I explained before, the other evidence acts to corroborate the history behind the events of that night. It gives context to your actions," I say.

"I get that. May I see my statement again?"

"Sure." I get it out of the pile and give it to her. She leans over and reads it, and I read another copy of it that's in the file. I know it backwards, the narrative I've given to the broken words she murmured to me as we sat together in Jasper's. I've studied it so much it's ingrained in my memory: the early stages of their relationship, the way the violence began, slowly, insidiously. The injuries, minor and major. The indignities, the undermining, the spitting and scratching and pulling at her hair and at her most sensitive triggers of shame and humiliation. The times she covered a black eye with makeup and said she'd bashed it on the car door. The excuses she made to her friends, to her doctor, to the other parents in James's class. How she had tried to protect James from it through the years, to keep him away from Edwin's anger and to carry the brunt of it herself.

I couldn't protect James anymore. He was getting too big. Taller than me, closer to Edwin's height. Edwin couldn't cope with having another man in the house. There was one time, at the beginning of May this year, when James stood up to him about something, I can't remember what. James went out and Edwin turned on me, slapping me and saying that I was turning James against him, that James was out of control and he needed to be taught a lesson. I thought I'd managed to talk Edwin down from his rage, said that of course James respected him, but when James came home that night, Edwin punched him to the floor and kicked him a couple of times. I pulled him off but I knew it was only a matter of time before it happened again. I sent James off on sports camps for nearly the whole summer holiday and when he went back to school in autumn I thought things would be all right, at least for a while longer. But he insisted on coming home that weekend for the party. I tried and tried to put him off but he wouldn't listen.

Edwin said he was going to be away for work and I stopped worrying so much, but the trip was canceled at the last minute. I told him on the Thursday that James would be coming home for the weekend and he was so angry, said the house wasn't a fucking kindergarten. Those were his exact words, "What the fuck did you arrange that for? The house isn't a fucking kindergarten. I'm not paying the fees for him to go to boarding school when he's never there." I tried to calm him down but he wouldn't listen to me. "Well, I'm fucking well going out tomorrow," he said.

James arrived home on the Friday around seven. Edwin did go out, and I felt very relieved. I made a fish pie for James, and we ate together and watched some TV. James went to bed at around half past ten, and I stayed up watching a film. Edwin came in at around midnight. He was drunk and when he smelled the fish pie he went mad, accusing me of stinking the house up deliberately. He stormed down to the kitchen. I followed him, not knowing what he was going to do, and as soon as we were both in the kitchen he picked up the fish pie dish from the counter and threw it at me. I dodged and it hit the wall. It didn't break but what was left of the pie slopped out onto the floor. Edwin grabbed me and forced me down to the ground and pulled me across to the mess, and then he pushed my face into the food. It got up my nose and into my mouth and it was difficult to breathe, bits of egg and sauce and smoked haddock. The smell was disgusting and I wanted to be sick. I struggled to break free but he leaned more heavily on me and it was getting harder and harder to get any air. My neck and shoulders were really hurting. Just when I thought I was going to suffocate he got off me. I started to sit up but he screamed at me to eat it up, saying "Clear up the fucking mess you've made, you fucking bitch." I leaned over and started eating. When Edwin's like that there's no point arguing. You just have to do what he says.

Madeleine's paused over that section, I can see from the page she's holding. It made me pause too, when she told me about it in the wine bar. To me she's the epitome of poise. Every time I've met her she's been immaculate. Patrick told me this too, that even when he saw her in prison, she managed to look groomed. Trying to imagine her on her knees, eating spoiled fish pie from the floor — it's a task almost beyond me. She sighs and continues reading to herself. I also keep reading the statement.

I ate as much as I could, but there was still some left on the floor. Edwin kicked me in the back. "You've left a bit. You'd better lick it up." I started licking the floor. I was feeling sick now, and really ashamed to be in that position. I was terrified as well that James might come down and see what was happening. Edwin moved away from me and then there was a big crash of breaking glass right by my head. A splinter flew up and hit me on the cheek. It stung.

A pool of wine spread out across the floor. "Thought you'd like a glass of wine with your dinner," he said, giggling. I didn't dare turn round or stop licking the floor but now I was terrified he was going to push me in the broken glass. His giggles grew more hysterical, until it was like he was crying, though I was too scared to check. He kicked me once more in the back and left the kitchen and walked up the stairs. I heard him go all the way up to the top floor. The door slammed and then it was quiet. I waited for about half an hour on the kitchen floor until I was sure he wasn't coming back down. After that I cleared everything up, piling the glass to the side in the kitchen. I wiped up the wine and the fish pie. When I went upstairs I could see through the banisters that our bedroom door was shut so I decided it would be better to sleep on the sofa.

The following morning Edwin woke me up early, about seven. He was a different person. "Did my snoring keep you awake? Is that why you came down?" he asked. He said that we should go out for breakfast. I said yes and washed and dressed quickly before he changed his mind. I didn't like leaving James without saying goodbye but it seemed better not to remind

Edwin about his presence in the house. We went up in a taxi to the Wolseley. Edwin likes it there. He had a full English and ordered me scrambled eggs and smoked salmon. I wasn't very hungry but I did my best to get through it, though the smell of the fish made me feel a bit sick. Edwin was lovely and kind and made lots of jokes and slowly I started to relax.

We got a taxi back after breakfast and arrived home at around eleven. James must have got up beforehand because all the glass had been cleared away in the kitchen. I felt very sad that my son was having to sweep away wreckage from our rows. I felt guilty because it was my job to protect him, not his to protect me by tidying up our mess in case it set Edwin off again. But Edwin was being calm. James came down and we chatted together about his sport and how he was doing in class. I made cheese on toast and actually it was all okay. I stopped feeling quite so much on edge.

We all got on with our own things in the afternoon. James had homework and I had some reading to do for the next exhibition coming up at the gallery. Edwin was in his study for the afternoon and I was careful not to disturb him. I booked a restaurant I know Edwin likes for us all to go out for dinner. We had steak and some wine. Edwin had a whisky afterwards, too. He might have had a drink already but I don't know. He drank a lot more of the wine than me.

After dinner James went to the party in Balham and Edwin and I went home. He drank some more whisky and started to get angry about the fact that James was out, saying he should be there to see us. I made the mistake of saying that I thought Edwin didn't want James around and so Edwin slapped me a couple of times for arguing with him. He was pacing up and down, up and down, waiting for James to come home. The moment that James opened the door at eleven Edwin jumped on him and punched him to the ground, kicking him repeatedly round the head and body. I was screaming and managed to pull Edwin off and James ran upstairs. Edwin was yelling, "I'm going to fucking kill him. I'm not having this." He stormed into the living room and drank more whisky while I sat on the stairs staying very quiet. Eventually Edwin's rage simmered down and he fell asleep on the sofa.

"Could I really get off the murder

charge?" Madeleine says, breaking away from her reading.

"I don't know. It depends on a lot of things. The best would be if the prosecution accept your account — we're writing to them with our psychiatrist's report and they'll get you seen by one of theirs. And even if the prosecution don't accept the plea, there's nothing to stop us from putting it in front of a jury. And that could go either way," I say. "But it's worth a try, surely. Given everything that happened."

She stands up and paces to the other side of the room. "It's true, though. I couldn't see any other way. It was the only thing I could do." She clutches her hands to her face and lowers herself down against the wall, squatting on the floor. I see an image of her juxtaposed above, bending over and licking food from the floor. I see a booted foot kick at her. She starts to sob, quietly. I keep reading.

I didn't sleep that night. I couldn't stop thinking about it all. I knew I had to do something, but I didn't know what. As soon as it was morning I woke James up and got him out of the house and back to school. I knew that he couldn't be hurt anymore. Then I showered and changed.

Edwin woke late morning and didn't talk to me all day. He locked himself in his study and I don't know what he was doing. I didn't dare go out because I didn't know what he wanted me to do. I waited in the kitchen for him, making some soup in case he was hungry. He came down at about six and started drinking again. I had a drink too, to try to keep myself calm. I was shaking with fear around him. He asked where James was and I said that he had gone back to school. This upset Edwin because James hadn't said goodbye to him. He punched my stomach a couple of times but then he left it. "You've turned him against me. I've lost my son for good," he said. "I'm going to make sure you lose him too."

At that comment something snapped inside me. "Don't you ever threaten my son again," I said. He laughed and laughed. "Or what, Madeleine, or what?" Then he punched me in the side of the head so that I fell down, and kicked me twice in the stomach. "There's nothing you can do to stop me," he said. "I can kill you both, any time I choose." I didn't reply. He drank some more and then went upstairs to our bedroom. I could hear him moving around upstairs and then it was quiet. I couldn't take it anymore. He had hurt me so often, and it was getting worse and worse. He wasn't going to stop. And he had hurt James so badly and threatened to kill him. I truly believe he would have tried to kill us both — I was terrified about what he was going to do next. I didn't feel I had any choice, I was so scared of him now. I checked to see that he was asleep, and then I took the carving knife and stabbed him time after time after time. I don't know how I found the strength. I wanted to make sure he was dead, so he wouldn't ever be able to hurt us again. Something took over in me and I kept going and going, big stabs and little ones. There was so much blood it was dripping off my hands and over my face but I couldn't make myself stop.

"Madeleine, are you all right?" I ask. She's still sitting on the floor, though her sobs have subsided.

"Yes. I suppose," she says.

"I can't guarantee the jury will accept what you say. But it's my view that what you're saying amounts to a defense of loss of control. It would bring it down from murder to manslaughter. We need to show that you feared serious violence, which you had every reason to do, and not just to you, to James too. And secondly, Edwin was making threats to kill both you and James. I honestly believe that there's enough evidence to put in front of the jury — you killed Edwin suffering from a loss of control, in fear of further violence from him. We've got the psychiatric report, the proper one, the one where you told the truth — it says you show signs of post-traumatic stress disorder and depression. We've got all the evidence about Edwin's violence towards you. We've got James's account too. We have to go for it. Don't you agree?" I'm standing by the end of this speech, my voice impassioned. I can't bear to see her give up on herself.

"I don't know, Alison. I honestly don't know. It means a lot that you believe so much in my case but I'm not sure. I'll think about it for a bit if that's okay — I want to talk it through with Patrick as well. I could change my plea to guilty if he doesn't agree." She stands up and comes over to me and hugs me. I hug her back, almost brought to tears myself. I can't bear to think of what she's gone through. She's shown more strength than I'd ever have been able to. We stand holding each other for a moment longer, then disengage. She goes over to the sink and starts rinsing out some mugs and I put the papers back together. Then I check my phone.

Ten missed calls. Five messages. What the fuck? God, it's Matilda. It must be Matilda.

It's not Matilda.

First message: Patrick. Call me.

Second, Patrick. Please call me.

Third, Patrick. It's all a big misunderstanding. Call me.

Fourth, Patrick. Please, call me. I'm begging you.

Fifth, Mark the clerk. Miss please will you call chambers urgently.

I duck outside and call chambers.

"You mustn't tell anyone," Mark says. "Don't mention it to the client. But Patrick is being interviewed by the police."

I stand in silence, unable to form a response.

"He's not been charged, Chloe says, but he's being interviewed under caution."

"Did they, has Chloe said why?" But I'm thinking about Patrick's text message, his use of the word *misunderstanding,* and a ball of lead is forming in my stomach.

"She was very circumspect. But I think someone's made a complaint about him."

"What kind of complaint?" I say.

"I think it was a woman. But that's all I know."

Mark tells me I have no case in the following day, and we agree I'll have the day off. He ends the call.

"Is everything all right?" Madeleine says as I come back inside.

"No. I mean, yes, of course. A bit of bad news about one of my colleagues, that's all." I'm surprised at how clear my voice is, how ordered my words. My mind's spiraling. "I'm sorry, Madeleine, but I'm going to have to go now."

"That's fine," she says. "I hope things are okay."

"I'm sure they will be," I say, hoping what I'm saying is true. My sense of panic is increasing and I say goodbye to Madeleine without really seeing her face, without hearing her voice. I walk automatically through the streets of Beaconsfield, unable to cope with the complexities of a cab. I sit on the station platform watching one train pass, then another. Much later it starts to rain and I get onto the next train that stops, not checking its destination. Not caring. It's dark and the messages he's sent and the messages I could send back ping together in my mind. *Call me fuck you I didn't did you not me call me fuck you you didn't did you not me I didn't I didn't I didn't did I? Fuck you.* Write, delete, write, but never send. I know I should speak to him but I don't know what to say. I try to call once but it goes straight through to voicemail and my phone dies before I can think of any message I could possibly leave.

When I arrive home I walk straight past Carl, straight past Matilda, straight into the bathroom, where I stand under the shower until the water runs cold. I think Carl is speaking but the words wash with the water down the drain and then I go to bed hoping that whatever terrors night might bring, tomorrow will never come.

17

But it does. Wednesday arrives.

Matilda jumps on me in bed.

I ignore her.

Carl shakes my shoulder.

I ignore him.

My phone doesn't beep, doesn't ring.

I'd ignore it if it did.

I'm rolled up tight in the duvet with my head pushed deep into the pillow. Tomorrow is here and nothing has changed. Nothing has gone away. Fragments of the conversation I had with Mark the clerk run through my head. *Not a charge. Just an interview.* That doesn't mean it's true.

Then I'm thinking back further to the Friday night in my house. "Stop," I said. "Stop."

But he did stop. Eventually. He's not a rapist. He's Patrick.

But what if he hadn't stopped?

What if this time, he hasn't?

It can't be true. Not Patrick.
I don't want to believe it.
I don't know what to believe.

"Alison, you have to take this call. It's chambers," Carl says, pushing the home phone into my cocoon. I want to tell him to go away but I can't, not anymore. I uncurl, put the receiver to my ear.

"Hello?" My tongue is thick in my mouth.

"Hi, miss. Sorry to bother you. I know we agreed you'd be off today but I wanted to give you an update," Mark says.

"An update?"

"Yes, miss. We've just heard from Chloe at Saunders and Co. She confirmed that Patrick has been bailed, as of seven o'clock this morning. He's got to return in a week. They're looking at a possible charge of rape. Obviously he'll be suspended from practice while this is ongoing, so she's picking up his cases. She'd like you to give her a ring later today to discuss the murder."

"Right. Okay," I say, sitting up and looking for a pen. I'm tricked into normal behavior but it only lasts a moment. I collapse back against the bed. "Rape. Are you sure?"

"Unfortunately so, miss. Yes."

"Do you know who?" I pause, think again.

"Sorry, of course I shouldn't ask."

"No, miss. We don't know any more. That's all the information we have. Chloe's on her mobile, she said. Or you can get her on the office number. I'd call soon. She's in a bit of a fuss."

Mark hangs up. I look at the receiver in my hand, trying to work out how those words could have made their way through the ether into my ear.

"Rape?" Carl says.

I jump. I didn't realize he was still in the room.

"Just a case," I say. "Something I've got next week."

"Right." He doesn't leave the room but looks at me closely. "You don't look well. You've gone kind of green. Are you hung-over again?"

"No. I'm not. I was working last night. I don't know, I've been sick a couple of times. I'm taking today off." The effort it takes to keep my voice normal is huge, tremors as big as Krakatoa threatening a tsunami of tears that I can't bear for him to watch.

"Sick? Oh god, I hope you haven't got that Noro bug. I'm going to keep Matilda out of here." He beats a hasty retreat. "Is there anything you need?"

"No," I say. Meaning yes. Meaning I want

the clock to be turned back and none of this to be happening, a nightmare I'm stuck in like quicksand.

I roll myself back into the duvet and shut my eyes.

I stay in bed for the rest of the day. Carl is kind to me when he gets home, making me soup and toast and bringing it to me in bed. When I'm finished he takes the tray away and I lie back in bed, my eyes shut. A bit later he comes back up and sits next to me on the bed, looking at his computer. I'm grateful he isn't talking, giving me space instead. But throughout the evening Patrick's face, gray and bloodshot, looms behind my thoughts. I try to call once again, my hands shaking so much I can barely get his number up, but his phone is still switched off.

At eight he texts, at last. I jump at the beep of my phone but Carl doesn't notice, too engrossed in what he's doing on his laptop.

She's lying, Alison. It's not true.

I delete the message. I reply.

I don't know what to think.

He replies immediately. Please trust me. You know me. I wouldn't do this. At least give me a chance to explain.

I delete this message too, and think for a while about what to say.

I'll listen to your explanation, but I can't promise anything. Let's speak tomorrow.

A long pause, then Thank you.

I turn off my phone and wrap myself up in the duvet again, no part of me exposed to the world outside.

Matilda comes in to see me, Carl now reassured that whatever's wrong with me, at least I'm not puking. I unwrap myself and she lies beside me on the bed and lets me hug her for a long time. Her breath is warm on my neck and her hair smells clean. The pain in my chest eases a little, the steel grip round my ribs loosening its hold. I catch Carl's eye over Matilda's head and he smiles, properly, fully, the first time he's done so in months. He sits down next to us and for a moment lays his hand on my arm. The grip on my ribs loosens further and I sigh.

"I've just got to go out for a bit, Alison. Are you okay?"

"Yes. I think it's passing, whatever it was."

"Good. I'll put Matilda to bed first — you'll be a good girl for Mummy, won't you?"

Matilda nods her head, clearly tired, and Carl picks her up.

"I'm seeing that client, the suicidal one. He's still not great," he says. "But I won't be too late."

It's not that I don't care but I'm too tired to engage. As long as Matilda's all right. "No problem. We'll be fine."

He takes her through to her room and while he sings to her, I tuck myself back into the duvet.

The next morning I head for chambers after breakfast. Carl, Matilda, and I walk to the end of the road until I see my bus coming and start towards it, waving goodbye to them. When I arrive at chambers, Mark is businesslike, handing a series of new files to me. They relate not just to Madeleine's case but also to the upcoming rape and a fraud that's been dragging on for months. They're getting closer to a date for trial now and as I look at the file I think how much easier it'll be when it's going on, three months at Chichester Rents down off Fleet Street, almost a normal nine-to-five. I'll be able to drop Matilda off and pick her up too. I think about it for a while and call Mark.

"Can we push for more frauds for me? Or an inquiry? It would be good to have some more predictability."

He says he'll see what he can do. I smile at the thought. It's the answer. Maybe I should even look at moving over to the Crown Prosecution Service. If my work were more straightforward, maybe I'd be calmer. And if I were calmer, my work more under control, I'd be able to concentrate fully on Matilda and Carl, and he'd stop being so angry with me too.

Patrick calls around lunchtime. I look at my phone for some moments before picking it up and answering.

"Patrick?" I say. "I've been trying to get hold of you."

"I know," he says. "I'm sorry. It's been . . . difficult. Can we meet?"

I wait for a long time before replying. Part of me wants to see him, be reassured that he's not the monster they're alleging. Another part of me wants to run for the hills. After all we've gone through, though . . .

"Okay. Where?"

He names a café near Waterloo, on the Cut, and I agree, trying to hide my relief that it's nowhere nearer Fleet Street. I walk down and cross over the river, my feet moving slower and slower as I approach.

He's sitting at the back of the café, both hands clasping a mug. He nods in greeting and when I get to the table, stands and reaches out to me. I pause for a split second, then let him hug me. The feel of him reminds me that it's him, Patrick, my friend, my colleague, my lover, and I put my arms round him and hug him back. I feel him take a sharp intake of breath and he sobs once, twice, wetness seeping onto my neck. I pat him gently, the tension from his body vibrating into me. Eventually he lets go and we sit down facing each other. He gets hold of his mug again, though doesn't drink from it, instead staring into it. The silence stretches beyond what is bearable.

"Patrick, you have to talk to me," I say, at the same time that he starts to speak.

"Listen, I want to try and explain. It's not what it looks like — she's stitching me up to try and get out of it," he says.

I open my mouth to answer but nothing comes out.

"I'm serious, Alison. You've got to understand." There's a note of panic in his voice.

"Why do I have to understand?" I get the words out with an effort.

"Because it matters what you think. I

don't care about other people, but I do care about you."

I sit in silence for a moment longer trying to get some resolve. I need to start connecting the dots.

"You're on bail," I say.

"Yes."

"They haven't charged you yet?" I say.

"I'm to go back to the station in a week. Next Monday. I guess they're reviewing the evidence at the moment. They said it would be expedited," he says.

"Why would it be expedited?" The dots are jumping round the page — I know I'm not approaching this with any order but I can't help parroting what he says.

"Because of who's involved," he says.

"What do you mean? Who is it?"

He puts his head in his hands.

"Tell me what happened," I say, my voice firmer.

"It's hard. It's really hard." He looks up but not at me. I see the pallor and the bags under his eyes. The life and soul of the party has lost his fire.

"Patrick, you need to explain. This is scaring me."

He takes a deep breath. "Okay. So it was on Monday."

"When on Monday?"

"Early evening," he says. "That's when I was arrested."

I'm trying to work out the timeline. I know we spoke on the phone on Monday morning about Madeleine, and in the afternoon we spoke again.

"But I was on the phone to you around half three, four." I say. "How does that all fit together?"

"Yes, I was. But I'd gone out for lunch with someone. I was pissed by then. Couldn't you tell?"

I shake my head, the movement slight. Patrick's always held his drink well.

"And then, well, we ended up drinking more. More than we should."

"Who were you having lunch with?" I say, my words slow, deliberate.

He doesn't reply.

"Who were you having lunch with, Patrick? I presume it's the same person who's made the complaint?"

He slumps into his seat, looking now like the man he'll be when he's sixty. Tired, gray. Spent. He spreads his hands out on the table before him, a fan shape in the slops of tea.

"Please," I say.

"You have to swear you'll never tell anyone this. I've only told Chloe."

"Yes, I promise. Please, just tell me."

"Caroline Napier. That's who I was having lunch with. Caroline Napier. And yes, she's the one who's made the complaint."

I throw my head back, winded. I take a long breath in, hold it, exhale. Fuck.

"As in the QC?"

"As in the QC," he says.

"But she's married. To that journalist . . ." I start to say. Caroline Napier is legendary, one of the youngest women ever to be made a criminal silk while maintaining her marriage and raising three children.

"He's left her for a trainee — she's in a real state. We got hammered, all right? We were both at the same court. Luton. We got the train back together late morning. I suggested lunch. She said yes. We got more and more drunk — her marriage is on the rocks, she's cutting loose. We ended up walking up into Clerkenwell and climbing over a fence into one of those garden squares. We've been there before, you and me. Remember? I didn't think anyone could see."

"You didn't think anyone could see what?" My hands are cold as I push away his invocation to memory. Special, that's what he'd said. I'd nearly believed him.

"Us. What we were doing."

"And what were you doing?" I say, my

voice calm, as cold as my hands.

"Do you want me to spell it out?" He looks on the brink of tears, his chin trembling.

"I think you'd better."

"It seemed really secluded. And it was dark. We were kissing in the restaurant. We kept kissing in the pub. We climbed over the fence and she was finding it all very funny and it was quiet and I know she wanted it just as much as I did . . ."

"Wanted what?"

"Come on, Alison. We were fucking. On a park bench. What's the point of making me say it?"

"Why wouldn't you want to say it?"

"Because you're just going to get jealous again and that's the last thing I can deal with right now."

His words settle on me thick as flies. I can't brush them off.

"I'm not sure that's the priority right now," I say, striving for calm.

"I'm sorry, I didn't mean it. I'm not thinking straight. That's not what I meant." He subsides into his seat. "We got arrested, Alison. Someone saw what we were doing and called the police."

He pauses and I think I'm meant to say something but the words aren't there.

"We were taken off to the nearest nick and they put us in the cells to sober up. Tuesday morning they offered us both cautions for outraging public decency. I took it but she didn't. Once she'd sobered up, she told them that she was too drunk to consent. She says she knew she was kissing me but that once we got into the garden it stopped being fun and she didn't want to do any more but I forced her to have sex with me. She says that she was trying to say no but she was too pissed. Whatever happens, she's guaranteed anonymity. My name could end up all over the press, soon enough, but she'll be protected."

I'm speechless. I can feel it all, every grope and tug and fumble. I've been there. I know the garden, the rhododendrons, the bench, the smell of dead leaves in the air. I leaned over the back of the bench, the wood rough under my hands, and Patrick pushed hard into me and within seconds it was over.

"Aren't you going to say anything, Alison?"

"I don't know what to think. It's such a serious allegation to bring. Surely she wouldn't make it up," I say.

"But I'm a liar? Thanks, Alison," he says with a flash of anger. After a moment he starts again, "Look, I get it. I understand how difficult this is. But all she's thinking about is herself," he says. "It's really clever, if you look at it objectively. My bet is they won't charge me — no way is there enough evidence to go ahead with a trial on this. Maybe she'll even withdraw her complaint so that she can have a clear conscience. But as a complainant in an allegation like this, she'll have lifelong anonymity. This'll never come out, not for her. As far as she's concerned, this is a win-win situation."

I'm gaping at Patrick. I remember again the evening at my house, when he wouldn't stop. I have to accept that he's capable of rape. I hesitate, though. What he's saying seems completely absurd, out of the question, but yet there's a logic in there. A logic borne of desperation, perhaps, but logic nonetheless.

"You really think . . ." I begin.

"I really think, Alison. I really do," he says, leaning forward towards me. His face is more animated than it's been all the time I've been there, some color finally creeping up under the gray. "It makes perfect sense. She's thinking clearly enough about herself, just not about me. All she reckons is that I won't be charged. Look at the stats. This would be an impossible rape to prove in court. She was drinking all day, highly inebriated, no physical evidence of force, eyewitness accounts of the sex with no suggestion there was a lack of consent . . ."

"Okay, okay, I get it. I see what you're saying. She's taking a risk, though — they could end up charging her with wasting police time. Or worse."

"Caroline Napier QC? Who's going to suspect her of that — no one would disbelieve her. The best I can hope for is that they take the view there's insufficient evidence, she withdraws the statement, and it's over before anything further happens. I'm almost sure that's what's going to happen. But I know what anyone who hears about it will say, there's no smoke without fire . . ." He pauses. "Do you believe me?"

My mind's spinning.

I know what Patrick's like. I've heard what Caroline Napier is like.

She wouldn't say it, not if it weren't true. Why would she put herself through it? I've defended a couple of rape trials in which she's been prosecuting before. Caroline knows exactly what happens when someone makes a complaint, the violation upon violation of the rape suite and the swabbing and the probing. A wave of compassion washes over me, the thought of what she's had to go through. No one would make this up.

"Please, Alison. Say something. Anything."

But on the other hand . . . Clearly she's in a mess at the moment. And people do really stupid things when they're in a mess. Broken marriage, too much booze, getting caught up in the heat of the moment. Getting caught . . .

"I can see it isn't clear-cut," I say. "But you put yourself in such a bad position." I don't even care about having a go at him about shagging someone else; I think we've moved past that.

"It should never have happened," he says. "Even without this. I know you don't like it, and I don't want to hurt you. I hate hurting you. You're the best thing in my life."

My heart jumps for a moment and then the reality of what he's said sinks in. I'm married to someone else. I have a daughter. Patrick and I don't exactly have what I would call a meaningful relationship, even with all the drama and turmoil. He's gotten off on it, and I have too, albeit in a different way. I've found it a solace and a refuge, a relief to be wanted rather than pushed away. But the best thing in my life? Under no circumstances is that Patrick. That's Matilda alone. I look at him. It feels as if a great distance has opened between us, an uncrossable chasm. He doesn't look like himself anymore; shrunken, unshaven, facing the loss of his reputation. If it goes badly for him, it means the loss of his freedom and his career. I want to find sympathy for him, but the thought of what Caroline has perhaps had to suffer is too overpowering.

"Please, Alison. Say you'll support me. I really need a friend right now," he says.

Pausing only for a second, I reach my hand out and take his, trying not to recoil at the touch of his fingers. Then I stand up and leave.

On the way to chambers I buy some fags and stand in a doorway smoking one. It's the stress, I excuse it to myself. If I'm ever going to buy cigarettes for myself, it'll be now. But the smoke crawls up my nose and makes my eyes water and I'm revolted by it, all of a sudden, the smell, the taste; everything. I take the pack and crumple it up, throwing it away in the nearest bin.

Once back in chambers I work on the files for a few hours and at three I tell Mark I'm going to go home. I text Carl to say that I'll pick Matilda up and he's pleased, saying he can fit in an extra client now. After that I turn my phone off. I don't want any texts from the threatening no-number. I get the Tube up to Holloway and do the Waitrose run again but this time I'm faster, zooming between the aisles like a pro. Not steak, not vegetables of seduction, this is plain home cooking: ingredients for fish pie and lasagna and a chocolate cake that Matilda and I can bake together, every bit as close as her and Carl's mother.

Matilda's happy when I collect her. I chat to the mums waiting at the gate and it's friendly and relaxed. I can't remember now why I hated them so much, why I thought they were so horrible. They're welcoming, a nice woman in glasses and a big jumper saying how much her daughter, Salma, likes playing with Matilda and perhaps we could arrange a play date. We talk about our mutual hate of swimming clubs and she laughs at an impression I do of Ms. Anderson, the scary after-school club teacher.

She puts her hand on my arm and says, "I don't know how you do it, working and looking after Matilda." She's so open as she says it, so guileless in her expression that for once the cliché doesn't make me flinch.

I realize there's a lump in my throat and I cough a couple of times to clear it before I say, "It's not easy, but Carl is great."

"She's a lovely little girl," the mum says.

"Thank you," I say, and I mean it.

The children start to stream out of the

school building and the mum and I drift apart in search of our own, but before she goes she says, "I'm Rania, by the way, really nice to talk to you."

"I'm Alison. Likewise."

"Some of us are going out for a meal in a couple of weeks. Do you think you'd like to come?" she says.

My immediate instinct is to say no but something else creeps in, a small shoot of green from the frost. It's been so long . . .

"I would, yes. I know I'm not around that much . . ." I say.

"All the more reason for you to come, then. We'd love to get to know you," she says. "I've got your email, I think — I'll make sure to add you to the invitation."

"Thank you. That's really kind." And it is. I really mean it. Her openness is thawing something inside me.

"Are you on WhatsApp? There's a class group, you know."

I shake my head, smile, the frost reforming. I'd deleted the app within days, the perpetual moaning about missing socks and homework robbing me of the will to live.

"Can't blame you, it's bloody irritating," she says, and the frost melts again.

"It was a bit full-on, all the notifications all the time," I say, and she laughs.

"I've turned the notifications off," she says, "but don't tell anyone I said that."

I almost want to hug her. It feels like the first normal exchange I've had in months. I've wasted so much time agonizing over stupid men, stressing about the politics of the school gate. Not anymore.

Matilda and I walk home hand in hand and I make the fish pie while Matilda draws pictures of dogs and writes a story about an elephant for her homework. When she's finished I let her have a go on her iPad. I've boiled eggs to put in the pie and I stand with my hands under the tap, peeling them. I'm going to cut them in quarters but then I remember the egg slicer that Carl's mother gave me three Christmases ago, when Matilda was still at nursery and needed to have lunches made for her every day. I unwrapped the box she gave me, the egg slicer and dinosaur sandwich cutters and cute little plastic boxes for fruit, the message so loud it was deafening. I forced a smile and put the box unopened in the back of the utility room cupboard.

Now I go through into the utility room, hoping desperately it's still there, rammed in behind cleaning products and plastic bags. I pull them all out and there it is, the domesticity I've been dodging all this time. There's a layer of dust on the top of the box but inside all the lunch box supplies are good as new. I get out the egg slicer and remove it from its packaging, take it into the kitchen.

"What are you doing, Mum?" Matilda says, looking up from her iPad.

"It's an egg cutter," I say. "I'm going to put slices of egg in the fish pie."

"That's nice. I like egg. Can I help?"

"Sure. I just need to figure out how it works."

We stand next to each other by the chopping board, the small white contraption before us. I pick up one of the hard-boiled eggs and put into the bottom of the cutter and then push the top part with its wires down over the egg. For a moment it doesn't look as if it's done anything, the egg still as perfectly ovoid as before, but as I take hold of it, it falls into thin, perfect slices, the yolk golden.

"That's really cool," Matilda says, and I nod in agreement. I can't believe I've been so resistant to it for so long.

"Can I do the rest?" she says, and I nod again, standing aside for her. She slices three more eggs, each time the illusion given that they're still intact before separating into their disparate parts. We put the rest of the pie together and bake it until the potato is golden on top, peaks and troughs of mash and white sauce and above all the aroma of smoked fish in the air.

When it's done I take it out to cool and at that point I turn on my phone. I want to see if Carl is going to be back soon. He should be impressed with this, I think, homework done and supper made. I leave Matilda with her iPad in the kitchen and go into the living room, shoulders tense, preparing myself for more messages. Threatening anonymous ones, or ones from Patrick. But there's nothing. Relief floods over me and my shoulders relax. I sit down on the sofa to check my emails. Again, nothing significant. Nothing frightening. The usual work things, that's all. I shut my eyes and lean back against the sofa, glad that the evening isn't being wrecked. The phone beeps to tell me there's a voice message and I look at it, tense again, but it's just one from Carl. *Going to be back around eight, don't wait for supper, see you soon.*

I go back to the kitchen to boil some frozen peas. Matilda and I eat our fish pie at the table and I cover the rest with cling wrap for Carl when he gets home. Matilda talks about the game she's been playing and her friends, and I tell her about being invited for a meal out with the other mums and she's pleased and I'm doing a good job, my voice light and laughing, no sign of the shades underneath. But they're there, Patrick's situation weaving its way through the weft of our chat.

After Matilda is in bed I go to bed too. It might be early but I'm cold and tired. The shock is passing and also the sense of unreality that's dogged me all day, however comforting and domestic my activities. I know where I am: in my bed, in my house, with my daughter asleep next door and my husband due home any minute. When I hear his key in the door I feel relief that we're all here, under one roof.

"Sorry I got held up," Carl says, sitting on the side of the bed next to me. "The fish pie smells good."

I smile at him and he goes downstairs to get some food and while he's gone I check my phone. Nothing. He brings his dinner back up and as he eats it I put my phone on silent.

"Do you want to watch some TV?" he says. "A new box set?"

I'm surprised but pleased. The last time we were getting on well was when we watched *The Wire.* "Sure. What did you think?"

"Some Scandi-noir? I'll get my laptop."

We sit together against the pillows, propped up in a halo of light from Carl's laptop. The series is subtitled, so I need to concentrate and soon I'm gripped. At the end of the episode we move on to the next with no discussion. After that it's nearly midnight and I'm too tired to watch any more but he doesn't mind, and we lie close together, arguments put aside for one night.

"I like it when it's like this, a quiet night in, just us," he says, and instead of saying anything I reach my arms round him and I know he knows I agree.

Friday passes, two bail applications and a mention at the Crown Court at Belmarsh. No drinks, I'm straight off home by four o'clock, pausing only to pick up my papers for Monday from chambers. Chloe and I speak briefly on the phone about Madeleine's case. I almost ask how Patrick is doing but I cut the words off before they leave my mouth and she doesn't acknowledge the pause.

It's another quiet evening, Matilda to bed early and a couple more episodes. Maybe we're going to be all right. And even though inside I know I doubt it, I don't let myself think otherwise.

18

Carl's working most of the weekend, so on Saturday morning I take Matilda swimming and it's not nearly as bad as I'd anticipated. There are enough chairs to sit and watch, and everyone is friendly. We go up to Hampstead Heath on Sunday morning as it's sunny and Matilda climbs the big oak trees near the entrance to Kenwood. I take photographs of her holding on like a monkey to the lower branches. The leaves have all fallen by now and she kicks through the piles that have built up under the trees.

"I like climbing trees with you," she says. "Daddy never lets me go high."

For a moment I wonder if I ought to stop her but she's enjoying it so much I don't want to spoil her fun.

"Make sure you don't fall off, then," I say. "We don't want Daddy to get cross."

She giggles and I suppress a flash of disloyalty. We walk up the hill to the coffee stall on the right and for once it's open. I buy a flat white and Matilda decides between hot chocolate or ice cream.

"It's too cold for ice cream," I say, and she thinks about it for a moment.

"It's never too cold for ice cream," she answers, and the lady behind the counter laughs and serves her two scoops of chocolate ice cream into a cone. We go back down to the oak trees and I laugh at the mess she's made of her face, licking a tissue and scrubbing at her cheeks to get rid of the worst of it. She starts running round in circles, away from me and back towards me, catching hold of my hands and spinning me round before throwing handfuls of leaves up in the air. I throw some too, and she sprints to catch them.

"Close your eyes," she says.

"What for?"

"I want to play hide and seek. I'm going to hide and you're going to find me."

"Okay," I say, putting my hands up to cover my face.

"Promise you won't look. Now you need to count to a hundred."

"It's a long time, sweetheart. Shall we say fifty?"

"That's what Daddy always does. It's not fair. You can't hide properly in fifty," she says. I hesitate, unwilling to disturb our alliance.

"How about seventy-five?" I say.

"A hundred. Please, Mummy." She stretches so much out of the syllables that I can't bring myself to say no any longer.

"Okay. A hundred. But don't go too far," I say.

"I promise. Do you promise not to look?"

"Promise. One, two, three . . ." I start counting.

Matilda giggles and grabs on to my legs for a moment to give me a hug. I hear her footsteps run away through the leaves.

Twenty-three, twenty-four . . .

"Are you still counting, Mummy? I can't hear you." She's still laughing, I can hear her somewhere behind me. I don't think the search is going to take long.

"Thirty-one, thirty-two," I call out.

Her footsteps go farther away, the rustling getting quieter and quieter. I can't hear her breathing anymore.

Forty-eight, forty-nine. I sneak a look around me.

"Mummy! I can see you looking!" I can hear her, not see her. I clap my hands over my eyes.

Other footsteps rushing past me, children, adults, a dog. They're laughing too.

Fifty-six, fifty-seven.

I'm getting bored. I haven't counted to a hundred in years and it's taking far longer than I'd have thought. I don't want to be standing eyes shut, blocking out the sun and the blue sky and Matilda's face.

But I promised.

Sixty-seven, sixty-eight.

Voices, close then moving far away. The only words I catch from their conversation are *football* and *meat pie.* Further away a murmuring, more laughter. A sudden shout from the distance, and the creaking of branches above me in the breeze.

Eighty-one, eighty-two.

My other senses are heightened. I'm surrounded by autumn. The faint scent of a bonfire and the mustiness of decaying leaves, the buzz of a plane high above, banking over north London towards one of the airports. It'll smell stale inside, sweat and feet, a whisper of ammonia from the loos. The passengers will be peering out the windows, ticking off the landmarks — Wembley, Kenwood House, the Heath, a mass of green and trees below, too far up to see the moving specks of people and dogs racing across Parliament Hill.

Ninety-nine, a hundred.

"Coming, ready or not," I shout out.

I open my eyes and look around. No sight of her. I circle the trees, keeping in mind the place where I stood counting as the center of my search. I go off, looking behind the trees, searching for a glimpse of Matilda's green-and-silver parka. Not there. I go diagonally, still looking, laughing at how good she is.

"You're hiding too well, Matilda. I can't find you," I say, and the wind replies, gusting through the trees. My pulse is rising, the adrenaline of the game kicking in. One tree, another, all merging into the same, their limbs outstretched to me. *Maybe I've got her,* says one, *No, it's me,* says another. It's as if a face is staring out at me from one trunk, a leer from another. I take a deep breath and stop running, look around me. The trees aren't alive, not in that way. They're not some malevolent force to have swallowed Matilda whole.

Yet I can't see her.

"Matilda, Matilda," I call out. "It's time to stop hiding now. You've won."

No reply. No small blond girl running up to me from behind a shrub. I'm turning round and round in circles, my breath quickening and something constricting my throat.

"Matilda. Matilda!"

A man in jogging clothes comes over to me.

"Are you looking for a dog? There's a spaniel over that way." He points. "I think it might be lost."

"Not a dog, no. My daughter. We were playing hide and seek." It's hard to get the words out. I'm entering full panic now, fear sparking through me.

"What does she look like?"

"She's about this high," I say, gesturing at my waist. "Blond-brown hair. She must be somewhere. I only had my eyes shut to a hundred."

The man starts running round the trees, calling out Matilda's name. Another jogger joins in. Two women walking their dogs see the commotion and ask me what's happening. I try to explain.

"It was less than two minutes. I had my eyes shut for less than two minutes. She was so keen for me to play the game properly — I should never have listened."

"Don't worry, love. We'll find her. She'll have gone into Kenwood, that's my guess," one of the women says. "Matilda, that's right?"

They head through the iron gate into the Kenwood Estate and I hear them calling her name. The jogger is shouting over to my left. More people join in, runners, dog walkers, two nuns, and a girl in platform trainers and a face full of black eyeliner. They've fanned out, pulling bushes apart and shouting. I'm stuck in the middle, at the last spot where I saw her, where she hugged me before running off. I take my phone out of my pocket and start to text Carl.

I can't find Matilda.

I look at the words and swallow back the acid bile that's rising in my throat. Then I delete them. She's bound to turn up soon. There's no need to worry him.

A small vehicle passes with two park rangers inside. They stop as soon as they see the commotion and speak to one of the searchers, who gestures at me. I run towards them, almost weeping at the reassuring sight of them in their green uniforms. They listen to me and call someone on their radio. I'm spinning round in circles, looking for a trace of her. One of the men puts his hand on my arm to get my attention and I nearly hit him.

"I've got to look for her. Let go of me."

"Please, can you tell us exactly what she was wearing," he says, his head close to mine. I think his voice is meant to be reassuring but he's in the way of me looking, stopping me.

"I've told you. Blue jeans, pink trainers, a green-and-silver jacket."

"Green and silver in what way?"

"What do you mean? Sorry, sorry, I know you have to ask. Block green on the bottom half, block silver on the top. The hood's silver," I say, pulling back the fear I feel, the sheer fucking terror of it, my daughter reduced to a list of her clothes.

Minutes pass. I don't know whether to stay where I am or to go into Kenwood, tearing my way through the bushes along the perimeter fence. I'd welcome the scratching of the branches on my skin, the whipping of the leaves across my face. But if I go, she won't be able to find me. This is the last place I saw her. Maybe she's wandered off through the shaded paths and has gotten confused, the way they turn back on themselves, the way that within minutes you're surrounded by dense undergrowth. I've gotten lost there myself, the time I tried looking for the old dueling ground, the icehouse. The icehouse . . .

"Could she have wandered into the icehouse? Maybe she's gotten trapped somewhere?" I say to the park ranger next to me. He's on his radio but turns to listen to me.

"The police patrol is on its way. We'll look into all the possibilities."

The word *police* punches me in the guts. No one's telling me not to get carried away, that I'm being silly and of course she's going to turn up in a second. They're calling the police and organizing people into systematic search parties. The bile comes up again in my throat, burning, sour.

Then the police are there, three of them this time, two young and one older. She's got short gray hair and a reassuring roundness to her face, though I can see from the brightness of her eyes that she won't let anything pass.

"I'm DC Murray from the Hampstead Heath Constabulary. You say your daughter is missing. How old is she?" she says, standing forward, flanked by the two younger officers.

"She's six. We were playing hide and seek. I had my eyes closed," I say.

"For how long exactly?"

"I counted to a hundred. I wasn't counting fast or slow, less than two minutes," I say.

"So you had your eyes off her for around two minutes?"

"About that."

"And you don't know where she went?"

"We were playing hide and seek. I promised not to look. She made such a fuss about having a proper amount of time to hide. I tried sneaking a look but she caught me." I'm trying to keep myself under control but I can't stop my voice from going into a wail. I want to put my head back and howl and howl until Matilda's safely in my arms.

"Does she know this area well?" The police officer's words break through to me. I wipe the snot off my face with my sleeve.

"We come here, not that regularly, though. I mean, she knows it, but I don't think she could find her way round."

DC Murray notes down what I say in her notebook.

"And you last saw your daughter at what time?" she says.

"I don't know. I didn't look at my watch. I counted to a hundred and then I started looking and when I couldn't find her I started shouting for her and then that man there started looking for her and then all of this . . ." I'm speaking so fast the words are falling out on top of each other but this is such a waste of time we should be in the woods in front of me and behind me looking under every bush and every tree until . . .

"We need to get an idea of how long she's been gone. Do you have any clearer idea than that?" the officer says, her voice kind but persistent.

"Maybe fifteen minutes?" I say, clutching at numbers in the air.

She backs away with the other police officers. They go to their car and one of them sits in the driver's seat and uses the radio. I'm about to go over to them but they're finished, they shut the car doors and one of them goes into Kenwood Estate, calling Matilda's name, and another goes down the hill behind me, doing the same. The group of searchers has gathered momentum, every passerby drawn to it like iron filings to a magnet. The urgency in their voices is rising. I stand still in the center, frozen to the spot, the frenzy of the search spinning round and round me until I'm so dizzy I could collapse.

DC Murray returns. She puts an arm round me and pushes me gently down into a kneeling position.

"You're very pale. Take some deep breaths," she says.

I try but I can't, my chest is too tight.

"We're on to it now. I'm sure she's just wandered off somewhere. Children of her age do this kind of thing," she says.

"She's never done anything like this before," I say.

"And I bet she won't do anything like this again, when she sees all the fuss she's caused."

I know that the woman's words are designed to calm me down but her eyes are flickering this way and that over my shoulder, assessing the situation.

"Who does she live with at home?" she says.

"Me, her father. The three of us."

"And is everything all right? Are there any problems?" she says.

"No, none. What's that got to do with anything?"

"Just checking if there are any problems with Dad," she says, the statement a question.

"What do you . . . oh, that he might have snatched her? No, nothing like that." I pause. A beat later. "I thought you said she'd just wandered off?"

"We have to cover all possibilities," she says. "Where is Dad?"

"He's a therapist, he's with clients all day."

"If you tell me where, we can send someone to pick him up," she says, her tone casual. The calmer she is, the more it's scaring me. There's depths of meaning I can't begin to understand. "What's the clinic address?"

I give it to her, the formula of words and numbers coming automatically out of my mouth. Matilda's name echoes around me and I'm straining to hear a response, anything at all that might give me some hope. A little girl runs along the path with her mother in front of me and it's everything I can do not to run after her and grab her and check it isn't Matilda though I know it isn't, she's in a pink coat and her dark hair is closely braided to her head.

The shouts get closer now and maybe they've found something, my heart leaps up into my mouth and the police officer runs out of Kenwood Estate holding something. For a moment I think it's her, Matilda, my daughter, my darling, back to me, but there's something wrong, she's all floppy as he carries her, all at a twisted angle, and then a huge relief as I see it's her coat not her body dead in his arms and I run up to him but the relief goes and then it's panic and no breath and a screeching somewhere that might be me as the policeman holds out a coat empty to me, part green, part silver, and as I clutch it to me the police officers look at each other with a grim expression I can read only too well.

The woman police officer reaches forward and takes the coat from me. I try to hold on to it but she pulls it firmly back.

"We need this for the search," she says. "You can have it back soon."

"I don't understand. She was wearing it. Where did you find it?" I look at the policeman who found it. He hesitates for a moment, as if searching for the right words.

"It was underneath a bush up through there," he says, pointing in the direction of Kenwood.

"Why would she take it off?" I say. "It's cold today."

"Maybe she got too hot when she was running round trying to find you," he says. "And it is distinctive."

I'm stone cold. The clock's ticking and I know exactly what he means. I've heard all the urban myths, the children snatched in department stores, their heads shaved, their clothes switched. I know there'd be nothing easier than to dump the coat and wrap her in something different to get her out of the park before anyone noticed what was wrong. I had my eyes shut for so long I basically handed Matilda over to them on a plate.

The adrenaline's kicking through me, keeping my heart so fast it might burst out of me, my hands twitching and clutching at Tilly's coat. And underneath, the knell of guilt growing louder and louder. This is all my fault. All my fault. I sinned, and she's paying for it. My shit mothering has lost her, lost her maybe for good. I sink down onto my knees, sick at the thought of everything I've done and everything I could have done and how now it's too late, I'll never be able to hear her laugh again or brush her hair or walk her to school or take her swimming. God, swimming. The pond at the bottom of Kenwood. I nearly shout it out but I stop — they know, they're searching up there. Even though I don't pray and I know I don't deserve any intervention, divine or otherwise, I bargain in my mind. *I'll give it all up, I swear, I'll be there for her. If I can have the chance, just once more, to see her, hug her, I'll stop being such a selfish cow. I'll relish every moment as I should have done from the start, instead of being so caught up in myself.*

The search continues. I stay glued to the spot where I last saw her. I'm losing track of how long she's been gone — my sense of time has gone funny, slow and fast merging into a spiral in my mind.

"Alison. Alison! What's going on?"

Carl's here — they've picked him up from the clinic and brought him up.

"Matilda's gone. We were playing hide and seek and then she wasn't there." I start crying again and go to hold him, to be held, to be told it's all going to be all right and that she's going to turn up any minute.

Carl pushes me back by the shoulders. "I told you to be careful, you can't be trusted to do anything." He's furious, I can see that now. "Have you told them what you do? Maybe it's one of your clients?"

DC Murray turns to me swiftly. "What do you do?" she says.

"I'm a criminal barrister. Defense, mostly. But I really don't think . . ." I say.

"And you're a therapist," she says, looking at Carl. "Any possibility that one of your clients . . . ?"

"None of *my* clients would do anything like this," he says, looking at me with contempt in his face.

DC Murray looks at me closely, back at Carl again. One of the other officers comes over and gestures to her, and they move off and have a brief conversation. He goes to the car and uses the radio again.

"We're calling out the helicopter," she says. "Sometimes it can help."

I was scared before but now I'm entering full-blown panic.

"Any idea of whether you might have upset one of your clients recently?" she says.

"I don't think so. Not like that," I say.

"And you, sir?" she says to Carl.

"Of course not. I can't believe you're wasting time on this. You should be looking for her, not trying to dig at us," he says, his anger overflowing. I inhale, exhale. I don't dare stand back up for fear I'll faint.

"We're doing everything we can," DC Murray says, trying to calm things down.

"Alison, how the hell could you lose our daughter!" He's screaming in my face now, bending down to my level. I put my head in my hands and rock backwards and forwards.

"This is all your fault, you stupid bitch! You've fucked up our marriage and you've lost our daughter. For fuck's sake!" He stands up and storms away from me before turning back.

"Where is my daughter?" he says to DC Murray. Then he leans forward and screams in her face too. "Where the fuck is she?"

"I'm going to have to ask you to calm down, sir," she says, not backing away but rather straightening herself into his fury. "I understand this is an emotional time, but —"

"An *emotional time*? My wife's so useless that she's lost our daughter and you think this is just emotion?" He squares up to Murray as if he's about to punch her. I'm watching him, holding my breath. If I say anything, if he notices me, it'll happen for sure and then he'll be inside for assaulting a police officer on top of everything else.

Murray stands firm and for a moment they stand locked in a stare. Carl lowers his hands and his face crumples.

"Sorry. I'm sorry," he says. He walks away again before coming back and aiming a kick at me. "Bitch," he screams.

I jump back and his foot misses. He almost overbalances and staggers to retain his balance. I'm frozen now, watching the fury on his face, suffused purple in rage. I know I should be frightened but I'm not. I don't have room to care. I deserve to be kicked. It would make me feel better to be kicked. But right now it doesn't matter. The only thing that matters is Matilda and the hole in my heart her absence has left. I don't understand how Carl can care about anything else.

"Stop looking at me," he says. "Stop fucking looking at me." He stands over me and takes hold of my shoulders and starts shaking me harder and harder. "You useless bitch," he says but the words get all caught up in his mouth. DC Murray has moved very close to him, an expression of deep concern on her face, but before she can intervene he stops shaking me and sits back on his heels, hands still on my shoulders, and starts to sob. "Where is she, Alison, where is she?"

"I don't know," I say. "I don't know."

We sit on the ground together, companions in fear. He's crying, snot and tears and sobs, wiping at his face roughly with his hand. I want to hug him, to tell him everything's going to be okay, but I know I can't. I reach my hand towards him and he recoils so sharply he nearly loses his balance. I try to think of something to say that won't make things worse but there's nothing.

Shouts from over to my right, and the sound of running. I ignore it at first but it gets louder and louder. I turn round to see what's happening and it's the same policeman who brought the jacket but this time the burden he's carrying is living and kicking and a beacon of hope lighting my darkness.

"Mummy!" Matilda cries and I run to meet them, grabbing hold of her and clutching her close to me.

"Mummy," she says again, and never have I been happier to hear her voice and to smell her hair. She curls up, her head safe under my chin. The pain in my chest eases and the emptiness fills.

Carl runs over and takes her from me and

I don't want to let her go but I know I have to. He hugs her for what feels like hours. She starts to move around in his arms and after a moment he puts her down and she runs back to me. I sit back down on the ground and hold her on my knee, her face to mine.

"You're freezing," I say, realizing how cold she is.

"I took off my coat because I got too hot when I was looking for you," she says. "I don't know where it is."

"Don't worry, sweetie, we've got it." I look around and see that DC Murray is holding it, standing at a distance from us, though closely watching everything that happens. I wave at her and point to it. DC Murray brings it over to us. She also kneels down on the ground.

"She was up at Kenwood House," she says to me. "She was a bit distressed and looking cold and a member of the public reported it to the staff. They'd obviously heard our callout, so . . ."

"It's just wonderful to have her back," I say. "Thank you."

"It's good to have a happy ending." Murray sits back on her heels. "Matilda, can you tell me what happened? How did you get lost?"

"We were playing hide and seek. I went up there into the woods. Then I got lost. The more I ran round the more hot I got so I took off my coat. And then I was up at the big house and the police came," Matilda says, all in a rush.

"You didn't talk to any grown-ups in the woods?"

"I didn't talk to anyone. My mummy tells me not to talk to strangers."

"That's very sensible. You're a good girl," Murray says.

Even though I've put her coat on her now, Matilda is still shivering, clutching on to me.

"Do you need to talk to her more now?" I say. "Because I'd really like to get her home."

DC Murray nods. "That's fine. We've got your details. We might come and have a chat later in the week — if you give me your phone number I can make sure to call in advance."

I tell her and gather myself and Matilda up. Carl is hovering nearby. He won't catch my eye.

"We should go home now," I say to him.

He shrugs but walks alongside me. We go back to the car and drive home. He's silent in the passenger seat.

■ ■ ■ ■

When we get home I run Matilda a bath. It's only four o'clock, but I feel as if I've been away from the house for years. Carl stays downstairs while I get her in the tub — I don't want to be in a different room from her. She's happy, showing no sign of stress. She splashes away and makes a wig and a beard for herself with the bubbles I've put in. I can't see any marks on her, any traces that her account of what happened to her might be anything but true.

"You're sure you didn't talk to anyone?" I say.

"I told you no." She disappears under the water. I don't want to push it any more.

After her bath she puts on pajamas and a hooded top. We go downstairs together. Carl is sitting at the kitchen table, staring into space. Matilda pushes herself onto his knee and he hugs her briefly before pushing her down.

"Go and hug your mother," he says.

I can't understand it. Normally he's all over her, no room for me at all. I know he's still in shock but this doesn't make any sense. I sit down next to him.

"Matilda," I say, "Dad and I need to talk

about something. Why don't you go and watch some TV?"

"Okay," she says, and goes through to the living room. Soon after, the sound of the TV starts up, a high pitch burbling in the background.

"Carl, do you have to stay so angry? She's home now — isn't that the important thing?"

He looks at me blankly. After a moment he clears his throat.

"All I can think about is how easily it could have gone a different way," he says. "It could have gone so wrong. It's only by a tiny stroke of luck it didn't. But this is the last straw." He pushes back from the table and stands up. "I've put up with your drinking, with your working hours, with the fact that you couldn't give a shit about my work or want to support me in any way. I could deal with all that. Even with what happened in Brighton."

I bow my head under the onslaught.

"But for you to be so careless, so useless as a mother as to lose my daughter . . . I can't do this anymore."

He's not shouting. He doesn't need to. The words are stripping layers off me like acid.

Then he shakes his head. "And what was

most unbearable? That when she came back, she ran to you. Despite you being so shit, she still loves you more. And I can't bear that. You've set her against me, I know it. It makes me so angry I can't even look at her right now."

"It's not her fault, Carl. That's not fair."

"None of this is fair, Alison. None of this is fair." He slams out of the kitchen and thumps upstairs. I hear him opening drawers and closing them before he thumps back downstairs again.

I go to the hall and watch him haul a carryall out of the door in one hand and a sleeping bag in the other.

"Where are you going?" I ask.

"I'm going to stay at my therapy room. For tonight. I don't want to be in the same house as you. I don't trust you with Matilda, but I don't have any choice. Not tonight. I swear to God, though, if anything goes wrong with Matilda, if she ends up with so much as a scratch on her little finger, I'll fucking kill you."

And with that he's gone, shutting the door quietly behind him. I stand in the hall for a moment, overwhelmed by his rage and the knowledge that something has irrevocably changed between us. It's all broken. And that's down to me.

Matilda comes out of the living room. "Where's Dad?" she asks, and I swallow hard before I can reply.

"He had to go away to do some work, poppet. He'll be back soon," I say, hoping it might be true. I sit next to her on the sofa and we watch some television. Later I cook us supper and put her to bed in our room, not for her benefit but for mine. I can't sleep for hours, the fear of the afternoon running over and over in my mind, but I hear her breathing and it soothes me, and I reach my hand out gently to rest on hers.

19

Matilda sleeps solidly, heavily, not disturbed by the car alarm that always goes off in the street, or by the yowling of foxes in the back garden that makes me start from my sleep at about five. My heart's pounding and there's sweat on my neck and chest. I don't sleep again.

When the alarm goes off I make breakfast. I'm lucky that my hearing that morning isn't until half past ten; I'll need to talk to the clerks about my cases until I know what Carl is doing. Surely he'll come home soon. Surely . . . I look at Matilda as she eats her scrambled eggs. I can trace my jawline in her face, Carl's brow. She looks up.

"Why are you staring at me, Mummy?"

"Sorry, darling. Just thinking how much I love you."

I go over to her and hug her tightly.

"Will Daddy be home tonight?" she says.

"I'm not sure."

When she's cleaned her teeth and I've put on my suit, we walk to school. She runs in, happy, and I wave at the parents I know before walking to the Tube station and getting on the train. I lean against the side of the carriage with my eyes shut. I've held myself so much under control for Matilda's sake, and now she's at school, I let myself sink under the sadness of it all, no need any longer to keep my face happy and my voice upbeat. I shift with the movement of the train, keeping my footing through every bump, swaying to the rhythm of the metal wheels on the track.

I keep my head down all the way to Belmarsh, not looking at anyone's faces, not catching anyone's eye. I robe up fast, avoiding getting stuck in conversation with anyone. A bail application on behalf of Robert in chambers, a sentence of my own from a trial that finished months ago. The pre-sentence report has been delayed three times, each time not because of my client.

"Is it going to be long? He's with my mum but she's got to go out," she says, fingers clutching the cheap electronic cigarette she's trying to suck on without attracting the attention of security.

I look at her blankly. "Who's with your mum?"

"My son, of course. Who do you think I'm talking about?" The irritation in her tone cuts through the fog in my mind.

"Sorry, yes, of course. I'm sorry, a bit tired this morning."

"Aren't we all, love, aren't we all," she says, placated. More or less.

"I hope it'll be fairly soon. There aren't that many cases up before you," I say. "And at least we've finally got the PSR."

"You think it'll be okay?"

"It should be. It's thorough. You've got that job lined up, you've moved back up to your mum's. It should be fine."

Mercifully, it is. The judge accepts the recommendations in the report without any need for me to say more than the basics. Twenty-four months of work in the community — my client's lucky, this time, but her drunken aggression was out of character. Her victim, a girl in the pub who showed a bit too much attention to my client's then boyfriend, will be wearing the scars of the attack for longer than two years but at least she's not here to object. I couldn't cope with that, not today.

I head back into town as fast as I can. With the hearings out of the way I can think about what to do next. Perhaps Carl will have calmed down overnight. Though I doubt it. My guts twist with the uncertainty of it. I take my phone out and turn it on, hoping Carl might have called, texted, *Let's talk about this.* Anything to break the impasse, put the clock back to before we were so unhappy. Nothing. I call him, it rings but no answer. I call again. It stops after two rings. I know that means he's looking at his phone. I text.

I'm so sorry, Carl. Please can we talk? Xx

I can see that the message is delivered, and for a moment my heart leaps as the bubble appears with the moving dots that show he might be composing a reply. But nothing. No reply, no beep. I try again.

Please call me. Please xx

Not even the moving dots this time. I put my phone in my bag and lean back with my eyes closed for the rest of the journey, exhausted at the thought of the changes ahead.

When I get into chambers I hand the briefs to Mark. I can see his face is sympathetic and that he's about to talk to me and I try to reverse out of the clerks' room but it's too late.

"Have you talked to him yet, miss?" he says.

"It's a very difficult situation," I say, batting him away.

"I think he's very keen to talk to you. He's called chambers a couple of times asking if you're in."

"Really?" My heart leaps. "But why hasn't he called my mobile?"

"Apparently he's tried, miss, but he can't get through."

I get my phone out and straightaway ring Carl again. Again it rings until it goes to voicemail.

"He's not picking up," I say, almost in tears.

"Well, he's left three messages for you here. I'm sure you'll get hold of him soon."

Mark hands me a wad of Post-it notes. I read them — *Message for Alison, Patrick called at 10:37 a.m. Please call back.* I crumple them up in my hand and throw them into the bin by the door. Patrick. Not Carl. Of course that's who Mark meant. The small flicker of hope I felt subsides, and the weight of it settles back on my shoulders.

"Yes, I'm sure I will," I say, and I leave the clerks' room and retreat into mine, door shut against all the reality of it. Even though I slept last night, the relief of finding Matilda outweighing even Carl walking out, today it's inescapable. He's gone and I'm going to have to deal with it.

At half two I leave chambers. I've told Mark that I need to work in London for the moment, until Carl and I have made proper arrangements as to who will have Matilda when. The calendar's quiet so I arrange to have the next couple of days off, unless anything urgent comes in. Following my earlier bullishness, my optimism has faded and I'm left hoping that when Carl has stopped being so angry he might be willing to talk. The one takeaway I have from what I've read is that mediation will be key. We are both Matilda's parents after all, we've shared so many years together — I can't believe that he won't be amenable to discussing this properly.

I'm on time at the school gate and chat to the other mums and dads waiting. When the bell goes the children stream out, each gathered up to their respective parent. Matilda isn't in the first flow, nor the second. She isn't even with the last boy, the one who's always late, trailing along with his jumper half on the floor and his books sticking out of a stained plastic bag. Everyone's gone and the playground is empty. It's like a replay of the day before and for a moment I'm struck by the same sense of fear — someone's stolen Matilda and isn't going to give her back. That shifts soon enough, recognizing the safety of school. She won't have gotten lost. But in the place of that nameless fear rises another, more precise, more specific.

I walk into the reception area and wait to be noticed at the desk. There's a young woman doing some filing in the room behind and I say "Excuse me" a couple of times until she notices.

"Can I help you?" she says.

"I'm here to pick up Matilda. Matilda Bailey, Year Two?"

"Hasn't she come out?"

"Not yet. I just wanted to check if she's still in the classroom. I can go through?" I say.

"Let me call." She picks up a list of names and runs her finger down it, stopping about three-quarters of the way down the page. She dials a number. "I'm after Matilda Bailey — Mum's here. Is she with you?"

There's a pause. I can hear a voice at the other end of the phone but not clearly enough to distinguish the words.

"That's great, thanks. I'll let Mum know." She replaces the receiver and turns to me. "She was picked up a bit early by her dad. Didn't you know?"

"I . . . I must have forgotten. Sorry about that." It feels like I've been kicked in the chest but I keep my voice steady. "I'd best get home, then." I smile at her but she's already turned back to her filing.

I walk home fast, heart pounding in my ears. Carl's being efficient, that's all. I'm being irrational, imagining that he's picked Matilda up from school early solely to make sure he's collected her and not me. I speed up even more, anxious to get home and stop the thoughts spinning round my head.

And as I unlock the door and walk in, for a moment everything is normal. Matilda comes running up and hugs me and we sit on the bottom stair while she tells me about what she's done that day and how her friends were impressed that she'd gotten to talk to some police officers the day before. We chat and I'm about to go through to the kitchen with her to give her some fruit when Carl appears, looming above me.

"Matilda, go up to your room," he says.

"Mummy was about to give me a snack."

"I'll get you an orange, then could you

please go up to your room." I stand in the hall and wait while he goes through to the kitchen, returns. He hands Matilda a plate and she takes it.

"What's this?" she says. "It looks funny."

"It's an orange," he says. "Can you go upstairs now?" Standing with the sun behind him as it streams through the window above the door he looks taller than usual, more imposing.

"It doesn't look like an orange. It's red."

"It's a blood orange, Matilda. Organic. Good for you. Just go up to your room and eat it," he says, pointing upstairs.

This time she does, pushing herself off my knee with a petulant sigh and stomping loudly up each step to make her reluctance clear.

"Alison, please will you come in here. There's some things we need to discuss."

I want to tell him to fuck off, to stop being such a pompous arse, but my bravado is short-lived. I stand up and follow him through, pushing my hands deep into my trouser pockets to hide their tremor. I sit down on the sofa, waiting for him to join me, but instead he takes a stance on the other side of the room, standing in front of the fireplace. I wait for him to start but he doesn't say anything. The silence lies heavier and heavier on the room. If my heart beats any harder he'll be able to hear it.

"Carl, I —" I can't keep quiet any longer but as I speak he starts speaking, too, drowning out my hesitant words.

"I've thought about this all night, Alison. And all of today. I've had to put up with so much from you and I can't do it anymore."

"What do you mean?" I say, my voice a bleat.

"Please, don't speak. This is hard enough but I've got to say what I think. It's gone too far."

I nod, muted. I realize I've put my hand over my mouth, though I don't remember making the movement.

"I'm going to file for divorce, Alison. There isn't a way back. I've spoken to a solicitor today and my case is overwhelming. I can divorce you on the grounds of unreasonable behavior. You know how much you've put me through, particularly during the last year or so."

"I —"

"No, you have to let me finish. This is very hard for me. The least you can do is let me speak."

I'm going to explode soon, words of self-defense, of accusation, of apology, of sheer pain roiling up inside me and writhing and twisting so that if they don't come out of my mouth they'll burst out of the top of my head. But I nod, quiet. It is the least I can do.

"I want you to move out. From today. Obviously you'll have to collect the rest of your stuff later but for now I want you to pack a bag and go. With the way you've behaved I'm going to have no issue going for primary custody of Matilda, and given I put down the money for the house with my redundancy payoff, I've got more right to be here than you."

I'm stunned. The words have disappeared. There's a seething mass of noise in my head and I can't process what he's saying.

"You'll be entitled to a financial share of the house, though, and I'm not going to begrudge it. You'll need somewhere to live, after all. But given this is Matilda's home, and I'm the one who's going to be looking after her, it's only right that it's mine. Do you understand what I'm saying to you?"

The confusion I'm feeling must be showing on my face. I swallow, breathe in and out. He keeps looking at me as if he's expecting a reply.

"You want me to move out?" I say eventually.

"That's what I said, yes."

"And you're going to have custody of Matilda?"

"Obviously. You're not trying to say you think you could look after her? You can barely look after yourself." There's nothing but scorn in his voice. Not even anger.

"But, but she loves me. She needs me." I'm crying now, tears slipping down my face.

"Okay, Alison, I'm clearly going to have to spell it out for you." Carl sits down on the edge of the armchair, leaning forward over the coffee table. I thought it might help for him to be at the same height as me but his proximity is more intimidating, not less. "Where shall I start?" He takes a deep breath and begins.

The drinking — tick.

The hours away from her — tick.

The smoking — tick.

My selfishness, always working on weekends and in the evenings — tick.

My emotional selfishness — tick.

I'm crushed under his list. Defenses spring up in my mind: I had to go back to work because he'd lost his job; the nature of being a barrister is taking work at the last minute and preparing it late into the night; the strains of dealing with clients and the constant cockups of the criminal justice system are such that sometimes it's better to drink it out with colleagues, with people who understand, than to bring it home with its fug of violence and grime. But before I can say any of them he's plowing on.

"And you might say it was necessary to do all this for your career, Alison, but you could have joined the Crown Prosecution Service, or become an in-house counsel at a solicitor's. You could have made it easier. But no, you're addicted to the attention you get when you stand up in your wig and gown. You like being center stage. Look at the way you try and hog the conversation, telling people about your cases. Look how much you showed off about being given your first murder." Carl's words are tumbling out faster and faster, years of resentment finally being voiced.

"Carl, look —"

"Will you shut up? All you ever do is talk. It's my turn now," he shouts.

I hold my hands up, shrink back into the seat, tucking my feet underneath me as I try to make myself smaller and smaller.

"And none of this would matter, you know, none of it at all, if it weren't for the way it affects Matilda. You're a dreadful mother. You never prioritize her, never take her to swimming or make sure she's got what she needs for school. You can't even be trusted to pick her up from school on time. You nearly fucking lost her yesterday," he says.

"But I love her," I say, my voice a whisper. "I love her. Doesn't that count for anything?"

"Not when the way you look after her is so shit, it doesn't. You're actively damaging her, I'm sure of it. And I'm not going to let it happen anymore. I should have known from the start you weren't fit to be a mother. At least I stopped us from having another, when I saw what you were like."

I'm silent for a moment, his words rushing over me. Then, "What do you mean, 'at least I stopped us'? What do you mean by that?"

"I had a vasectomy, of course. I wasn't prepared to risk it again. And you're hardly reliable enough to be trusted with the pill." He's looking at me as if I'm mad to think otherwise.

"You, you had a vasectomy? When did you have a vasectomy? Why didn't you tell me? You let me think . . ." I say, stumbling through the words.

"Soon after we had Matilda," he says, "and I'd do it again, Alison. It didn't take me long to see how hopeless you were with her. There's no way you could have coped with two. Now, you're going to do the right thing and you're going to walk away without fighting. You can have her at weekends, but I'm going to make sure she's properly looked after."

"You can't do that, Carl. I won't let you," I say, finally finding some strength to argue, stunned by what he's said.

"I'm not giving you a choice, Alison. I'm telling you what's going to happen. Actions have consequences, you know, actions have consequences." I've never seen him like this before, so calm yet so furious at the same time. His head's nodding abruptly in time with his words. It's clear I won't get anywhere with him right now.

"What do you want me to do?" I say.

He nods, satisfied, sitting back finally into the chair. "I'm going to take Matilda out for a meal. While we're out, you will pack some stuff and go. I'll tell her you've had to go away for work."

"Can I say goodbye to her?"

"I don't think it's a good idea, not now. You're too emotional and I don't want her to be upset. You can see her next weekend, we'll make arrangements in a couple of days."

"And what about my things?" I say, though I don't really care about my belongings.

"We'll sort it out in time. You can always pick more up next weekend. Actions have consequences, remember that. All this is of your own making."

He's got it all worked out. I go upstairs and fill a suitcase with clothes, pushing items in randomly. I force myself to think about what I'll need for work, grabbing clean collarettes and white shirts. At least my robes are in chambers so I don't have to lug them round. I hear the front door open and shut, Matilda's voice moving into the distance as they walk away from the house. I look round our bedroom, aware suddenly that it's the last time I'll be here when it is ours. Carl always likes to push me over to the side of the bed, sleeping sprawled out across the middle. He'll be able to do that with impunity now — it's all his. For a moment the enormity of it all buffets me, a G-force of intensity such that I have to sit on the side of the bed, breathless. I'll never sleep here again, never feel Carl's warmth up against me. But I compose myself and keep packing.

I call a taxi and wait for it downstairs with my case. There's a Travelodge near Covent Garden and I'm going to stay there. I used to have friends, once, before trying to fit Matilda and work and Carl and Patrick all into the same small space. But I haven't spoken to anyone except at the school gate or chambers for what feels like months. I think fleetingly about calling Rania but it's too soon, we've only chatted a couple of times. I can hardly descend on her laden with my suitcase and my broken marriage.

The taxi arrives and I haul myself into it. As it drives forward I stare out the window. It's all slipped through my fingers: house, daughter, husband. Lover, though that hardly seems to matter now. I arrive at the Travelodge and check in, thumping my case up every stair to the third floor, as the lift is out of order. There's a smell of fried food in the air and a sticky patch of something on the headboard of the bed. Without bothering to undress I roll myself up in a blanket on top of the bed and stare at the wall for what feels like hours until I sleep, and when I sleep my dreams are all of Matilda, running ahead of me, just out of my grasp.

20

I wake at three a.m., cold. The air-conditioning has been set on high and the blanket has fallen off me. I go to the loo and take off my suit trousers and shirt and turn off the air before getting into bed properly. I try to get back to sleep but it's not happening, too many thoughts chasing through my head. I get my phone out of my bag and turn it on, wishing that I hadn't been so firmly against social media. Maybe this would be the time that something like Facebook would be good. I could post a status update saying something vague about being unhappy and suddenly I'd have little friendly strokes from all my friends across the world. I bring up the website and almost sign up but the futility of it stops me. Hauling back through all the people of my past has limited appeal when my present is so empty.

A number of texts have arrived while I've

been looking at Facebook. Resisting a sudden urge to delete them all, I go into my messages, part of me hoping that Carl might have sent something to say it's all been an awful mistake, *Please come home darling, we miss you.*

I know it's too late, though. It's not going to happen. It's all fucked up and it's pretty much all my fault. I lie straight, looking up at the ceiling. The smoke alarm is glowing red in the corner and there's a glare from the exit sign on the other side of the door. It's time to be honest with myself about it all. I love Matilda, I've always loved Matilda, but I struggled with motherhood at the start. I rushed back to work, and maybe I should have given it more time. Okay, yes, Carl had lost his job and we needed my income, but surely we could have managed? And if I'd been at home, maybe I could have paid more attention to him and then he wouldn't have turned away from me, making me feel so rejected and unloved that by the time Patrick came stalking into my life I was so desperate for affection and human contact I let him into my bed and sometimes even into my heart . . . If, if, if . . . So many variables, all of them leading to the same conclusion. If I had been less selfish, less focused on myself and more on my daughter, this could all have been avoided.

The cold in my feet has gone, though something chill is still gripping at my stomach, a sense that the chaos around me is only going to get worse. I huddle myself round a pillow, willing it all to go away, and eventually fall back asleep again, the dreams of Matilda only more vivid than before.

I'm woken by the ringing of the phone. I'm finally deep in slumber and at first I'm confused, thinking I'm at home and reaching my hand out to pick up the handset only to find an empty space where it should be. It stops ringing and starts again and I find my mobile under the pillow, pulling myself upright to look at the display.

It's Patrick.

"Alison. You're there," he says.

I can't speak for a moment.

"Alison? Are you there? Can you hear me?"

"I'm here. I can hear you."

There's a long pause. Then he says, "Something's happened."

"What do you mean? What's happened?"

"I mean they've charged me. They picked me up last night and brought me into the station. Then they charged me with rape. I've been bailed and there was a photographer waiting outside my house. It's going to be in the papers."

"Jesus, Patrick. I thought you said this wasn't going to happen." My jaw's rigid with tension.

"I didn't think it was. Can we meet? Please? I could really do with some support, to see a friendly face."

I want to say no. I ought to say no. I should be out of this as fast as I can run.

"Yes," I say. "Okay, I'll meet you. Where are you?"

"That pub round the corner from you. The one with the restaurant," he says. "I came up, hoping I'd be able to talk to you."

An image of him walks through my mind, pacing round the shops of Archway, stopping for coffee in the greasy spoon and hovering outside the Tavern until its doors opened. I push it away.

"There's a bit of a complication," I say. "I'm not at home. You'll have to come down to Covent Garden. I'll meet you in the Delaunay in forty-five minutes."

"Not there, Alison. It's too . . . I'd rather go somewhere more low-key."

Fair enough, I don't say. I'm not sure why I've suggested it, other than it being the first place to come to mind.

"I'll meet you in that Wetherspoon's on

High Holborn. You know the one? I'm going to the Tube now," he says.

I do. I agree, and hang up. It seems appropriate, somehow. We started in the Wetherspoon's on Kingsway, so why not finish at one. There's a circularity that's almost pleasing. Almost.

I pull a brush through my hair, throw on jeans and a big jumper from my suitcase. I find a scarf and wrap it round my neck twice, covering the bottom half of my face. As I walk to the pub, the sleeves of the jumper fall down to cover my hands and I keep them tucked in for warmth. Patrick is standing by the back entrance, unshaven. He approaches me as if to kiss me and I duck, motionless as his hands reach to my shoulders and drop again. We stand facing each other but I don't look him in the eye.

"Do you want to go in? They've got loads of tables," he says.

I shrug and follow him inside.

"Let's sit here," I say, going to a table in the corner.

"What do you want to drink?" he says, too normal again.

"Don't care. Water. Whatever." I wait while he gets the drinks, pulling at the bits of wool fraying from the cuffs of my jumper.

"What are your bail conditions?" I ask

when he sits back down.

"Not to contact any prosecution witnesses, residence at my flat, weekly reporting. And I lodged fifty thousand pounds with the court."

"Blimey. They're not messing around."

"No. No, they're not." He's bought himself a pint and drinks a third of it in one gulp.

"Have they got some new evidence?" I ask.

"I don't know. I mean, I've told you what happened. But they were different with me, this time. The fact they didn't wait for me to come to the station, that they arrested me last night. That's all a bit odd. I don't know what's happened." He's checking his phone the whole time he's speaking to me.

"Why do you keep looking at your phone?"

"I'm checking to see if it's been reported."

"Right." I pull my own phone out of my pocket. There's a couple of texts about work and a voicemail from Pauline in chambers.

Patrick starts to say something but I hold the phone up to him. "I just need to listen to this. She doesn't normally call. It might be important." He subsides into his pint.

I don't bother listening to her message but call her straight back. She picks up.

"Alison, hi. Thank you for calling. I . . ."

"I didn't listen to your message I'm afraid, I thought I'd better get in touch. Is everything all right?"

"No, no it isn't. I'm afraid this may come as a bit of a shock."

"You absolute fucking bastard," I say a few minutes later, spitting the words at Patrick across the table.

"What are you talking about?"

"You fucking bastard."

"Alison, you need to calm down. What's going on?" He takes another long drink of his pint. It's nearly finished. He needs all the Dutch courage he can get.

"Right," I say, "Caroline Napier is a liar. You're misunderstood and too easily led astray. Is that your version of events?"

"Yes, yes of course it is. I told you."

"Then how do you explain someone else going to the police over the weekend to make an allegation of rape?"

The color drains from his face. "Alison, I can explain. It's all a misunderstanding."

"That's not what I've just been told. Did you think I wouldn't find out about it?"

His chin is wobbling, his eyes welling up with tears. "I didn't think it would get to charge."

"Which one? The QC? Or the pupil?"

He puts his head in his hands, shoulders shaking in sobs. "It was all a misunderstanding. I thought she wanted it. She seemed up for it the whole night we were out."

I look at him, full of contempt. Not even an attempt to deny it. I could punch him. I could punch myself. I'm overwhelmed with rage, but also with remorse. How many times have I thought dark thoughts about Alexia the pupil and the way she laughed at Patrick's jokes, sat just that bit too close to him? I was too blinded by jealousy to understand the dynamics there, that he was too much an egotist to hold back from taking advantage of her. He shouldn't have had anything to do with her, let alone do what she told Pauline all about last week when she heard he had been arrested in the other matter.

They were out a couple of months ago, Alexia told Pauline, and got drunk. They went back to her flat, a scummy flat share on the Holloway Road. They started kissing, she decided she didn't want to go further, he didn't want to stop. So he didn't. She didn't tell anyone because she knew how important his work was to chambers; I was given my murder the following week, she says, illustrating her point. She didn't want to make trouble. She didn't think anybody would believe her. Pauline believed her, though, and Pauline said they both sat and cried before Alexia called the police.

And I believe her too. I know how close it came to rape when Patrick was in my house, how nearly he didn't stop then. And all the other times when he pushed it just that bit too far, but I was willful in my blindness to what was really happening. *You like it rough* was his mantra and I didn't disagree, a craven Anastasia to his cut-price Christian Grey. My throat closes up with a wave of nausea and I have to be on my own. I run to the loo, slamming the cubicle door behind me. The desire to vomit recedes but there's a stale taste of acid in my mouth and I spit it out. I wipe my mouth with toilet paper and spit and spit again until the taste goes, before leaning my head against the seat with my eyes closed. I'd stay here forever but I have to face him again. Only once more though, that's it.

As I come back to the table I can see that he's still crying, making no attempt to wipe away the snot trailing down his top lip.

"I know you." I stand next to him, righteous with rage. "I know you. I can't do this anymore."

"If you know me, surely you know I'm not capable of this? Please let me explain," he says, sobs breaking through the words.

"There's no point." I stay standing. "The thing is, Patrick, I do know what you're like."

He's crying properly now, more snot, tears trickling down his neck. The pub is still mostly empty but we're attracting glances from the barman, a bearded man in a checked shirt who's wiping the glass in his hand intently.

"I think I'd better go," I say.

"Yeah, go. Go back to your lovely family, your lovely husband." He's raising his voice, veering between anger and tears. He pauses for a moment and I think that sadness has won as he puts his head in his heads but then he raises it and nothing but anger shoots from him, his eyes bloodshot and glaring straight at me. "You fuck off home."

I'm about to walk off but something inside me snaps. I lean over the table towards him. "I don't have a home anymore. I can't see my daughter. And my husband is filing for divorce. So you know what? I don't care about you. This is on you — you did this. I should never have started seeing you in the first place."

I thought he was gray already but he loses even more color. "Look, Alison. I'm sorry. I'm so sorry. What happened?"

"Matilda went missing yesterday when I was looking after her, and Carl lost it with me. He's right too — I've been a shit mother all these years, totally distracted. This, this *relationship* hasn't helped. I should never have got involved with you. I should have looked out for myself. I should have looked out for Alexia." Indignation is making my voice rise higher and higher. It's anger with him but also anger with myself, that I could have been so blinded by him to ignore what he was really like.

"I'm sorry, Alison. Please, will you sit down? Can we talk about this?" he says.

"There's nothing else to say." I've had enough. "I'm leaving now. Please don't call me again. I want you to leave me alone."

Patrick says nothing for a moment, then stands up next to me. "Alison, please. We're good together. I know it's all a mess right now but we could make it work."

"You're accused of raping two women."

"It wasn't like that," he says, his voice pleading.

"I know you, Patrick. I know."

I'm trying not to cry but I can't hold it back anymore. Patrick is standing close now, too close, and I back away but he moves with me, trying to reach my shoulder. I'm blocked in by a chair, a table, he's getting closer and I know I don't want him to touch me but he's nearer and nearer.

"Is everything all right?" says the barman.

Patrick looks at him and picks up his glass. He tries to take a drink but realizes that it's empty. He looks at the glass, at me and at the barman, before raising the glass to his shoulder and throwing it hard onto the table. It smashes and a piece hits me on the cheek. The barman moves forward as if to block Patrick from hitting me but he's already sat back down, head in hands, shoulders shaking.

"Sir, I need you to leave now or I'm going to call the police," the barman says, and Patrick looks up at him and starts to laugh. I want to walk away but I'm scared if I leave the pub first he'll come after me. He looks at me once more and stands, moving at me. The barman blocks him but he pushes past and, putting his hand under my chin, leans in to kiss me.

"I've lost everything now," he says. "Everything."

I'm pulling away but he's already let go, shoving me out of his way and leaving the pub.

We stand in silence, the barman and I. I realize that my face is wet and I put my hand up to wipe away what I think are tears.

He's gone to the bar and comes back with a clump of white tissues and I scrub at my cheeks, my eyes, scrubbing his kiss off my mouth.

"Are you all right?" the barman says, and I nod. "Your face, I mean. It's bleeding."

I look down at the tissues and he's right, they're splotched with blood. And as the adrenaline wears off, I can feel the sting from the cut increasing. I put the tissue back to my face.

"It'll be all right," I say. "I'm going to go now."

"Do you want me to walk you? He might be waiting for you," the barman says. I nearly take him up on it but the knowledge is there inside me that Patrick won't be waiting, he'll be gone. I shake my head and leave.

I walk past Holborn Tube on my way back to the Travelodge, keeping my head down so that I don't see anyone I might recognize. There's a newspaper board leaning opposite the station.

TOP SOLICITOR CHARGED WITH RAPE, it shouts. I take a copy of the paper, a grainy picture of Patrick on the front cover with one hand up trying to cover his face. I start reading it but throw it in the next bin I see.

I know enough.

Once I reach the Travelodge I spend the rest of the day sitting in the hotel room trying to call Carl, but his phone is switched off. At around five it rings and my heart lifts, especially when Matilda answers, her "Hello" too close to the mouthpiece and utterly beautiful to hear, but then Carl takes the phone from her and it's turned off again, her voice still ringing in my ears.

21

Mark calls me early on Wednesday morning to ask if I mind going down to Inner London Crown Court to deal with a plea in a theft — it's Sankar's case but a trial he's doing has overrun. I've had enough of the Travelodge and even though Inner London is a bit close to Patrick's flat I say yes. It's not like I can keep turning down work. I shower and dress, ignoring the calls I can hear on my phone until I'm ready to go. I get into the lift and as I wait for it to start moving, I look at the screen to see who it is.

Chloe, three times in a row. I pull my wheelie bag out of the lift, exhausted. It doesn't stop. I've got so much on my mind already, what Carl has done, missing Matilda. Patrick. I don't have any space left in me.

"Yes, it's me," I answer, negotiating my way out of the hotel lobby and into the street. I'm early enough I'm going to walk.

"Something terrible has happened," she says.

"What?" I'm still thinking about my route, whether I do actually have time to go on foot.

"It's Patrick," she says, her voice disappearing.

I bristle. "I don't want to talk about that," I say. "I don't want to have anything to do with it."

"Alison, please will you listen. He's dead. Patrick's dead. He threw himself under a train at Holborn yesterday afternoon."

I stop. Someone walking behind me bumps into me, swears as they swerve to avoid me. A man bashes his foot on the wheelie bag. I stand stock still in the middle of the pavement, trying to absorb what's she said.

"Patrick is dead, Alison. He texted me saying sorry, I didn't know why."

"Are you sure?" I say.

"Yes, I'm sure. His sister identified him last night from his belongings, his wallet, his ring. There wasn't much left of him. It'll be in the paper soon enough." She's firing the words at me fast; I can't take them in. "Alison. Alison? Are you there?"

I take the phone away from my ear and end the call. I don't understand what's happening. Someone else bangs into me, so hard I stumble across the pavement into the wall beside a sandwich shop.

"Are you okay?" a woman asks.

I can't reply for a moment, words and sobs mixed up stuck in my throat. She touches my shoulder, makes as if to take my arm. I pull myself away before she can help me further.

"I'm fine, thanks. I'm all right." I start to walk away, wheelie bag dragging at my heels.

"Are you sure?" she's saying but her voice fades away the farther I walk, the tap of my heels hammering down on her concern. My footsteps take on a beat, *off to court, off to court,* and I sniff up my grief and wipe it off on my sleeve.

It's late now and I don't have the energy to walk — I'll have to take the Tube. I turn round and head down towards Embankment. I wait at the platform until the Northern line train arrives and as it pulls in I'm drawn towards it, walking closer and closer to the edge until someone shouts and grabs my arm. I pull away from them and almost run to the other end of the platform, images tripping through my mind of Patrick and wheels and tracks and metal through flesh. Would they have been able to gather all of him up or would there still be clumps, traces of him clinging to the subway at Holborn, a meal more appetizing by far for the rats than the usual dregs of McDonald's and KFC. I shake my head clear but not in time to board, stepping back as the train pulls away.

The next train arrives in minutes and this time I'm prepared, all thoughts of gore and Patrick tucked away. I lean against the side all the way to Elephant and Castle, looking at the Northern line stations on the map in front of me. London Bridge. I'm not going to think about London Bridge, or the night so recently when Patrick cooked me dinner and we were happy. I pull myself together and walk to court.

The robing room is busy and I could swear it falls quiet as I walk in but that could as easily be my nerves talking, jangling so loudly I can't hear anything else. Robert from chambers is there and he walks over to me and puts his hands on my shoulders.

"Awful news, Alison. I take it you've heard," he says, his voice low.

I nod.

"I know you did a lot of work for him . . ."

I'm stiff with control. I look at Robert closely but there's nothing in his face or voice to suggest he's getting at any more. There's only distress on his face, his eyes pink and bloodshot.

"I just can't believe it," I say.

"I know. I spoke to a couple of people earlier, Alison. Sankar, some other people out of chambers, Patrick's team — we thought we'd go to the pub tonight. Remember him. I mean, I know there was that stuff in the *Standard,* but . . ."

I nod again. "Where?"

"The Dock, we thought. Do you think you can make it?"

"I'll do my best," I say.

A barrister from another chambers comes up to us. "Sorry to interrupt, but I take it you're talking about Patrick? Patrick Saunders?"

Robert steps aside to tell her the plan for tonight and I take the opportunity to unpack my bag, put on my wig and gown, adjust my face to something more professional in the mirror. I collect papers from the prosecution for the case, aware it's not prepared. I've looked at it, but the details have gone out of my head. I check the name and head over to Court 7, trying to concentrate.

It's a prosecution brief, at least, and it's a plea hearing, and at the point at which the defendant pleads guilty, I click into the present moment and read out the Crown Prosecution Service summary of facts, hoping that no one will ask me for any additional information. The defense brief is young and earnest, mitigating well past the point that the judge has already agreed for a pre-sentence report to be prepared — "though I must point out, Mr. Ketteridge, that I'm minded to consider *all* the options" — and only sitting down and shutting up when the judge says he's almost heard enough to sentence immediately.

I note down the date for sentence on the brief and endorse it. As I disrobe, Robert comes back in and we go together for the bus. He can't stop talking about Patrick, his voice wearing down my resistance to the point I could lie down in the road and scream for the rest of the day.

"I just hope the allegations were true," Robert says, "not because I hope anyone was raped, of course, but because if they made him kill himself and they were lying . . ." and I'm hit with the knowledge that if I don't get off the bus now and walk away from him, I'm either going to punch him or throw up all over him. I stand up and push past, wheeling my bag over his feet. I mutter something about needing air and get off at the end of Waterloo Bridge.

I walk back to the middle of the bridge and stand looking down at the water, over at the London Eye and Westminster. Best view in London, Patrick once said. I turn to look over past Blackfriars at London Bridge and Tower Bridge beyond. A bit over to the right is where Patrick should be in his flat, pale and compliant, pleading his innocence. Not in bloody bits in a morgue somewhere.

I turn back to look down at the river, wondering why there isn't a bronze plaque screwed onto the edge, engraved with the number for the Samaritans. There is on the other bridges. It's as much use to Patrick as I'd been, refusing to talk to him or listen further to his explanations.

A man stops next to me, and I realize he's looking at me. For a moment I glare and then I realize he's concerned. I've been standing here too long, looking too hard at the water.

"No, not that," I say, and walk away, head hunched. He's shown me more care in one look than I showed Patrick, and that knowledge lies heavy on me as I walk to chambers.

I see Pauline on my way in.

"I've told Alexia to take a few days off," she says. "It's categorically not her fault, but she's feeling dreadful. We're going to have to look after her, make sure she gets some counseling."

"It's all just awful. I hope she's going to be all right. If you think it's appropriate, could you pass on my best wishes and say that I'm offering the fullest of support?"

Pauline nods. "I will do. She was worried about what you'd think. I assured her that you'd be on her side, but she wasn't sure. She seems a bit hostile to you, if I'm honest, but it's been a difficult time."

It's a kick to the guts. I've always seen myself as an ally — now I realize the depths of my ignorance, the damage my selfish stupidity has done. Then a different thought occurs to me.

"I can see why she'd think that, but I've learned a lot in the last few days. She can count on me for whatever she needs, please make sure she knows. But Pauline, there's something I'm wondering. I've been getting anonymous text messages recently. Unpleasant ones. Do you think . . . ?"

Pauline doesn't reply for a long time, then, "I don't know. From some of the things she was saying, I don't think it could be ruled out. If I can, I'll have a word. But she's in quite a state."

"Of course. And it's okay, it's not urgent. I'd just quite like them to stop."

"Understood," she says.

"Thanks, Pauline. And please tell her I'll

give her any support she wants or needs from me," I say.

"I'm glad, Alison. I think we need to have a proper look at how we in chambers support pupils — would you be up for that? I can set up a meeting."

"Definitely. We can do a whole lot better."

Once I've said goodbye to Pauline I hole up in my room for as long as possible, unable to cope with the idea of people pressing round me. I've got a gnawing feeling at the pit of my stomach and a shake in my hands. I go to my phone to listen to Patrick's voicemails again, to see if I can divine any clue to the state of his mind from the tone of his voice. Then I remember I've deleted them, automatically. Same with all his texts, even the ones that skirted somewhere close to love in the short window we had between lust and death. I remember the force of him, how sore he left me, how I'd feel it for hours after we'd fucked. The idea he's dead seems absurd, but when I go through my phone, there's no trace he existed. No photos together, no memories shared. We never had Paris. We never deserved Paris, either.

Bangs on my door. It's Robert. Yes, I'm going to the pub, yes, I'll come now. No, I don't know any more, haven't heard from anyone else. He stops me at the doorway for a moment and hugs me.

"I know you were close," he says.

I pull away and frown at him.

"No, not like that. I'm not suggesting . . . He gave you some good work, though."

I nod. He did. It's all that's left.

We're the first in the pub, sitting in the corner of the downstairs space that Robert has reserved. It's the same table we sat at the night I was first instructed in Madeleine's case, the night we fucked and I broke Matilda's photograph. Damn it, it was only glass, not a mirror. This shouldn't be happening.

I buy a bottle of house red and we drink it, fast. Robert's face is grim and I know mine is the same, our jaws clenched against the weight of it all. Other people from chambers come in, clerks, solicitors, one after the other ordering cheap bottles of wine. It's no time to worry about vintage — we're necking the vinegar. I'm a bottle down and still steady, words not slurred. Some people have heard about the news report, and it ripples round the room. The poor train driver. The poor women. Poor Patrick . . .

The room's shimmering, a haze of light playing around people's heads. It's like it was when we could smoke indoors, the bulbs from the overhead lamps glowing through the fog. I push upstairs with Robert and have one of his fags, neither of us finding anything to say. When I get back downstairs someone else has laid on a bottle of whisky — Famous Grouse, moderate like the wine. I have a dram and then another, still seemingly unaffected. I look round the table and the light has moved on to people's heads, pulsating in the evening like jellyfish. Sankar turns to me with something really important to say but stays suspended in the gloom, his mouth part open. Chloe walks past him and I raise a hand to her and she waves and sits at the far end of the table and I turn back to Sankar but by now he's closed his mouth and Robert's poured me another dram so I drink that and stop thinking about talking.

There's still a shimmer, a calm not warranted by the occasion. Patrick's sins have been temporarily expiated by his suicide and the odd anecdote is emerging; a flawed character, but one we loved. We're swaying with the rhythm of shared emotion, telling tales of Patrick in court or dealing with clients, each story different but merging into one.

". . . that gang, they all had his business card — that was one of the pieces of evidence against him . . .”

“The time he told DJ Connor to fuck off, in Greenwich. You should have seen the judge’s face.”

“. . . one of his clients threatened him with a knife, do you remember that? And he just laughed until the guy realized what a twat he was being and put it away . . .”

Someone else has joined in the whisky supply but now it’s a Lagavulin, the peaty fumes catching in my throat. The war stories go on, the mood shifting maudlin as the evening lengthens. I stand to go to the loo, still convinced I’m sober, but my legs nearly give way beneath me and I half collapse onto Robert’s lap. He steadies me and pushes me up, laughing. I walk carefully over to the ladies’ but it seems a long way, farther than I’ve noticed before, and the walls are spinning around me. Once I’ve been to the loo, I sit for some time with my tights round my ankles, head in my hands, hoping if I shut my eyes the spinning will stop.

“Alison. Alison? Are you in here?”

It’s Chloe. I rouse myself, pulling up my tights and calling out to her, “Yes, I’m here. Just coming.” The break from people has cleared my head, a little. My eyes are hurting and I fish out my contact lenses, vision blurred but not stinging anymore.

Chloe's waiting for me by the sinks. She goes to give me a hug and I hug her back, awkward in her embrace. I'm nearly smothered by the scent she's wearing, something sweet and cloying. It's strong, but as I get used to it, I can smell her own scent underneath, sour sweat as if she hasn't washed for a couple of days. I extract myself gently. God knows what I must smell like by now. I dig through my handbag and take out my glasses, put them on.

"Terrible. It's just terrible," she says.

I nod my agreement.

"At least he won't have suffered," she says. "It would have been quick. The poor driver, though . . ."

I try not to visualize it again.

"Still, we must be brave and carry on. It's what he would have wanted."

This I can deal with more readily.

"Have you told Madeleine?" I say, the words coming out surprisingly clearly.

"Yes. She was extremely distressed." Chloe looks into the mirror, applies lipstick, and then turns to face me with what's meant to be a smile. It's more of a rictus grin and I can see the effort it's costing her. I don't comment on the lipstick traces on her teeth. "She wants to come and talk to us as soon as possible."

"That's fine," I say.

"I'll get her into the office and maybe we can discuss it beforehand." She dabs again at her nose. "God, I look awful." She scrubs at her teeth with her finger.

"It's very difficult . . ." I take my turn at the mirror, pushing my glasses up on my head. My eyes are as bloodshot as Chloe's. The blue of my eyes is blurred behind a watery film, my hair lank against my forehead. I turn the tap on and dash water against my face, desperate to see if I can wake myself up at all, get rid of the blurred pain lodged at the front of my head.

"It's so sad . . . He had so much to offer, so much to live for. Well, if only he'd been able to control himself better. A fatal flaw. He was such a good boss — I was due to become a full partner soon too."

The pain of it all is exhausting me, Chloe's sadness, my own sense of guilt. It's heavy and difficult and all I want to do now is go home, shower off the whisky and fags, sit with Matilda on my knee and read her a story, drinking in her warm, clean smell, untainted by grief and betrayal and lies. But that's the last thing I can do. I swallow down a lump in my throat and hug Chloe again, trying not to inhale too much the stench of her perfume.

"We don't know the full story yet," I say.

"Come on, Alison," she says, not needing to say more.

I can't deal with it anymore. "I might go now actually," I say. "It's been a long day."

She puts her arm round me and pulls me close again, turning us round to look in the mirror.

"I really do look fucking awful," she says. "Especially next to you. Even with this going on you look lovely."

I grimace. We're clearly not looking at the same reflection — we look as tired as each other. "I look done in," I say. "I'm amazed we're still actually standing."

"No, Alison. I mean it. You've got one of those faces. Patrick always said how beautiful you are." She pulls me in even closer before releasing me. "Oh, what does it matter now . . . I'll see you in the office tomorrow."

I leave the loos and retrieve my bag. The group is down to single figures now, Robert and Sankar propping each other up, Mark to their side looking considerably more sober. I wave to them and leave, climbing the stairs slowly to avoid any potential stumble. I'm surprised by how dark it is when I exit the pub, streetlamps glowing orange in the night, but then I check my phone and see it's nearly eight.

I walk on up the hill, one foot after the other, my bag heavy behind me. I'm trying to walk straight but I'm drunk, more drunk than I should be. Finding the words to comfort Chloe has taken my last reserve of control, the streetlights dancing above me and the dull reflections of those lights on the damp pavement in front of me from where it's rained earlier. I get back to the hotel and huddle up in bed still in my suit, remembering just before I pass out that I haven't even tried to contact Carl today.

22

I arrive at Saunders & Co. at ten the next morning. Chloe takes me into what was Patrick's office.

"Do you think she should change her plea to guilty?" Chloe says, straight to the point.

"I think it would be giving up a bit easily. I'd be happy with a plea to manslaughter, though I don't think the prosecution are keen. We should write to them, though, with the defense case statement, and offer it, see what they say. I know Madeleine has reservations about her son giving evidence."

"Right." Chloe leafs through the papers in front of her, finding a statement and reading through it. She's sitting behind Patrick's desk. The usual clutter has been cleared away, and it's been dusted. He normally kept the window and door blinds down, and these have been fully opened. The room's much brighter than I've ever seen it.

"Do you believe all of the stuff about her

husband?"

"It's credible. She's got scars. And the doctor's statement backs it up."

"I imagine she's very upset by what's happened to Patrick," Chloe says, and rubs a hand across her eyes. The dark bags are pronounced. I'm about to comment on how tired she looks but think better of it. I know I don't look any better.

"At least he left a plan in place," she says.

"A plan?"

"Patrick nominated me to deal with his cases in the event of something happening. He did it a year or so ago, to be organized. I don't think any of us would have anticipated this, though." She bends her head down and breathes deeply, rubbing her eyes again.

"No. It's all been very difficult," I say, aware of the lameness of the words.

"All of the last week . . ." She inhales deeply one more time and looks up at me. "Do you believe the allegations? What they said he did?"

Her eyes are suddenly sharp, and I don't know what the right answer is. But at the same time . . .

"It's one of those things . . . You can never tell . . ."

Chloe shakes her head at me. "Come on,

Alison. You can do better than that. We both know what Patrick was like."

I'm still not sure what she wants from me. I shrug, feeling helpless.

"I don't think they would make it up," Chloe says. "Last night I wanted to pretend everything was all right, that we were simply mourning the passing of a friend. But when I woke up this morning I knew it wasn't."

I know what she means. Last night was full of eddies and flows, moments of laughter with my colleagues and his as they remembered him, moments when I remembered again what he was said to have done.

"I don't know. But you know what Caroline's reputation is too. I can't see why she would make up such a thing," I say. "Nothing would be worth going through that, surely."

I've been talking down to my hands clasped in my lap. I don't want to upset Chloe but it is what I think. As I finish speaking I look up at her.

"I agree with you," she says. "I don't want it to be true, but . . . And there was something he said to me on Tuesday afternoon."

I haven't even thought to ask whether she saw him before he went under the Tube.

"I'm sorry, I've been all over the place. I should have asked if you saw him," I say.

"I couldn't get hold of him at all on Tuesday morning," she says. "I don't know what he was doing."

I say nothing. Meeting me, being rejected by me. Not something I want to put into words.

"It was annoying, there were a couple of things I wanted to ask him about other cases. But I managed. And he came in late morning. We had a long conversation and went through every one of his cases. He got me up to speed on all of them." She starts sobbing, wiping tears off her face.

"I'm sorry, this must be very difficult," I say, not wanting to interrupt the flow of her words.

"No, this is silly. It's thinking about how thoughtful he was being, how organized . . ."

"Organized?"

"He didn't want any of his clients to suffer. He made sure I knew everything, and then he said goodbye. He thanked me for all of my support, for everything I was doing to help him, he tried to give me a hug, and he left. And before he walked out of the door, he turned round and said that he was the only person to blame. He had always known what a complete shit he was, and now the rest of the world knew too." The effort to finish her sentence without sobbing has left Chloe bereft of control. She's crying in earnest. I think about the last time I saw Patrick, how ill he looked, how I turned my back on him.

"Do you know the worst thing, Alison? The absolute worst thing?" Chloe says, fighting for breath through her sobs.

I shake my head.

"I didn't want to believe Caroline Napier. Of course not. I've worked for Patrick for years. He's always been a perfect gentleman to me. But after what she said . . . it made me think less of him. And he must have known it. I wouldn't hug him back. I was the last person he ever spoke to, the last friend, and I wouldn't hug him back."

I bow my head. I can't give her the absolution she seeks. I wouldn't hug him either; I stood impassive for his last kiss. But he alone stood on the Tube platform, he alone made the decision to jump. And he alone decided to take advantage of Alexia, a girl less than half his age; he alone decided to ignore Caroline when she said no to him.

"This is all on him, Chloe," I say. "He's the one who did it, he's the one who threw it all away. Not you, not Caroline Napier."

"Unless —" Chloe starts to say but she's interrupted.

"What's on him?" It's Madeleine. Chloe

and I both jump, pulling ourselves together quickly.

"Hi," I say, standing up and walking over to her. I put my hand out to shake hers, and she clasps it. I usher Madeleine through into the conference room, Chloe making noises of welcome in the background, and sit her at the table.

"It's obviously come as a huge shock to us all, Patrick's d—" I start.

"Don't say it," Madeleine interrupts. "I can't bear it. I know what they're saying about him but he was so lovely to me." Now I look at her, I can see that her face is even more drawn than usual, her eyes red too. Hers, mine, Chloe's — Patrick's regiment of women, all weeping at his passing. Or something like that.

"I know. It's terrible."

"And it was really suicide?"

"That's what they're saying, but of course there hasn't been an inquest yet, a coroner's report," I say.

"I saw the *Evening Standard,* but surely the accusations can't be true?" Her voice is shaky but there's an edge underneath, something very slight that makes me unwilling to discuss it any further.

"I don't know any more at the moment," I say.

"Surely you must have some idea." She's not letting up.

"I really don't, Madeleine. I'm as shocked about this as anyone else," I say.

She opens her mouth and shuts it again. I've had enough of her questioning.

"We have to think about your case," I say.

"I don't care about my case. What's the point?"

"You know what the point is. Think about how much work Patrick put into it — he wouldn't want to see you give up on yourself," I say. I'm feeling impatient. If the rest of us are able to keep going, why should Madeleine find it any harder? She's known him the shortest of any of us. Not that she even knows him either.

"I suppose not. But without him there to support me, I'm not going to be able to go through with it," Madeleine says. She's twisting her hands together. To be fair, she does look genuinely upset. For once her clothes are disheveled, jeans and a cream shirt that's creased and has a stain on one side of the collar.

"I'll be there, and Chloe too," I say.

"I don't like her. She doesn't understand. She hasn't been in it from the start. He saw me in prison when I was at my worst."

A flash of anger overtakes me. I'm not being paid enough to deal with this. She's got the same barrister still, and a perfectly competent solicitor, even if it's not the one who dealt originally with her case.

"Look, Madeleine. I appreciate this has come as a shock but we need to be pragmatic about it. The defense case statement is due in at the end of this week. I've been the person working on your case, primarily. Patrick's death is very sad, but it doesn't actually affect what happens with you."

"I can't believe you'd be so heartless. I'd have expected you, of all people, to understand," she says, seemingly determined to milk maximum drama out of what's happened. But then she starts crying, quietly but properly, her face contorting. My anger disappears, replaced by a sense of shame. I should be more sympathetic.

"I'm sorry. I'm just trying to keep it together too. It's been an awful shock," I say.

She sits up straighter, seemingly pulling herself together. "I'm sorry too. I'm not helping. I don't want to drag everything through court, especially James. I'd do anything to protect him, I really would."

"We may not have to. There's a small possibility the prosecution may accept the manslaughter plea. You'll have to speak to their psychiatric specialist too, but if they come to the same conclusion as ours . . . And if not, James's account isn't that contentious," I say. "We won't be putting him through difficult cross-examination."

"I don't want him being examined at all," she says. "By us or anyone else. I hate the idea of him giving evidence."

I pick up my notebook and leaf through it, buying myself a moment while I think about what to say next.

"I know he's a prosecution witness but his evidence is helpful. He backs up the overall account of domestic violence. And of course, Edwin's assault on him that final day is crucial. So . . ."

"I'm very unhappy about it," she says. "It'll destroy him, giving evidence against his own mother." She shakes her head. "I can't do it, I don't want him to have to. I don't want him to have to lie."

"He's telling the truth, though. Isn't he?" I say, shifting on my chair. I don't quite understand. I look at her, a steady gaze, and she meets my eyes for a moment before looking down. Something changes on her face.

"Madeleine," I say.

She takes a deep breath. "I don't want James to have to give evidence. I have to protect him," she says. "I think I'd better change my plea to guilty."

"Okay," I say. "I understand that. I just want you to think about something, though. You want to protect James. I get that. Being in court, it's intimidating. Especially for a child. But —"

"Enough. Enough! I've made my decision!" Madeleine pushes up out of her chair as she shouts and then turns her back to the room, looking out the window. Chloe comes into the room but Madeleine doesn't acknowledge her.

The room's silent and I start to notice the sound of the streets, sirens and horns and the rumbling of an airplane. Madeleine keeps looking out the window, past the grime encircling the frame down onto the roofs and courtyards below.

"I'm sorry that you're upset," I say. "But given that we've been working from a plea of not guilty to murder, and that we've been preparing your defense on that basis, it's important that we go through all of the implications in detail. I need to ensure that you understand it all."

She turns round to me, her face flushed. She moves so fast I flinch, thinking she might be about to hit me. Instead she pulls back and sits down again. When she finally speaks her voice is as scornful as Carl's was on Sunday.

"I understand it all perfectly," she says. "So did Patrick. But he's not here anymore."

I look at Chloe and her expression is as confused as mine.

"Patrick was the only person who could keep this whole case under control. Without him there's no hope. So talk me through it, tell me about the implications, and then I'll plead guilty, okay?" Madeleine says.

I do as she says, explaining that I won't be able to mitigate fully if she pleads guilty to murder, that the remorse I can express on her behalf is limited, that we won't be able to put it in the context of the violent relationship as we would like to because I'll be so restricted in what I can put forward to the court. As I run through the legal formulae, spelling each out in turn, my mind's elsewhere. The phrases she's used, the talk of protecting her son . . . Patrick's part in the trial and his insistence on instructing me to represent her rather than someone more experienced. There's a eureka thought slightly out of reach and a large part of me doesn't want to know, doesn't want to ask. All I want is for her to say that she understands the explanation that she's been given and sign the endorsement on the brief to the effect that she knows that if she pleads guilty, despite asserting the existence of a defense, then all our hands will be tied. The other defense that might be out there is huge in its magnitude and utterly terrifying.

As a mother, I hope it's a situation I'd never have to find myself in. As a mother, to a fellow mother, I know the best thing I can do is leave it alone, let Madeleine make her maternal sacrifice. But as her barrister . . . I know there's something that doesn't feel right, something I'm missing, just out of the corner of my eye. I stop telling her about the limitations of mitigation and steel myself.

"What exactly is it that you're protecting your son from, Madeleine?" She looks up, startled. "Do you really just want to stop him from giving evidence, or is it something more than that?"

Chloe's standing behind her looking equally startled, a hand held up as if to stop me. Nevertheless, I persist.

"What exactly has Patrick's role been? Because this isn't making sense, not at the moment, and I'd like to have a better understanding of exactly what it is we're doing here."

Madeleine's face goes entirely still. The

fury in her eyes is such that in a different story I'd be turned to stone, no question. I look back at her, my eyes level with hers, refusing to let her anger beat me back. I've weathered worse than this: Carl, Patrick, all of it. I'm not going to be beaten by my client, even if I have been misled all the way through.

"I'm going to ask one more question. The answer you give will be the last answer I ask from you. After that, we're going to proceed in whatever way you instruct. I want you to think very carefully about this and about all the implications of it," I say, my voice cool.

She stares a moment longer and drops her eyes, with a nod of assent.

"Did you stab Edwin," I say, "or did James?"

The silence in the room stretches longer than any silence we've had before. I can hear the traffic noise again and closer, Chloe's breathing, the scuff of my feet on the floor and the catching of my tights as I cross and uncross my legs. Chloe scratches her arm and the noise is as loud as the motorbike in the street below. Only Madeleine is utterly still, so quiet the absence of noise and movement becomes almost palpable. I turn my head and the cracking of my neck sounds like a gunshot in my ear. I count the beats, one, two, three — she's still quiet. I want to speak but at the same time I want to swallow the words I've spoken, pull them back and ram them down my throat. Chloe's shifting from foot to foot, I can hear the rubbing of the fabric on her suit as if she were ripping Velcro apart. I hold my breath.

I'm going to suffocate in the silence but then Madeleine lifts her head and looks at me again. She meets my gaze squarely and this time it's me who has to look away, my body washed with a flush of heat and a desire to leave this room, run away, pretend I've never seen her before in my life. She inhales and I feel my heart rate rise, my nails clawing into the palms of my hands.

"Yes," she says. "Yes, James stabbed Edwin. His father. Edwin beat me once too often, hurt James for the last time. It was James who snapped, not me. And as a mother, *what do you suggest I do now?*" It's a hiss but it cuts through the air as loud as a shout.

One crack in the silence and the edifice collapses. Chloe moves to the table and sits down, I shift backwards in my chair and take in a deep breath. It's what I've been waiting to hear. It's the only explanation that makes sense.

"I told Patrick," Madeleine says. "I told Patrick, when he came to the police station. He knew. That's why I did a no-comment interview. We were trying to work it all out."

"Patrick was prepared to mislead the court?" Chloe says.

"He didn't see it like that. He knew I needed help."

Chloe and I exchange glances. It's obvious now that Patrick was in far more of a mess than either of us had realized.

"That's not something I'm prepared to do, though," I say. "Now that this has been said, it can't be unsaid. So we will have to go through the options."

"Go on, tell me. But I know they're all fucking awful," Madeleine says. I'm shocked for a moment — she barely swears.

I lay it out for her, trying to focus. "You can change your plea to guilty to murder, as I explained before. Your mitigation will be limited and you will receive a life sentence. You can maintain not guilty and while we can't put forward an alternative defense for you, we can put the prosecution to proof. That means that they present their evidence and try to make it add up to a convincing case against you. All I will be allowed to do is point out if they make any factual errors. I won't be able to suggest any alternative scenarios to them, or put forward any defense on your behalf. So if the prosecution can't put together a convincing case, it might, but only might, result in an acquittal. Or you can stay not guilty and go ahead with a trial on the basis that we discussed before, only Chloe and I wouldn't be able to represent you. Or, you can give us permission to put this new piece of evidence in, which would complete your defense case statement on the basis that it was your son, not you who committed the crime. Cross-examine him to that effect. The jury might not believe you, but it would be a defense."

I say it all calmly, in order, relieved that I can salvage some professionalism from the situation. But the horror of Madeleine's situation sits large before me, clutching at my chest.

"What would you do, Alison?" Madeleine says. "What would you do?"

I shake my head. "I don't know. I'm sorry, but I can't tell you what to do. And I don't know what I would do."

"Chloe?" she says, but Chloe shakes her head too.

For another long moment Madeleine sits silent before speaking again. "You talked about entering a plea of guilty to manslaughter. What would that entail?"

Another pause. Chloe looks at me and I at her, the longest conversation we've ever had without words.

"You would be telling the court what you've told us before, what you told the psychiatrist. But what you've said now, you could never say that again." Pools of sweat are forming under my armpits, the room too hot, too stuffy.

"If I did that, would you represent me?" she says. "Even though . . ."

And I know what the right answer is, I know what the professional obligation is upon me. I know that if I give her the nod on this, I'm breaking the most fundamental rule in the code of conduct of barristers. It's not my job to interfere with justice in this way. But the thought of the violence, the fear, the anger, the heartbreak that she's suffered and her son's suffered, the thought of all the men through all the ages who've gotten away with this kind of shit time and time again . . .

"We could try," Chloe says. "We could see if they'll accept it without a trial. But if not, if you want to avoid the risk of James giving evidence, then you'll have to plead guilty to murder. And take the consequences."

Chloe feels the same as me, I know it. At least we're in this together.

"This is going to be very difficult," I say. "But we'll try and sort it out."

Madeleine leaves shortly afterwards. She looks exhausted, but there's less strain around her eyes. She's handed that stress over to Chloe and me now, relying on us to work out how best to approach it all with the court.

"This is a nightmare," I say to Chloe.

"Yes. You did ask. I sometimes think that was one of Patrick's greatest strengths."

"What?"

"Knowing which questions it was better not to ask. That old chestnut, never ask a question to which you don't know the answer."

"Or don't want to know," I say.

"Quite."

I put my notebook and pen away in my bag and stand up. I'm exhausted too, now that I'm not focusing on Madeleine's case anymore. The realities of my own situation settle back around me.

Chloe shuffles papers together into a pile and ties them with a pink ribbon before staring into space briefly. She takes the papers and puts them heavily on top of a pile at the edge of the desk. Then she takes another pile and starts to look at it before pushing it away from her so hard that it and the other pile fall onto the floor.

She picks up a graduation photograph of Patrick from the shelf behind her and gestures at it. "Look at him, just look at him. He had everything going for him, the job, the practice, but it wasn't enough for him. He had to keep flirting with people, fucking them, pushing them too far. He could have had everything, but he was just another fucking rapist." She throws the picture against the opposite wall and it bounces back against the desk before falling to the floor on top of the strewn papers.

I'm so shocked at what she's saying, so amazed to hear this come from her, that I laugh, a sound that bursts out from me before I can stop it. I put my hand over my mouth but she's heard it.

"No, it's fine. Laugh. It is fucking laughable. I'm a solicitor and you're a barrister, both of us moving up to the top of our game, and we're stuck with this shit? He's put us in the situation where we're going to risk everything professionally because he took on a case like this. It makes me so mad."

She moves round the desk and picks up the papers, straightening them into a pile and putting them down. Then she picks up the photograph. I think she's going to throw it in the wastepaper basket but she looks at it for a moment, a twist to her mouth, before she opens a drawer and puts it away. I'm still standing motionless by the door, not sure which way it's going to go.

"So, um, what happens now?" I say.

"We're going to get on it. I have a load of clients to inform that their solicitor is dead and we've got to try and work out how the hell we're going to manage this defense now that Madeleine's let the cat out of the bag."

"It's going to be very difficult," I say. "I wish . . ."

Chloe sighs. "You did the right thing," she says. "There were clearly inconsistencies in what she was saying, and it was going to fall apart at some point or another. We needed the truth, regardless of what we do with it. Especially without Patrick to hold it together. It does make me worry about other cases, though, how much he's been doing behind the scenes with those clients too."

"I was thinking the same thing," I say. "There's a lot to do."

She shrugs, nods. I shrug back. But despite it all, there's a sense of kinship in the air, a feeling that we are developing into a team. There's too much between us to throw away, an entire practice of cases.

"I think we can do it," I say. "I think we can sort it out. But if this comes off, if we actually mislead the court in such a major way . . . I'm not sure I can keep practicing as a barrister."

Chloe considers my words for a while. "I'm sure people do it all the time."

I shake my head. "I'm not. We take it seriously, you know. It's not the Hippocratic Oath but it's important. If it were for anything less . . . But if I do this, I don't want to keep being a barrister. It's the trade-off. Do you see?"

She looks as if she's about to laugh. "How high-minded of you," she says.

"I know, I know. But I mean it. I've had enough of breaking promises. I don't know what I'll do, but I'll find something. I just can't lie in court and go back the next day like normal."

Slowly the smile fades from her face. "I see your point. You could always join me as a solicitor."

It's my turn to laugh. "God, you're so practical."

"Yeah, but I don't like to see good talent go to waste. I'm going to need someone to help me sort out all of this. And if you don't want to go court, I'll do it. I've got my higher rights of audience, just don't use them much. Or hell, we can always brief someone from chambers."

I don't move for a moment, caught by the idea. Considering it. Regular hours, an office in central London. Predictability.

"You know what, that's not a bad idea. It's not a bad idea at all."

We shake hands and she pulls me in and hugs me.

"We'll speak soon," I say as I leave, pulling my wheelie bag behind me. "Tell me what you need me to do."

23

I walk down to chambers, noticing as I'm halfway down Kingsway that my bag is sticking, not running smoothly along the ground. I can pull it, but it's stiff and increasingly irritating. I push people to the side and reach a doorway next to a pub. Here, I turn the case over on the pavement to look at it. It's only one of the wheels, which has become bunged up with a large wad of chewing gum that's worked itself all the way up round the mechanism. It's gray and viscous and revolting, bits of hair and cigarette ash mixed up in it. Even dog shit would be easier — at least I could rinse it off. I don't know what I'm supposed to do with this. I remember something about freezing it off clothes but a wheelie bag is different. It's not that new, the bag, but it's in good enough condition apart from this. I zip it up, muttering swear words under my breath, and keep walking down into chambers, giving up trying to pull it and carrying it instead.

Once I reach chambers I head into my room and chuck the bag down on the floor. I unpack it, sorting through the papers in a way I should have done weeks ago. It's a complete mess. I've been carrying round old bits of work and law reports, empty cigarette packets, and even a sandwich wrapper, a bit of lettuce stuck brown to the edge. I dump all the papers in the confidential shredder bin and poke at the gum with a screwdriver I find at the back of one of my desk drawers. The gum doesn't budge, and impatient, I thump the screwdriver in at an angle to try to break off the lump. There's resistance, initially, and then the whole thing gives way, the screwdriver flying out of my hand and the wheel coming off in its entirety.

I pick up the bag and try wheeling it — it's uneven but goes pretty well. It's good enough. Just because it isn't perfect isn't any reason to throw it away. Putting it down I sit at my desk and leaf through the briefs, my notes on Madeleine's case. Chloe's right, it really is a mess. Her accounts have been inconsistent, the conferences with her trying and overemotional. But in her position, what would I have done differently? I believe what she's said about Edwin's abuse of her, and I understand her fundamental desire to protect James. It may not be enough, though. James is in trouble whichever way it goes, either with his mother inside for life, the killer of his father, or on trial himself, dealing with police and social services and court even though he's only a child, only fourteen years old. I imagine cross-examining him, putting to him that it was he who stabbed his father repeatedly, and acid rises in my throat. Even if she gets away with pleading guilty to manslaughter, she'll still go to prison, albeit for a shorter time. There are no good outcomes here.

Madeleine used the phrase *as a mother.* It's never a phrase that goes anywhere good, usually crowbarred in to justify some particularly conservative or repressive piece of thinking. I've always tried to avoid thinking about myself as a mother at all. But now I make a conscious effort to put myself into that place. I'd like to think I'd have stuck to my story if I were Madeleine, kept telling the lie, risked the life sentence. I realize that I'm angry with Madeleine, livid that she hasn't done more to protect her son.

I look at my anger more. I might think that she's failed — what about what I've done? I've failed *as a mother* every day, every month of Matilda's life, or at least that's what Carl would say. And looking at it honestly, in my own view too. But one thing I know is that I've always loved her, even if I haven't always been good at being her mother. I could change, though. I've already started to be more present, cooking and picking her up from school, not going out drinking to escape from whatever the misery was I felt. Even though I've fucked it all up so much, maybe it's not too late. Matilda certainly seems to love me, and I know how much I love her, her absence from me a nagging pain that underlies everything else.

And what about Carl, his role as a father? Is he as good a parent as he thinks? Kicking me out isn't acting in Matilda's best interests — it's because he wants her all to himself. Instead of shutting them out, I force myself to remember all the things he's said to me, all the times he's tried to undermine my relationship with Tilly. He even took away my chance to give her a sibling, put me through the misery of believing we couldn't have another child. Anger bubbles up in me at the thought. I remember one of the first stories Madeleine told us about her abusive husband, how he fed her the pill without her knowledge. What

Carl has done isn't that far off. She and I have both let our husbands tell us how to feel bad about ourselves, carrying all the guilt for failures that belong to them too.

I'm not going to let Carl push me out. I've been a shit mother to date, but it's going to change. I'm going to make sure that Tilly has the love and the care she deserves, no more conflict and silent wars of attrition. I'm going to stand up to him, fight for what's best for my daughter.

I leave chambers and run for the bus, leaving my bag behind. Carl doesn't usually see clients on a Thursday so he'll be at home, most likely. With Matilda at school we'll be able to talk properly and iron all of this out. The bus gets stuck in traffic at Angel and I run out, heading down into the Tube. Now I've decided I'm going to fight for her I'm alive again, all the indecision and worry lifted from me.

I run down the road from Archway and get to our house, my house. I'm about to let myself in with my key but I stop myself. It's courteous to let Carl know that I'm here, it's appropriate. I'm going to handle this calmly. I ring the bell and wait for him to come to the door. There's no sound for a few moments and I ring again before I hear footsteps heavy down the stairs. He opens it and looks at me, silent.

"Carl, I want to talk to you. Is that all right?" I say.

Still nothing.

"I know you're angry but there has got to be a way to work this out. I'm not going to let you do this."

A long pause again and he replies, "You're joking, surely."

"No, I'm not joking. I may not be your idea of the perfect mother but I can be good enough. Matilda loves me, you know that." My voice is getting louder and louder. Carl gestures at me to quiet down but I keep going. "You can't push me out like this. I wasn't fighting, but now I'm going to. I'm not just going to let you break up the family this way — we have to talk about it, see if there's anything we can do."

He looks around. I know what he's thinking about the neighbors, what they'll think about me standing here shouting at him from the doorstep. He moves as if to shut the door and I stick my foot in fast.

"If you don't want a fight on the doorstep, Carl, let me in. Because I'm not going anywhere." I push my body into the door and as I hit it with my shoulder he stands back, releasing it. I fall heavily through the doorway and onto the floor. Rather than reaching to help me up he looks at me with an expression of pure contempt. None of the old Carl is there. I pull myself up, rubbing my shoulder, and stand in the hall. At least I'm in the house.

He looks at me and says, "I think you'd better come in here," gesturing me into the living room as if I'm a stranger, as if this isn't the house we've fucked and fought in for all these years. I walk behind him, running my hand along the wall, remembering the feel of the wallpaper and plaster, the hole I gouged out the time we tried to drag a new chest of drawers into the house, the bad paint job I did on the banisters. He points to the sofa in front of the TV without saying anything and while I sit down he leaves the room before returning with his laptop. He plugs it into the television.

"Would you like a cup of tea?" he says. "A glass of water before we begin?"

"No thank you, I'm fine."

"Are you sure? Come on, I'll get you some water." Carl leaves the room and comes back with a glass. I take it and sip at it. The television screen comes on.

"What are you doing?" I say. "What does this have to do with anything?"

His face is sad as he turns to me. "I didn't

want to do this, Alison, but you haven't left me with any choice. Just like the vasectomy."

"Didn't want to do what?" I say.

"Just watch," he says.

I am watching. But I don't understand what I'm seeing. The television screen is reflecting what's on his laptop. It's a Mac, there are windows open, a background picture of Matilda playing in the garden. It's what's in the window at the front I can't comprehend.

"Carl, what is this?" I say, panic leaking out of my voice.

"Come on, what do you think this is? You know perfectly well."

He's right. I do know. But I can't believe it. It's a video of our front hall, the front hall I've just walked through. It's taken from ground level, from near the bottom of the stairs.

"I'll rewind it, in case you missed something."

I look up at Carl and see he's smirking.

"Why don't you describe what you're watching? I'd love to hear what you think of it."

"I, no. You know what we're watching," I finally manage to push out.

"Alison, tell me what we're watching." There's such malice in his voice I can't withstand it. He pauses the video and sits next to me on the sofa. Then he takes hold of my jaw, fingers locking into my chin. He plays the video again for a few seconds. The two people on the screen come close together, kiss, move apart.

"Who's this, Alison? Tell me who we're watching." His fingers tighten so much it's difficult for me to open my mouth to speak. He's hurting me.

"It's me. And it's . . . it's Patrick."

"Who's Patrick?"

"He's my solicitor," I say.

"And doesn't he look solicitous. Is he the one that's just died?"

"Yes. But how do you know that?"

"You'll find out. Shame. I heard a little rumor he's a rapist. Know anything about that?" he says.

I try to shake my head but he's holding me too tight.

He starts speaking again, "Funny, it was all over the *Evening Standard.* Anyway. Keep telling me what's happening. Why don't you describe what you're wearing?"

I don't want to look at the screen anymore but Carl won't let me move my head. I look at myself in the freeze frame.

"I'm wearing tracksuit bottoms and a T-shirt," I say.

"Not made much of an effort, have we? Still, easy access, as we're about to see." The cruelty in his voice is breathtaking — I've never heard him use this voice before. He starts the video again. "What's happening now, Alison?"

"Patrick's, Patrick's . . . He's ripping my T-shirt."

"Ah yes, so we see. Why don't you tell me what you're wearing underneath?"

I try to move my head but his grasp won't shift. He moves the other hand onto my neck and squeezes. I was already struggling, panic and stress making my inhalations shallow, but now I can't breathe at all. I feel my face redden and I bring my hands up, pull at his. He doesn't budge for another few seconds before he lets go of my throat.

"I'll do that again for longer next time," he says. "Tell me what you're wearing underneath."

I try to inhale, compose my voice.

"Sounds like you've got a frog in your throat," he says. "Have a drink." He hands me the water and I gulp at it.

"Let's try again," he says. "What are you wearing underneath?"

It's useless to resist further. "Nothing," I say. "I'm not wearing anything."

"How convenient for your gentleman

caller. And what's he doing now?"

"He's pulling off my tracksuit bottoms."

"No, not that. Before that. Shall we say, what's he doing with your top half?"

I want to lower my head so far down that I can sink into myself, slide under the sofa and lie there undisturbed for the rest of time. I've come to fight and ended up in a nightmare. Carl puts his hand up to my throat again.

"He's playing with my breasts," I say.

"That's right," he says. "Good girl. In fact, that gives me an idea." He pushes me back on the sofa and still without letting go of his grip on my jaw, moves his spare hand as if to pull up my top. I'm looking at him, trying desperately to see some trace of the Carl I know, but it's as if he's a different person. Bluebeard's pulled off the mask.

He moves back. "On second thoughts," he says, "I don't think I can be bothered. I've seen enough to last me a lifetime."

I'm pushed back into position to watch the rest of the video. I sit poised, ready with my descriptions for what we watch. Here Patrick's undressed me, here he's turned me round, here he's pushing into me from behind. But Carl doesn't ask again. When it's finished he lets go of me and moves over to the armchair. I rub my jaw.

"Where did you get this from?" I ask.

"That's not important," he says. "But it's not a bad recording. Wouldn't you say?"

I close my eyes, trying to shut out the vision of my tits and arse, Patrick's hands on me.

"It was only once," I say.

Carl nods as if I've made a minor observation about the state of local government. He clicks through on his computer.

"It's certainly the only time so far I've found on film," he says. "But all of this would indicate it was a lot more than once."

The screen that comes up now on the television is full of records of calls and text messages, from me to Patrick, from Patrick to me. Carl clicks on one of them and shows the full text, an arrangement to meet after court.

"Fairly conclusive, wouldn't you say?"

"Where, where did you get all of this?"

"Ah, well, I was quite pleased about that, actually. It was after you got so pissed you spent the night in chambers. Remember?"

I nod. I do remember.

"And you smashed your screen?"

I nod again.

"They're very helpful, the people in those phone shops, especially when they're helping a concerned dad with his wayward teenage daughter. They showed me exactly what I needed to do with the phone to track what you were up to. Every call, every message, every email. Everything."

I rummage through my handbag and pull out my phone. It looks entirely normal. Like Carl looks entirely normal, mask back on. I pull off the case and poke at the back of it.

"It's an iPhone," I say. "You can't hack into an iPhone."

"Apparently that's what everyone thinks," he says. "But you can. You can jailbreak it, install spyware easily."

I turn it over in my hands. "That's illegal, Carl. This is illegal. You can't hack into people's phones like this. It's not admissible evidence."

"Who's talking about evidence? I'm not trying to take it to court."

"What are you trying to do, then?" My hands are so cold now I'm finding it hard to hold the phone. I put it down on the coffee table and rub them together, my face tense.

"If you don't fuck off and leave Matilda and me alone, I'll email this video to every contact in your address book," he says. "Your naked tits, your pubes, your instructing solicitor taking you up the arse the moment your husband and child aren't in the house. I think that would cause a bit of a stir, don't you?"

"But that's blackmail. You're blackmailing me," I say. I reach for his laptop and he grabs it away and holds it above his head, laughing.

"Yeah, it probably is. But are you really going to go to the police? Actions have consequences, you know. I can destroy you, Alison."

I reach again for the laptop before recognizing the futility of my movement. I sit back on the sofa.

"How long have you known?" I say, curling myself up as small as I can in the corner.

"Since I hacked your phone," he says, and the matter-of-fact way in which he refers to his behavior nails in its reality more clearly than anything else he's done. "That's when I knew for sure. But I had my suspicions well before. I know when it started now, of course. You had one particularly tedious conversation about it." He goes through the call record. I watch the mouse arrow move down the list on the screen. "Ah yes, here."

He double-clicks on a date and the sound of my voice and Patrick's fills the room. I put my hands over my ears. He laughs.

"I didn't think you could handle the truth," he says.

I keep shaking my head, wanting to push it all away.

"You wouldn't . . . I know you wouldn't. I'm her mother," I say.

"I thought about that, and quite honestly, I've decided it's not important. It wasn't important to you. She'll get over the embarrassment. It'll be less damaging than having you in her life."

"I don't understand how you can do this to me," I say. "We loved each other, once."

"We did, but not anymore. You've made that abundantly clear. And I think you're a damaging, toxic person, Alison. You're entirely selfish. Almost narcissistic. Matilda needs to have you out of her life, and I'll do everything in my power to ensure that happens."

The shock of it is starting to wear off. I can't rub my eyes and make it all go away. I knew I'd angered Carl but I had no idea how much he hated me, not until now. I look at the screen showing all my calls to Patrick, all my messages, and past the horror of it, the truth sinks in.

"Why didn't you say all of this on Sunday?" I say. "Why did you save it?"

"I didn't think I'd need to. I thought you understood how bad a mother you are. You lost Matilda. I hoped you'd get the message then."

"I might have lost Matilda," I say, standing up. "But it was me she ran to first. It's always me she wants. I might not be much good but she loves me. You can't take me from her."

"It's for the best, Alison. It's for the best."

He unplugs the cable that's connecting the television and the laptop. I'm about to lunge at the laptop again but he catches my eye and laughs.

"It's all backed up, ready to send. Doesn't matter if you get the laptop, you can't delete the files. If anything happens, then poof, they'll be off. Sent to everyone you know and everyone you've ever met. And it'll be all your fault."

"Carl, please . . ." I say but it's too late. He's walking out of the living room, laptop under his arm.

"I need to collect Matilda from school now," he says. "I'd like you to leave, please."

I look at him but his eyes are blank, reflecting only the light from the window above the door. There's nothing behind them, no hint of love or affection or anything that we used to share. I stumble backwards towards the door and open it, going outside. It's bright, much brighter than inside the house, and my eyes sting and water.

I'm out of the gate now and Carl's shouting something at me about the keys but I turn and run, feet pounding the pavement and the exhaust-heavy air thick in my mouth and my throat. A taxi passes and I hail it down, ask it to drive me to Covent Garden, and I huddle up in the back seat, hoping he won't follow. I get back to the hotel without further interruption.

When I get to the room I go for my phone automatically but the thought of Carl watching stops me. I turn it off and shove it under a pile of clothes. The day has caught up with me now and all I can think of is how tired I am, how exhausted, how the only thing I can do now is to make myself so small under the covers that I disappear from everyone's view. Only stopping to remove my shoes, I climb under the covers and sleep comes down fast to release me from the horrors of the day.

24

I wake slowly, my head thick. There's light round the side of the blinds, and outside, the streets are awake. I reach for my phone and as my hand comes back empty I remember, thought after thought crashing down. I nearly cover my head back up with the duvet and go back to sleep but that won't solve anything. I find my watch and am amazed to see how late it is, nearly nine. I get up and shower, standing under the water as I try to make sense of the day before.

I would never have thought Carl had it in him to treat me like this but I know that now he has, he'll see it through. I've seen that resolution in his eyes before: when he stood down the dog that threatened Matilda in the park when she was three, when I was being hassled by a group of youths on the Tube years before. He didn't budge then and he won't budge now. Spyware, though.

That's underhanded, even if he is claiming devotion to Matilda as his justification. Even if I was having an affair. I climb out of the shower and dry myself, dressing in jeans.

The video Carl played me yesterday is running through my mind. I try to become more analytical, think about how he's done it. He must have put a hidden camera in the hall somewhere. I think about the angle. It's been shot from lower down, somewhere near the bottom of the stairs, I reckon. I look around the hotel room. A camera could be hidden anywhere in here. It could be anywhere. There could be more than one. My head's pounding.

As soon as I'm ready I go through Covent Garden to the Apple Store. I've wrapped my phone in a sock, not sure if Carl's managed to infiltrate the camera on it too. I go into the shop, pushing through the crowds of foreign-language students, and look for someone in an Apple T-shirt. A woman in her twenties approaches me, three earrings in her right ear and five in her left. Counting them calms me down and when she's finished asking if she can help I'm ready to speak, hoping I don't sound too mad.

"I think someone has put spyware on my phone," I say, holding out the sock to her.

"What makes you think that? Is there a

problem with the phone?" she says, not taking the sock. I realize it looks a little odd and pull the phone out of the sock. She takes it and looks at it.

"Is there any way of telling if it's been interfered with?" I say.

"Not really," she says. "And it looks fine to me."

"He said something about jailbreaking it and installing spyware."

"Who did?" she says, giving it and me a closer look.

"Just someone. Anyway, can you do anything?"

"It's not really my area," she says. "But if you want to wait, someone at the Genius Bar could help you. I can make you an appointment."

"I don't have time for an appointment."

She looks again at the phone. "You know, I have read a bit about this. I can't guarantee it'll fix the problem, but if you do a full factory reset, it should clear it."

"Can you help me?"

She nods and gestures me towards a stool. She goes through some processes and gives me back the phone, empty as when it was bought.

"Do you know how to set it up?" she says, and I nod.

"Is there a laptop I could use, please?" I ask, and she unlocks the one in front of me.

"You can use this. If I were you I'd change my passwords. All of them. Especially for your phone."

"That's exactly what I'm going to do." The code has always been the date of our wedding anniversary. No wonder Carl could crack it so easily.

While the apps are downloading onto my phone I log into my email account online and change the password. Once that's done I call my mobile phone provider and ask if it's possible to change my phone number too. A text arrives while I'm on hold waiting for a reply. I switch on speaker.

You can lock me out now but it doesn't change anything. I've still got the video.

Carl. I look at the message and something clicks, an explanation for something that I would have realized last night if I hadn't been so shocked and tired. I think about it and send a reply.

Was it you?

He replies soon after.

What?

I know the answer already but I want to see it.

It was you who sent those anonymous texts. Why?

I send the message and at the same time am taken off hold to speak to the operator about my phone number. I tell her not to worry, it's fine. I know who the problem is now. Carl sends a reply.

You deserved it.

I thank the woman in the Apple Store and leave. I think about blocking Carl's number but what's the point? All the damage is already done.

I walk through Covent Garden, past Swish the nightclub, past the alleyway where I got shit on my hand all those weeks ago. I cross Kingsway. Everyone around me is dressed for work, carrying briefcases and disposable coffee cups. The traffic's stuck in a queue going down to Aldwych and I dodge between buses. There's Holborn, where Patrick chose to end his life. Do I know how he felt? I hope I don't find out. I've lost Carl, Patrick too, and my reputation is hanging by a thread, but the thought of

Matilda keeps me going.

Now I'm in Lincoln's Inn Fields, the rumble of traffic reduced in the green. I walk down to the café and buy a coffee, sitting on the terrace. It's cold, but the sky is bright and I need the quiet and the calm. I look over at the roofs of Lincoln's Inn and remember dining there, the old traditions of Latin and candles and port, the chapel where John Donne preached. Once my face appeared in Carl's eye, and his in mine, our hearts plain and true to each other, as I thought, but now those reflections are as contorted as in a funhouse mirror. I start googling family law and custody arrangements but stop, putting my phone down on the table. I know that Carl isn't right in law, that no judge would prevent me from sharing custody of Matilda, but I also know he'll make good on his threat the moment I put up any argument. I rub my hand across my face, my head hurting from the spikiness of all the conflicting thoughts.

"Alison."

The sound of my name catches my attention. I look around.

"Alison."

I can't see who it is for a moment. There's a bit of wind and it's blowing my hair across my eyes, confusing me.

She comes forward and takes my arm. I push my hair out of my face and see it's Caroline Napier. For a moment, an abyss opens at my feet and I topple over the edge. Then I regain my footing. She doesn't know I know. It's okay.

"Caroline. Hi. Sorry, I was miles away."

"I saw you and I was going to leave it but I really need to speak to you."

I look at her more closely. She's not looking good, her hair greasy, her skin blotchy with spots on her chin. It's like looking in the mirror.

"Is everything all right?" I say, hoping I sound more professional, more detached than I feel.

"I'm fine," she starts to say, stops. "No, I'm not. I'm not at all. Do you mind if I join you?"

I want to tell her no, but I can't bring myself to do it.

"Sure," I say. "I was just having a coffee."

She sits down opposite me, her scarf wrapped tight round her neck. She's wearing fingerless mittens and she traces a line in the water spilled on the table in front of her.

"I expect you're wondering why I want to talk to you," she says.

"Well, um, yes. I suppose." I look round

the gardens, focus on a little boy holding a balloon, desperate to look at anything other than her.

"You see, the thing is, Alison. God, this is hard to say . . . The thing is, I know. And I know you know. He was bound to tell you."

The abyss yawns in front of me again but I look her straight in the eye. "I have literally no idea what you're talking about." You could chip ice off my words.

"Come on, we're past that now. I think Patrick made sure of that when he threw himself under the train."

I can't help but flinch. "What did he tell you?" I say. There's no point denying it.

"That you were having an affair. That you were the most meaningful relationship in his life." She shakes her head, apparently baffled at the notion. "There was something very lonely about him, though I don't think I realized at the time. Too drunk . . ."

"Christ . . ." I say.

"I expect he told you he didn't do it, that it wasn't like that?"

I don't say anything but I incline my head once in assent.

"It was true. But I didn't know it would affect Patrick this badly," she says. "If I'd had any idea . . ."

"Would you still have reported him to the

police?"

She looks down at her hands and pulls at a bit of the mitten. She's wearing a wedding ring, a plain band of silver.

"Yes. I would have done. I think," she says. "I mean, it was so open to interpretation, what happened. But it seemed right to tell the police and I talked it through afterwards with my therapist and he was clear that if I thought it was rape, then it was. Actions have consequences — Patrick knew how vulnerable I was with all the problems with my husband."

I gesture at her hand. "You're wearing your wedding ring."

"My husband's been very understanding. He can see now how much damage he's caused, that the way I was acting out, the drunkenness, the uncharacteristic behavior, it was all a cry for help. He feels really bad about what happened to me — he's moved back in," she says.

"So you're not breaking up anymore?"

"I don't know. But we're going to do counseling together."

"Good. That's good," I say. I'm in two minds as to whether I should ask but I can't help it. I take a deep breath. "Do you want to talk about what happened with Patrick?"

She lowers her head. "A lot of it was as

much my fault as his," she says. "I got hammered. No one made me drink all that wine, no one made me go into the garden. I wanted to kiss him, I wanted to go further. Until I didn't. And he wouldn't stop. He was hammered too. But I said no, and he didn't listen, and after that I didn't have a choice, I had to say yes."

I reach over for her hand and after a moment she takes it. Her fingers are cold. She keeps talking.

"And then we were arrested. It was the most humiliating moment of my life, being dragged off like that to the police station. I slept it off, and when I woke up, I knew what I had to do. That's when I made the allegation of rape."

Her hand is making mine too cold and I pull it away gently.

"I was going to retract, almost the moment I said it. But then I went to see my therapist. I really wasn't sure I'd done the right thing, but he made me feel much better. I was all set to withdraw it but he made me see I was right. If I thought it was rape, it was. And actions have consequences. I know I keep saying that phrase, but it's one of my therapist's favorites, and I think it's a really good one to bear in mind."

The chill from my hands is spreading up

my arms and through my body. My feet are rooted to the ground. There's a ringing in my ears, a feeling that there's something I'm missing in what she's saying to me.

"It sounds terrible," I say. I think about what Patrick said to me about anonymity but I don't want to say the words. It's not fair. Maybe there was something in that, but I think she's telling the truth.

"It was. It really was. And then to find out that Patrick had killed himself. But I suppose that other girl had come forward. And it was all over the paper. His career was over." She puts a hand across her mouth and bows her shoulders. I stay seated as I am, tucking my hands into my pockets. I say nothing.

"Oh, I'm sorry, Alison. You don't need to hear me going on." She squints over at me. "You don't look great either. It must be very hard."

She could be lying, but I know exactly what Patrick was like. And I don't believe Alexia was lying, not for a moment. He was always right on the edge of what was acceptable, even with me. Blurred lines, indeed. I exhale.

"It is. But I agree with your therapist — you did the right thing. Actions do have consequences." And as I say that, I realize what I've missed.

I know that phrase. It was said to me only yesterday. My mind whirs while she keeps talking.

"I'm staying married, I tell you, if I possibly can. I'm not up to dealing with it out there."

"I might not have the choice," I say. "Mine's just fallen apart."

"I'm so sorry," she says.

It comes to me. "You know what, I could do with some therapy. It might be exactly what's needed for me, for us. What's your therapist's name? He sounds good."

"I've got a card," she says. She picks up her handbag and rummages through it, pulls out her wallet. Removing a card she hands it to me. "He's so good — I'm sure he'll be able to sort you out."

"Thank you," I say. I take the card and shove it down into my coat pocket without reading it. "I'll definitely think about it."

She looks at her phone. "I'd better go. I'm due at Southwark soon," she says. "Maybe we could meet up? Have lunch?"

I nod, say yes. It might even happen, though I doubt it. She touches me once on the shoulder as she passes and I listen to her walk away.

■ ■ ■ ■

I sit at the table for a while longer before walking back into chambers. I'm caught in a short moment between suspicion and knowledge. The answer's on a small piece of card in my pocket. I want to ignore it, pretend that everything's normal, but I'm not sure I can manage normal for much longer. Once I'm in my room I sit at the desk and take some deep breaths.

I'm going to lose my daughter. In many ways, I've lost her already. Unless I develop a bit of backbone. I know what I've done to Carl is bad but what he's done to me is awful too — lying to me, spying on me, and taunting me from behind an anonymous shield. Is this who I want to bring up my daughter? Maybe I could scoop her up from school and run away with her? If we went to the north of Scotland, one of the islands, he'd never find her. We could go to New Zealand, Australia — I've looked into it before, as a barrister I'd get permission to emigrate. But he'd stop me. He's got the ultimate threat to hold over me.

One final deep breath and it's time. I take the card out of my pocket and I read it. Read it again. Put it down on the desk, side parallel to the edge. I flatten my hands down on each side of it before closing them into fists so tight my knuckles whiten. It's time to fight.

25

The words on the card dance in front of my eyes.

CARL BAILEY — PSYCHOTHERAPIST
RELATIONSHIP COUNSELING/SEX ADDICTION

He was Caroline's therapist. He was Caroline Napier's therapist and from her own mouth it was he who backed her up in reporting Patrick. He knew exactly who Patrick was when she told him about what had happened to her and rather than being objective, recusing himself from treating her due to a conflict of interest, he counseled her. He supported her in her claim of rape without telling her what good reason he had to dislike Patrick, gleeful, no doubt, rather than supportive of his client. A chill spreads over me as I start to realize quite how much he knows, how far his reach has spread.

I grab my broken wheelie bag from the

side of my room and throw it down on the floor. I pull it open and look at the lining, searching for rips or holes, anywhere an opening could have been made. Frantic, I turn it over and look at the outside. There it is, what I'm looking for. A hole in the top, small enough to be disregarded but big enough for its purpose. I put the bag flat again and rip the lining out, pulling with both hands. And there it is, small, black. A red flashing light. A camera. A miniature camera, lens poking out of the hole. I pull it out of the housing that's been made for it and sprint out of the room.

I'm running out of chambers, pushing past Robert, shutting the door in Mark's face. I'm sending pedestrians this way and that as I sprint towards the bus. Someone shouts at me but I ignore them. There's no bus but there's a cab.

"Archway, please," I say, and he accelerates off.

I push my feet against the floor, willing the cab to go faster.

I don't care anymore what he's got on me. Some dirty pics, a video? So what. So fucking what. Patrick was my instructing solicitor, not my opponent. *We* were consenting adults. There's millennials the world over showing off their bits on social media

— I can weather it out. There's no way I'm going to let Carl raise my daughter. I'm difficult, I'm self-obsessed. I've lied and cheated, drunk and smoked my way through the hours I should have spent with her, playing with her, reading with her, being her mother. But I'm not twisted. It's sick, to have known about my affair for all this time and said nothing, to have spied on me and seized the opportunity like that to get his revenge on the man fucking his wife.

Carl must have felt pure glee when Caroline told him what had happened. He must have leaned forward, all caring and solicitous. "What was that name, again?" he'll have said. "Yes, terrible situation. Definitely rape. Definitely." He'll have laughed himself sick inside thinking the damage that could be caused. And it's not like he was necessarily wrong either, helping the situation along like that. He wasn't to know someone else would make an allegation — but he didn't care. Carl wasn't being an engine of justice, he was making mischief, pulling the strings of my life from behind the scenes.

We hit traffic at Highbury Corner and I try to control my impatience. He doesn't know I'm coming. He might not even be there. But if he isn't, I'm going to sit, and I'm going to wait, and when he comes in

I'm going to tell him to send the email. I'm going to tell him that I'm staying in the house and that he can't kick me out, that I'm going to be Matilda's mother and that he can't stop me. I'm going to tell him that I'm going to report him to his professional body for dishonesty and for failing to report a conflict of interest, I'm going to report him to the police for blackmail, for installing spyware illegally on my phone and for filming me without permission in my house. He's put a hidden camera in my wheelie bag. In my fucking wheelie bag, the one item he could be sure I would always have with me. And God knows how many other cameras there are squirreled around the house.

The taxi pulls up outside the house and I thrust money through the window at the driver, thank him, rush off. He's calling something but I wave my hand and struggle with the keys to the front door. It seems like it's not opening and fine, that's fine, I'm not going to let it set me back, I'm going to sit here on the doorstep and wait for Carl to come home from school with Matilda and then I'm going to take her safe in my arms, push past him into the house, refuse ever to leave her again, but it's all right, the key's going in okay now and it's turning and the door's opening and I'm in. I slam the door behind me.

I'm in. I hear a heavy thud and then it's quiet, a strong smell of cigarette smoke in the air. Music's playing from the living room.

I look round the side of the door but I don't see Carl.

The curtains are drawn and the room is dark. The only light is coming from the television screen, which again is connected to Carl's laptop. I can see it dimly, resting on the coffee table. My eyes adjust to the dark, to the screen. I look at it more closely, trying to make out what it is I'm watching.

The woman on the screen looks dead. A man moves her first this way, then that, props her belly-down on the bed. The camera zooms in from behind, her body filling the screen. She's almost naked, wearing only bra and garters. No underwear. In the background, music, a rhythmic beat in which he joins, slapping her bare arse in time to the music, gently at first, then harder. He's laughing. I know that laugh. It's Carl.

His hand appears in front of the camera, fingers splayed. The penetration starts, the camera focusing closer and closer.

The muscles clench at my jaw. Images

flash before me, rush past as fast as the blood in my ears. I cover my face with my hands, then force myself to move them away. I need to see.

Sated, Carl picks the woman off the bed and drapes her arms over his shoulders. He starts to waltz, moving her from side to side as her head flops over. She's dead and he's singing, *bada-bada-bada*-ba-*bada bada-bada-bada*-ba-*bada . . .*

I can't take my eyes off him.

The song ends and he puts her back down, legs sprawled open, head over the edge of the bed. She's dead. She must be dead.

She can't be dead.

She can't be dead because it's me only it can't be me because I'm here not there on the screen and I can't have been there because some of the things he did I'd never have let him do and it's the hotel room in Brighton but I don't remember a moment of it and why couldn't I even lift my head up let alone cry the way I'm crying now, clawing at my face before wrapping my arms tight round myself and rocking, rocking until I'm back in myself again, here, safe, in body at least, though my mind is racing.

The music's loud. It's coming from the

stereo, not the video. Too loud, I can't bear it. I walk farther into the room to turn it off, try to gather myself. And that's when I see him.

Carl.

He's there.

I breathe in, out, in, calming myself. I'm not dead, I'm alive. I'm a witness. I bear witness to what he's done to the me that's not me on the screen, the limp doll that he's manipulating, the puppet.

I turn on the light. And I see it's gone wrong. However many times he's done this before and got away with it, it's failed now.

He's the puppet now, half-naked, slumped off the sofa, his head at a grotesque angle as it dangles sideways in a noose, the rope attached to the bookcase behind. His mouth is contorted out of shape, something sticking out of it. I take a step in. His face is purple, his eyes bulging, a small flicker of movement the only sign that he's still alive. He's pushing with his arms against the coffee table as if to get some purchase but he's not quite close enough to stop the process of strangulation.

I'm not dead, I think. *I'm alive, back in control. No more puppet master.*

He groans, a noise of desperation. I look again at the screen.

If he takes his eyes off me, just for a moment.

I get hold of the coffee table and pull it towards me, away from him. He reaches out once more but he's losing strength. He collapses into the noose, gravity too much for him. I can smell fag smoke, an ashtray knocked on the floor, stubs and ash on the carpet. Above it a tang of citrus — I see the eighths of red-fleshed orange left on the coffee table, the piece he's put in his mouth.

The video plays on a loop, his trophy. I think about how many times it could have happened, all the nights I thought I'd passed out because I'd drunk too much.

Now there's a smell of shit in the room. Carl's face has gone from purple to blue.

Time passes. I sit back on my heels and wait. It won't be much longer. Then I'll call for an ambulance, the police.

A moment is all it'll take.

Five Months Later

"I dreamed about Daddy last night," Matilda says as she's eating her breakfast.

"Did you?" I say. "What kind of dream was it?"

"It was a good dream," she says. "We were walking on the beach and we made a sandcastle and he said he'd have to go but that he'd be back soon."

I walk round the table and hug her. She turns and hugs me back.

"I miss him," she says, her voice muffled against me. "I wish I could see him in real life."

"I know, sweetheart. I know."

I hold her for a bit longer, until she shifts. She starts eating her breakfast again. They told me this is how it would happen, bursts of grief, stretches of normal routine. I'm with her nearly every moment she's not at school, and she's coming through.

We walk to school together.

"You're going home with Salma this afternoon," I say. "I'll pick you up at six o'clock. Okay?"

"I like going to Salma's," she says. "I like their cats. Could we get a cat?"

I almost say no, instinctively. That's always been the answer before. But then I remember. It was Carl who was so against it. I stop walking and crouch down beside Tilly.

"I think that would be lovely. Let me do a bit of research, and I'll see what I can find out. Maybe we should look at getting two, so they can keep each other company."

She flushes up with pleasure and hugs me. "Really?"

"Yes, really. I think we could give some

cats a very happy home."

After I've dropped Tilly off, I go down to Holborn. Chloe's in the office already, sorting through paperwork.

"All set?" she says.

"All set. And I mean it, this is the last time I ever open my mouth in court."

"Yeah, yeah, I know. You've told me."

"I mean it, though. I'm not doing this again," I say, firmly. We lock eyes until she concedes defeat, laughing.

"It's okay. I only love you for your paperwork, anyway."

I know it isn't a problem for her. She loves being a higher court advocate and I'm more than happy running the office and keeping on top of the cases. I work a lot from home — it's been a godsend, really. I can be there for Tilly and keep the roof over our heads, just about.

"That suit's falling off you," Chloe says.

I pull at the waistband of my skirt. It's true. I've dropped nearly two stone since finding Carl. Since letting Carl die . . . He's pursued me out of sleep, closed my throat to food. Night after night I've sat by Matilda, watching her sleep, playing out the last two years in my head, wondering what I could have done differently to change the way it's turned out. So many times I've wondered if I should have known, what I missed. I never saw the shadow in him, not until it was too late. What I'll never know is how long it was lurking before it started to take form and emerge from the darkness. For so many years I believed he loved me, but now I can never ask when that love left him, or if hate had been there all along, biding its time.

Madeleine's arrival pulls me out of my reverie. I offer her a coffee but she shakes her head. She stands near the door of the office, a wheelie bag standing next to her.

"You brought everything," I say.

She gestures at the bag. "Yes, I'm all ready."

She and Chloe embrace and the two of us walk along to the Old Bailey together. I crane my neck as we approach the building to look at Justice, standing astride the court. Some statues of Justice are blindfolded, but not she. She weighs the evidence, impartial. And she wields a sword.

"Here goes," Madeleine says as we enter the building.

"You okay? You're happy with what's happening?"

"I am, yes. And Alison, thank you. For everything you've done on this case and for all the support."

We make our way to the custody suite and she surrenders to the security guard.

"I'll see you in court," I say, and raise my hand to her in farewell.

Chloe called me a month ago. I was at a swimming practice, watching Tilly swim front crawl. I ducked out of the building to take the call.

"They'll take the plea," she said, excitement bursting from her voice.

"What plea?"

"Madeleine. They're going to take the plea," she says.

"You're joking . . . Seriously?"

"Seriously. That shit Flynn, the barrister who was prosecuting — he's been suspended for drunk driving. So his cases have all been dispersed. It's gone to Alexandra Sisley — you know her?"

"I do," I say, relief coursing through me. Karma's a bitch.

"She's very sensible. I've instructed her in a couple of cases in the past. But anyway, she looked at it all. I told you their psych report was good, didn't I?"

"You did," I say.

"Well, it's all worked out. It's going to be okay."

■ ■ ■ ■

Sisley is opening the case. She runs through the facts as we've agreed on them, adding, "It seems clear to the prosecution that the defendant was the victim of an abusive relationship."

I look round at Madeleine. She's crying, I can tell by the slight shaking of her shoulders, but she's composed. Even though she's facing a custodial sentence, she looks better now than I've ever seen her before, fuller in the face, her neck less tense. She knows James is safe; that must be what's taken the strain off her.

Now it's my turn to rise to my feet. In my mind is the ring of the "Guilty" that Madeleine answered when the charge of manslaughter was read to her. The judge nods through my remarks, and I conclude, "As I know your Lordship is aware, the loss of control defense to murder is still a comparatively new piece of legislation. And one for which my client is most grateful. She understands, as do I, that your Lordship's hands would have been tied in earlier times, and that she would most likely have been convicted of murder and sentenced to a mandatory life sentence. But the evolution of the law allows for a more merciful disposition. My client knows that there is no alternative to a custodial sentence. She comes today to court prepared for that outcome. But I would urge your Lordship to bear in mind all the events leading up to the commission of this offense, and impose as light a sentence as might be commensurate with the whole series of events, not just the actions of my client that night."

Madeleine is crying properly when I go down to the cells after sentencing. She flings herself at me, wiping her snot all over the shoulder of my gown. I don't care.

"Five years," she says. "Five years! When it could have been life."

"You're all right, then," I say.

"I'm all right. I saw James a couple of days ago," she says.

"How was he?"

"He's doing all right too. He says he misses his dad sometimes, but other times he's glad . . ."

"Is he going to live at Francine's when he's not at school?"

"Sometimes. But he's got a really good friend in his boarding house and they've offered to have James whenever he wants to go. I've met them — the mum's lovely.

Dogs, cats, horses, big paddock and woods round the house. The kind of family home we could have had . . ."

"You'll make your own family home," I say, "your own unit. You and James. You'll be out in less than three years, if you just keep your head down."

"Yes. And how are you getting on, you and your daughter?"

"All right, we're doing all right too."

Of course Madeleine knows. There's no one who knows me, knew of me, who doesn't know. News of Carl's death spread like wildfire. ANOTHER STEPHEN MILLIGAN, screamed all the headlines. The police didn't give all the details away, though.

I've run through that day a thousand times, trying to talk to Carl about it in my head, trying to understand what he was thinking as he set up his noose, cut up his orange, lit his cigarette. I've looked it up, read all the articles I can find.

Autoerotic asphyxiation. A method of enhancing sexual excitement by restricting the supply of oxygen to the brain. More common than you'd think.

More dead than you'd know.

It might seem silly but it's his preparation that gets to me, the paraphernalia of it. The way he'd strengthened the bookcase and fixed it to the wall. The precise cut of the rope so that as long as he stayed in the same place on the sofa, it would be at the right length, choking him enough but not too much. Even the orange — he'll have read the same pieces online as me. Done his research. Carl wasn't one to take chances. As he bit the citrus fruit, the tang would jolt him back into his senses before anything could go wrong.

It must have worked, time after time. Until I slammed the door shut and he jumped, fell.

The hanged man.

How did he get into it? When did normal sex stop being enough? I've read about sex addiction — perhaps that's what he was suffering from, driven by the need to push himself into more and more extreme situations, the normal stuff too boring to give him any thrill. Perhaps.

But I know he hated my job, hated his financial dependence on me. He wanted his power back.

The police took his computer away. They asked if I wanted to look at any more of the video clips they found of me, but I said no and asked if they could be destroyed. They told me there were other clips, of other women. They're looking into his men's group. Other arrests have been made. Most of me doesn't want to know.

It's a cold comfort, but the earliest clip of him raping me is dated a year before I started sleeping with Patrick. What I was doing was wrong. What he was doing was so much worse.

And I'm doing my best to make amends to Matilda, be the mother I always should have been.

"This is exactly how you found him?" they asked when I let them into the house.

"Yes," I said.

"Did you know about these cameras?" they asked a few days later, gesturing at all the secret holes in the walls they'd uncovered, the hiding places behind books and photographs. Even a thermos mug was a hidden camera, the one that always sat on the counter in the kitchen.

"No. I didn't know," I said.

That was true.

And maybe they looked at the recordings on all of those cameras, maybe they saw a time stamp. Maybe they knew I came in earlier. Just a little earlier. Only a moment. Maybe they even saw a mark on the carpet when the coffee table wasn't pushed exactly back into its original position.

Maybe.

But they've never asked. And I'll never tell.

"Mummy, Mummy!" Matilda runs to me when I arrive at Rania's house to pick her up.

"Have you had a lovely time?"

"Yes!"

"Thank you for having her," I say to Rania. "She loves playing with Salma."

"It's great to have her. She says you're going to get cats?"

"Yes, as soon as I've worked it all out. With any luck in the next couple of weeks. That's the plan. You'll have to come and visit them."

"We'd like that."

They wave us goodbye as we walk down the path and back to our house.

"Are you hungry?" I say once we're in.

"A bit," she says. "Not much. Do we have any oranges?"

"We do."

I get one for her, put it on a plate. I give her a table knife to peel it.

I watch her cut into the rind, carefully marking a circle round the top and two more circles crisscrossing it. Her hands are slow and steady. She knows how to do it now.

This time, there's no blood.

ACKNOWLEDGMENTS

I owe great thanks to many people, to my agent Veronique Baxter for her early and constant faith in the book, and to Henry Sutton for his astute supervision and unwavering support. Huge gratitude to my brilliant editors, Kate Stephenson at Wildfire and Lindsey Rose at Grand Central Publishing and their teams, and to Alex Clarke and Ella Gordon. To Jason Bartholomew, Nathaniel Alcarez-Stapleton and the Hachette Subsidiary Rights Team, more gratitude for their phenomenal work in selling my book across so many international territories. You've all given me the opportunity to realize a dream of a lifetime, and I can't thank you enough.

Thanks to the UEA MA in Creative Writing — Crime Fiction, to Laura Joyce and Tom Benn, and the 2015 cohort, Caroline Jennett, Trevor Wood, Kate Simants, Geoff Smith, Suzanne Mustacich, Merle Nygate,

Marie Ogée, Jenny Stone, Steven Collier, and Shane Horsell.

I am very grateful to Dan Brown and Helen Hawkins for the inspired title suggestion. Daniel Murray and Richard Job have been extremely tolerant and generous in providing replies to my numerous questions about legal procedure — any errors are mine alone. I never was much of a barrister . . .

I have been given much support by my friends and early readers: Sarah Hughes, Pinda Bryars, Louise Hare, Maxine Mei-Fung Chung, Anya Waddington, and Petra Nederfors. Katie Grayson, Sandra Labinjoh, Norma Gaunt, Susan Chynoweth-Smith, Russell McLean, and Neil Mackay have kept me going with wine and encouragement, Amanda Little and Liz Barker with regular fresh air and exercise, Jaynee San Juan and Viktoria Sinko with a huge amount of practical support. My heartfelt thanks to you all, and to Damien Nichol and Matt Martys for making sure I don't stop moving in the right direction.

And to my family. My parents for giving me a lifelong love of reading and an abiding fascination in crime fiction and criminal law, my brother for being a solid source of motivation. My parents-in-law for being lovely and never rearranging my ornaments. And above all, my husband and children, my *sine qua non,* an essential respite from the misery and dysfunction of my fictional world. I couldn't have done it without you.

ABOUT THE AUTHOR

Harriet Tyce was born in 1972 and grew up in Edinburgh. She studied English at Oxford University and law at City University in London before working as a criminal barrister for nearly a decade. She left the Bar after having children and recently completed an MA in Creative Writing — Crime Fiction at the University of East Anglia, where she is now studying for a PhD. She lives in north London with her family.

The employees of Thorndike Press hope you have enjoyed this Large Print book. All our Thorndike, Wheeler, and Kennebec Large Print titles are designed for easy reading, and all our books are made to last. Other Thorndike Press Large Print books are available at your library, through selected bookstores, or directly from us.

For information about titles, please call:
(800) 223-1244

or visit our website at:
gale.com/thorndike

To share your comments, please write:
Publisher
Thorndike Press
10 Water St., Suite 310
Waterville, ME 04901